THE WIDOWS' GUIDE TO SKULDUGGERY

AMANDA ASHBY

Storm

Ebook ISBN: 978-1-80508-800-4
Paperback ISBN: 978-1-80508-802-8

Cover design: Emily Courdelle
Cover images: Shutterstock
Map design: Yopi Kwb

Published by Storm Publishing.
For further information, visit:
www.stormpublishing.co

Midnight Reynolds and the Agency of Spectral Protection
Midnight Reynolds and the Spectral Transformer
Wishful Thinking
Under a Spell
Out of Sight

Young Adult – paranormal adventures

Demonosity
Fairy Bad Day
Zombie Queen of Newbury High

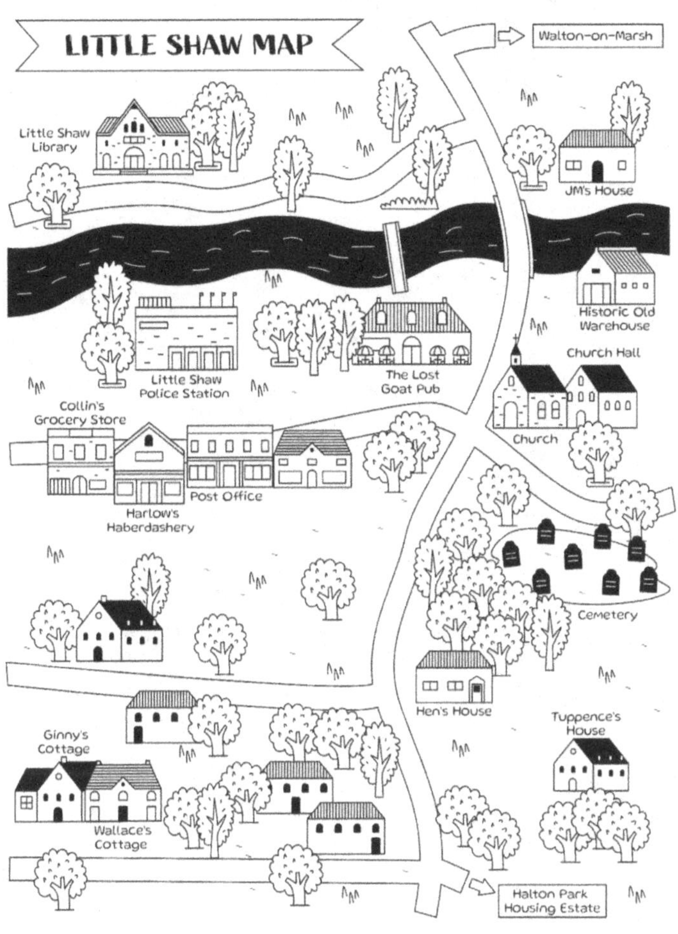

LITTLE SHAW MAP
Walton-on-Marsh
Little Shaw Library
JM's House
Historic Old Warehouse
Church Hall
Little Shaw Police Station
The Lost Goat Pub
Church
Collin's Grocery Store
Post Office
Harlow's Haberdashery
Cemetery
Hen's House
Tuppence's House
Ginny's Cottage
Wallace's Cottage
Halton Park Housing Estate

ONE

It was a perfect day for a wedding. The sky was blue and cloudless as a faint breeze rustled the lavender and rosemary bushes that surrounded the sandstone chapel, while a yew tree shaded the grass, keeping the heat away from the guests as bees lazily drifted past. In short, it was the kind of late July weather that any bride would kill for.

That was if the bridal party didn't kill each other first.

Ginny Cole winced as the best man and the maid of honour screamed at each other over by the lychgate, while Colin, a Jack Russell-slash-ring-bearer, dug up yet another rose bush from the churchyard garden that ran down the side. It was dotted with wooden benches for people to enjoy the meditative silence. Unsurprisingly, no one was sitting on them today.

'What did you call me?' the maid of honour squealed.

'You heard me,' the best man retorted as Colin barked at a small flower girl who had wandered over. The child promptly burst into tears. The tan and white coloured dog barked a second time for good measure, then returned to his digging as the other flower girl began to cry. The wedding photographer, a woman in her mid-thirties wearing a deconstructed black dress and Doc Martens, was standing on the flagstones with an unimpressed expression on her face as she took in the argument. A phone was clamped to her ear, and she was explaining to whoever was on the other end that she hadn't signed up for a circus and had no intention of staying.

Ginny glanced at the church doors.

Why aren't they open yet?

Next to her Connor West chewed his lower lip. His long dark hair was brushed off his face, and his usual outfit of jeans and a hoodie was replaced with a suit. They were unlikely friends, considering Ginny had just turned sixty-one, and Connor was nineteen. But after working together in the Little Shaw village library for eleven months, Ginny had grown close to him and his family, and especially to his sister Grace, who was an avid reader and often came into the library with the two small flower girls, who she nannied for. And so, while Ginny hadn't expected an invitation to the engagement party and the wedding, she'd been delighted to accept.

The screaming increased, and she willed the thick oak doors to open so the guests could be ushered into the cool interior. The change in temperature might calm the rising tension.

The problem was that Grace's fiancé, Theo Faulkner, came from the famous mill-owning Faulkner baronetcy – a family whose wealth and title stretched back generations. And while Theo's father was only an honourable younger son, it was still a far cry from the rundown housing estate where Connor and his siblings had grown up. Never mind the fact that the Wests were notorious. Not only was Grace's uncle, Joey, on the run from the law, but her grandmother, Maureen, had her own chequered past, and while she had insisted on paying for the wedding, she'd refused to come, saying that it was the last thing Grace and Theo needed on their big day.

All of this was compounded by the fact that the Faulkners were from Walton-on-Marsh – a place that everyone in Little Shaw seemed to feel a strong aversion for. The two villages were only five miles apart but were bitter rivals in everything from cricket through to how many times *Antiques Roadshow* had visited. And while Ginny hadn't lived in the area long enough to fully understand the feud, she knew Connor was worried about keeping the peace between the two families. Especially since Theo's mother had insisted the wedding take place in the Walton-on-Marsh chapel, instead of on the lawns of a modern spa in Little Shaw, much to the chagrin of the bride's family.

'Yeah, well, you'd better take it back or you'll be sorry.' Nina, the maid of honour's voice hit a pitch so shrill that it made Digby, the best man, roll his eyes and let out a mock snort.

'Are you threatening me?'

Oh dear.

Bracing her shoulders, Ginny silently looked at Connor. In general, she was better at fading into the background rather than breaking up fights, but she liked Grace and wanted to help.

Probably best if she talked to Nina and Digby, while he dealt with the dog. Connor gave a nod of understanding and moved off, while Ginny walked to the lychgate.

She tentatively placed a hand on the maid of honour's heavily tanned arm. 'Let's join the others and get ready to go inside. Grace will be here soon.'

'Tell that to Lord Muck. He thinks my dress is too short and that I should go home.' Nina didn't budge as she pressed her full lips together.

Sighing, Ginny pulled her hand away and swallowed at the orangey-brown smudges that now coated her fingers.

'I said it was too short *and* too tight,' Digby clarified. He had an angular face with dark hair that brushed off his brow, while his aristocratic accent was in sharp contrast to Nina's Lancashire burr. 'It's a church, not a bleeding nightclub.'

'Lucky for you, since you wouldn't get past any doorman with *that* haircut,' Nina flung back, but Ginny saw tears glittering in the corners of her eyes. Her voice was so loud that everyone turned to stare at them, while a low whisper rang through the waiting guests.

It's the curse.

Ginny winced. Ever since Grace's engagement became known, all Little Shaw could talk about was how misfortune always fell on anyone who crossed the village lines. It was accompanied by a long list of those who had tried and failed, which ran from some poor soul who had gone to buy a cabbage forty years ago and never returned, through to a couple whose tragic love story made the War of the Roses seem like a childish pantomime.

It was clear by the hard-set countenance of the groom's family, who were standing in the shadow of the spire, that they took it all as seriously as everyone in Little Shaw. Or maybe it was because they considered the Wests beneath them.

Regardless, there was no reason for the best man to be rude.

'I'm sorry, but you owe Nina an apology,' Ginny said. Despite her dislike of confrontation, she couldn't tolerate injustice.

'An apology?' Digby spluttered, chest expanding.

'Yes. Imagine if someone spoke to your mother or sister like that.' Ginny refused to let herself wilt under his looming presence.

They stayed locked in a stalemate before his shoulders dropped in acquiescence.

'Fine. I'm sorry I commented on your dress,' he muttered.

Nina's jaw opened but Ginny shook her head and mouthed: *Think about Grace.*

It had the desired result as Nina gave a final sniff and

stalked away. The effect was slightly ruined by her towering silver heels that kept sinking into the freshly mown grass. She came to a halt next to Connor's mother, Jo, who was clutching an enormous lavender hat, while talking in a loud voice about how much the wedding breakfast had cost.

'I didn't mean to cause a scene,' Digby said to Ginny, still simmering slightly. 'I'm sure they're decent enough in their own way. But curse aside... Theo's a Faulkner, and we're almost like brothers. It's hard to watch him throw himself away like this. Especially when he could've—' Digby broke off as Connor materialised beside them, clutching the dirt-covered dog.

Ginny wasn't sure if he'd overheard Digby or not, but if he had, he didn't let it show. Instead, he thrust Colin at the best man. 'I think you'd better take him back to Mrs Faulkner before he digs up the entire garden.'

'At least he's not digging for gold,' Digby snapped, seeming to forget his manners again. He glanced at Nina, who was now swigging sparkling wine straight from the bottle. Then he wrapped his arms around the wriggling dog and strode over to the clutch of Faulkners.

Most of them were wearing black, their solemn faces more suited for a funeral than a wedding. It was in stark contrast to Grace's side of the guest list, who looked like they were on their way to the Grand National, complete with hats, heels and an air of hopeful excitement.

Digby stood next to a willowy girl in her mid-twenties with a severe haircut. Unlike the others around her, she was wearing a blood-red dress that clung to her slim frame, but her face was partly obscured by a black veil. It was quite dramatic, and not in a good way.

Ginny was just pleased her own wedding had been a lot less stressful. She and Eric had been married in a registry office with only the clerks to act as witnesses. It had been followed by thirty-five years of happiness before his death eighteen months ago.

Stop it, she chided herself, pushing back the familiar grief. It still managed to slip under her skin at times, but it didn't bury her the way it once had. Her friends in Little Shaw had helped with that, and she was learning to enjoy the new life that she'd never planned to have.

'It's only eleven in the morning and I'm already shattered.' Connor ran a hand through his dark hair, tousling it into its usual style. Then he looked down at his suit and wrinkled his nose at all the dog hair that was now covering it. He groaned. 'Seems I'm shattered *and* hairy.'

'At least I can help with that.' Ginny retrieved a small lint roller from her handbag. She'd taken to carrying it, now she had been adopted by a cat. 'Hold out your arms.'

'Thanks.' Connor did as instructed.

Ginny had just begun removing the worst of the hair when a low moan came from behind them.

They turned to see the girl in the red dress clutch the groom's arm.

Theo Faulkner was twenty-seven, with a firm jaw and a sweep of dark hair that hung across an equally dark brow. He looked deeply uncomfortable.

'Please, Theo. Don't do it. It's not too late,' she cried, before turning to the best man. 'Tell him, Digby. Tell him what a mistake he's making.'

'What the actual hell?' Nina broke in from where she was standing. And Connor's brother, Jake, who'd spent the morning on his phone, suddenly looked up, eyes blazing. He flexed his scar-covered knuckles and Ginny knew him well enough to guess what he was thinking.

Oh dear.

Connor's jaw went rigid, clearly worried about what his hot-headed brother, or Nina, might do. But before either of them could act, Theo said something in a low voice to the girl then stepped away, leaving her in Digby's care. Moments later, the heavy oak doors creaked open and two solemn-faced ushers stepped out.

'Saved by the doors.' Connor wiped his brow as the groom's friends and family walked into the church. 'That could have been bad.'

'Do you know who she is?' Ginny asked, her stomach tightening with unease as Digby led the now sobbing girl into the church.

'Yeah, that's Digby's sister, Jacinta Theakston. I've never met her, but I know that her coming today was a whole other argument, because she's also Theo's ex-girlfriend.'

Ginny bit back a gasp. Why would Theo invite an ex to his wedding? Particularly one who appeared to still be in love with him? Though it did explain Digby's furious rant at Nina, as well as his broken-off conversation. What had he said?

It's hard to watch him throw himself away like this. Especially when he could've—

'Does Grace know she's here?'

'Yeah.' Connor nodded. 'They're family friends. That's the parents over there.'

'What an awkward situation for Grace.' Ginny followed his gaze to a glamorous couple who were hurrying after their distraught daughter. Their faces were set in matching scowls. Had they hoped Jacinta would be marrying Theo as well?

'Mum and Nan were fuming but Grace didn't want to upset anyone,' Connor said, though his brow was furrowed and it was clear he didn't like the idea.

As a long-time people-pleaser, Ginny could understand Grace's reluctance to go against Theo's mother, but still, it was hard to imagine any bride being happy about having an ex watching on.

'I hope she doesn't try anything during the wedding.'

'Me too. I'm starting to think it's a good thing Nan refused to come. She has even less impulse control than Jake.'

Ginny still thought it was a pity the West matriarch hadn't attended, but she could see Connor's point. 'It won't be much longer,' she assured him.

'Thanks, Mrs C,' Connor said, as a long white limousine pulled up outside the church. Ginny used the lint brush to remove several more stray hairs from his jacket.

'You're welcome.' She kissed his cheek as Grace climbed out of the limousine.

Her dress was pale ivory and had a simple straight skirt and scooped neckline that perfectly framed her long brown hair. She was the same height as Connor with a gentle smile and large eyes that made her look like a frightened deer. It was clearly nerves, though Ginny wasn't sure if it was because she was having second thoughts, or because she really was worried about the curse.

Still, once they said, 'I do', all the talk about curses, and ex-girlfriends dressed in red, could be put to rest. At least, she hoped so.

Ginny passed the photographer, who had obviously decided to stay. The woman peered over the top of the tripod and waved in the direction of the bride.

'Perfect, Grace, just lower your head and give me a bit more Princess Di energy.'

'Princess Di?' Connor looked up and frowned, and even Grace blinked.

'I'm going with the shy-girl-marries-aristocrat narrative,' the photographer explained, just as something small and furry darted past, almost knocking the tripod over. 'What the hell?'

Colin had no interest in the photographer or the teetering equipment and zoomed on, half running, half jumping his way towards Grace and Connor. His white furry nose was smeared with soil and mud as he gripped something round and white in his jaw.

Was it a ball?

'Stop.' Digby appeared from the side of the church, in quick pursuit. His chest was heaving and there was dirt down his morning suit. 'Stop, I say.'

Colin suddenly seemed to understand what the word 'stop' meant and came to a skidding halt at Grace's feet. He leaned forward and dropped the ball, his muddy fur smearing the hem of the white dress.

Ginny let out a low cry and fumbled for her lint brush. What had induced Digby to play fetch moments before the wedding? And why were he and Connor both just standing there?

Ginny reached their side as the wedding photographer let out a high-pitched scream. 'It's the curse. The *curse*. I knew this would happen. People always say not to work with children, animals or *anyone* from Little Shaw. And here's proof.'

Colin barked in agreement as Ginny stared down at the object at Grace's feet. *Oh no*. Her throat tightened in horror. It wasn't a ball at all.

It was a human skull.

TWO

'Grace has gone straight into nanny mode.' Connor slid along the wooden pew inside the church and gestured to his sister, who was encouraging their distraught mother to take off the over-sized hat, while at the same time keeping a firm grip on Jake's arm, no doubt to stop him getting into a fight with someone.

Her hair was pulled back into a practical bun, and the stunning ivory wedding dress was hidden under Theo's suit jacket. It was in stark contrast to the beautifully decorated church that had been filled with garlands of eucalyptus hanging from the pews, while large urns were overflowing with white roses, peonies and dahlias.

Ginny's heart ached for the young couple and the dark turn their wedding had taken. The police had turned up half an hour ago, and after getting a statement from Digby, they'd directed everyone inside while the scene of crime officers scoured the garden where the skull had been discovered. And now an uneasy tension was filling the air as the Wests took up one side of the church and the Faulkners the other.

Jake, Grace and Connor's mum, Donna, let out a hysterical sob and Jake made a growling noise in his throat.

The rector, the wedding photographer and a delicate woman with a towering beehive stood by the altar, their glowering frowns matching. As if feeling the heat of their collective gaze, Donna wailed even louder.

'For goodness' sake. Could you please exercise just a modicum of decorum?' Theo's mother suddenly snapped. Annabel Faulkner had none of her son's cheerful countenance. Her face was long and narrow with large navy eyes and a curtain of straight brown hair. The only hint of colour was the red lipstick that covered her pursed mouth. 'You are creating a scene.'

'Pots and kettles,' Jake growled, fists clenched. 'It was your dog that caused all the trouble, so I don't know why you're looking at us like that.'

'How dare you blame Colin?' Annabel snapped, two circles of colour forming on her cheeks. She got to her feet and stepped into the aisle, but was cut off by a thick-set woman in her sixties who had been talking to a gaunt man in a wheelchair.

The woman was wearing a pale apricot dress made of taffeta that looked straight from the 1980s. It was a far cry from Annabel Faulkner's immaculate outfit, but her presence had a calming effect on the groom's mother, and Annabel dropped her head and allowed herself to be led back to the pew. She was soon joined by Colin, who must have still been foraging around somewhere.

Ginny's eyebrows pushed together at the sight, before she twisted to face Connor. 'How did Jake know who owned Colin?'

'Because there was an argument about that as well.' Connor sighed. 'Jake wanted his dog to be included, but Mrs Faulkner insisted that it was family tradition for a Faulkner dog to deliver the rings, and that Colin doesn't play well with others.'

'That's a strangely specific family tradition,' Ginny said, with a frown. Colin hadn't struck her as territorial. Though if he *was*... why bring him to a crowded church?

She sucked in her breath, trying not to let herself jump to conclusions. She didn't like to think ill of anyone, but considering how against the wedding Theo's family and friends seemed to be, it was hard not to wonder about the timing of the discovery.

Had someone given the skull to Colin on purpose?

She peered at the best man, who was sitting at the end of a pew, arms folded. Digby had been at the side of the church when Colin had dug up the skull. Was it a coincidence? Or had he led the small dog there to stop the wedding? Next to him were his parents, talking in low voices, while Jacinta stared at her phone from behind her black lace veil. It wasn't thick enough to conceal her wide smile.

She's clearly happy with the outcome. Ginny shivered.

'My poor girl,' Donna wailed, which earned her another furious glare from Annabel Faulkner.

Next to her, Connor flinched. 'Never thought I'd wish Wallace was here. The longer we're stuck in this place, the worse it's going to get.'

Ginny couldn't share Connor's sentiment. Due to her accidental involvement in two murder investigations, she had no desire for the short-tempered but brilliant Detective Inspector James Wallace to find her at yet another crime scene.

Thankfully, Wallace, who was also her next-door neighbour, had gone on a three-week trip to New Zealand with his father to visit friends and watch rugby. Which meant Ginny would be spared a lecture. It was also a reminder to not overthink what had happened.

After all, it had nothing to do with her. This was a case for the police.

As if on cue, the oak doors opened and two uniformed officers appeared, followed by a blonde-haired woman in her mid-forties. She was tall with broad shoulders, wearing a navy trouser suit that seemed too heavy for the time of year. Yet, despite the outfit, an air of glacial confidence clung to her, making Ginny suspect she must be the lead detective.

The woman ignored the left-hand side of the church and swept across to Annabel Faulkner and the woman in the apricot taffeta. Theo joined them in a whispered discussion. Moments later, Annabel gave an imperious gesture to a tall muscular man who looked like he'd once been a sportsman. With his firm jaw and thick hair, Ginny guessed he was Theo's father.

He strode across to Annabel and they disappeared out of the door. The act had a Pied Piper effect as everyone on that side of the church quickly followed, including the woman in apricot who steered the wheelchair-bound man down the aisle.

'What the hell? Where are they going?' Donna West stopped crying long enough to glare at the detective, but the DI just joined the procession outside, leaving only Theo. His eyes were clouded with worry as he put an arm around Grace and whispered something in her ear.

She pressed into his shoulder, as if needing the support, before she nodded up at him. Theo kissed her mouth and then addressed the remaining guests.

'My uncle is far from well so DI Sterling has decided it's best for everyone to go home, where police will visit to take statements. Which means you will need to give them your details before leaving.'

'Yeah, but why is *your* lot going first?' Jake growled.

'Because she thinks we're scum. I'm surprised they don't handcuff us,' Donna snapped. 'And what about the wedding breakfast? Your mother was the one who insisted we have it at

Hawthorne Hall, and she didn't even have the decency to ask what was going to happen with the booking. But I suppose all that wasted food and money doesn't mean anything to her.'

'Mum.' Grace's voice quivered. 'There can hardly be a breakfast when there hasn't been a wedding.'

'I don't see why not.' Nina patted Donna's arm in agreement. 'It might be our last meal if that copper has anything to do with it. It's clear what she thinks of us.'

'I'm sure the detective doesn't think anything of the sort.' Grace was wringing her hands, clearly agitated. 'Plus, Theo's right – Sir Spencer's been poorly. I'm sure the detective was only trying to help.'

'Helpful my arse. Besides, this doesn't have anything to do with us. They can't stop us from going to Hawthorne Hall.' Jake ground out the words.

'Please, I just want to go home,' Grace said, and Donna West burst into tears again.

Theo's expression was bleak as he tried to comfort his fiancée and future mother-in-law. 'Come on, let's get you both out of here. Jake, could you and Connor help everyone else?'

Connor grimly got to his feet, while giving his brother a warning look. Then he turned to Ginny. 'Mrs C, do you want a lift? Nan paid for the limo for the entire day, and it's massive. Or Hen could collect you.'

Hen was one of the three widows who had welcomed Ginny when she first moved to Little Shaw and was now one of her closest friends. She was also spending the afternoon teaching a knitting class at a local craft barn and the last thing Ginny wanted to do was to disturb her. Besides, compared to the two bodies she'd previously stumbled across, seeing a skull for several seconds didn't have the same impact. Which, of course, was a dreadful thing to think. Maybe it was because Eric had also been a GP and, over the years, she'd become quietly friendly with Elliot, the replica skeleton who had resided in the corner of her husband's consulting room? Or because long ago she had studied archaeology, and from what she had seen of the skull, it was several decades old at the very least.

'I'm parked around the corner and am fine to drive,' Ginny assured him. 'Is there anything I can do to help? Have you contacted Hawthorne Hall yet?'

He frowned and shook his head. 'I tried but there was no answer, so I left a message. Mum has a real thing about food wastage. Probably because of how many meals she skipped when we were little... just to make sure we had enough to eat.'

'Oh, poor Donna. No wonder she's so upset, on top of everything else.' Ginny bowed her head at the struggles Connor's family had gone through. 'I'll call them, and if there's no answer, I'll drive over to explain. Maybe I could take it to a food rescue charity, so it isn't wasted.'

Gratitude flooded his face. 'Mum would like that.'

'Leave it to me. And try not to worry about giving a statement. Whoever the skull belonged to, it's nothing to do with your family. Or the curse.'

'I hope you're right.' Connor rejoined his sister and brother as they escorted a still-weeping Donna out of the church. As the four bridesmaids followed, along with the rest of the guests, Ginny fished out her phone and searched for the number for Hawthorne Hall, pleased to be able to help in some small way.

The call went through to a machine. Frowning, she tried again, and this time was put on hold. A jazz instrumental played in the background. The track looped around twice before the line went dead. The third time was just the same.

Ginny would have to drive there after all.

Slipping her phone away, she left the empty church and walked out into the sunlight. Shielding her eyes from the brightness, Ginny caught the tail end of the white limousine disappearing down the street, while the last of the guests were escorted past the police tape. Two uniformed officers stood by the lychgate and police vans were parked on the footpath.

She couldn't see the special crime scene officers, but movement came from down the side of the church. An older man appeared, pushing a wheelbarrow, his face set into a scowl. Was he angry that his garden was being dug up? Before she could consider it, a woman in her mid-thirties with thick red hair hurried past. It was Imogen Smith, the police pathologist.

Despite Ginny's intention not to get involved, curiosity prickled her skin. *Had* Colin really managed to dig up the skull, or had Digby or his sister had something to do with it?

And, who did the skull even belong to? Unless—

'Hey, you shouldn't still be here.' A young officer stormed over.

'DI Sterling's orders.' A second officer joined them.

'Oh, I'm sorry.' Her spine stiffened, like it always did when she talked to the police. It had been that way for as long as she could remember, and despite her recent involvement with the grumpy detective who lived next door, she'd still not conquered it. 'I-I was calling the caterers about the wedding breakfast. But I didn't mean to linger.'

'We'll need your name, address and phone number,' the officer said, not bothering to respond to her excuse. Ginny recited her details. At the mention of her address in Little Shaw, his face darkened, and he gruffly escorted her past the police tape without saying a word.

That's me told.

Sighing, Ginny walked towards her small car parked two roads away. It was on a beautiful tree-lined street, with several stone cottages tucked behind thick hedges. Not that they needed the privacy, since the street was all but deserted.

She came to a halt and looked around.

Where was everyone? In Little Shaw, if there was a murder – or even an altercation between library patrons – a crowd would instantly appear as if from thin air. But apart from the police and someone who looked like a journalist, not a single person was trying to get past the cordon or even standing in their gardens discussing the matter.

The silence was broken by the clatter of metal hitting the ground, followed by several swear words. Ginny turned to where the woman in the apricot dress was staring at a large serving tray on the ground, along with what had once been finger food, but was now a deconstructed pile of bread, salmon and pastry flakes.

'Here, let me help. Are you hurt?' Ginny joined her and started picking up what looked like pigs in blankets. *Goodness, how retro.* She hadn't seen one of the small pastry and sausage hors d'oeuvres in a long time.

'Only my pride. It was silly to think I could still carry a tray like a waitress. What a terrible waste. Though I suppose the dogs will be happy.' The woman returned the last of the food onto the tray in a no-nonsense way. 'But thank you for helping. I didn't realise anyone was still here.'

'I'm the last to leave.' Ginny blinked. Apart from her conversation with the best man, she hadn't received so much as a smile from Theo's side. However, the woman didn't seem satisfied with the answer, and she let out another soft curse.

'I told Angie... I should say Detective Sterling... not to segregate the guests like that. If anything, Grace's family should have been allowed to leave first. Problem is that we're such close friends with her father – he was a detective as well, you see – so when Annabel begged to be allowed to leave, DI Sterling thought she was doing the right thing. I tried to tell them how it would be,' she said, before her face broke into a rueful smile, 'and I need to stop trying to manage the world. I'm Theo's aunt, Kitty. I would shake your hand, but I don't want to drop the tray again.'

Kitty spoke with the kind of energy that reminded Ginny of

a whirlwind. The kind of whirlwind who was close friends with the lead detective's father. It highlighted how different the two families were, since the Wests also knew the police well but for very different reasons. None of which she could explain to the woman in front of her.

'Lovely to meet you. I'm Ginny. I work with Grace's youngest brother, Connor.'

'Oh, you must be the librarian.' Kitty's eyes widened and she broke into a smile. 'Grace told me how much you've helped her brother. Sounds like he's really blossomed in the last year.'

'I can't take any credit for that, but he's a wonderful young man. As is the *whole* family.'

Kitty let out an embarrassed sigh. 'I'm afraid not all of *my* relations have behaved well today. I'm usually on top of these things, but Spenny has been in hospital... not that it's an excuse.'

'Theo mentioned his uncle had been poorly,' Ginny replied, realising the man in the wheelchair must be Kitty's husband. It would explain the greyish tinge that lay below Kitty's weather-kissed complexion. It was one Ginny had often seen in her own mirror in the last few months of Eric's life. 'I hope it's not serious.'

'He had pneumonia, but he's on the mend now.' Kitty's stoic expression faltered and she sucked in a breath. 'As he tells me, it will take a lot more than that to slow him down. He was deter-mined to make it to the wedding.'

'I'm pleased he's feeling better.' Ginny nodded, hoping that the cancellation wouldn't push back his recovery. Then she frowned, wondering where he was.

Kitty seemed to follow her train of thought. 'Don't worry, I haven't left him stuck in the car. Theo's taken him home. He and Spenny are very close, and we don't have children of our own, so we both adore him. I was about to follow in my car when the staff from Hawthorn Hall arrived – I called and arranged for all the food to be dropped off to the night shelter in

Bacup, but asked them to come via the church so we could give a tray to the officers.'

Ginny's mouth dropped open. 'I was heading there now. Donna was worried about food waste, but no one was answering the phone.'

'That's my fault, I'm afraid. I called them immediately, so they were probably already hard at work packing everything up to be driven over. But I'm pleased to hear Donna had a similar idea. I haven't met her very often and from what Annabel has told me... well, it doesn't matter. Do you think Donna will mind what I've done? I didn't mean to overstep.'

'I'm sure she will be happy to know it's gone to a worthwhile cause.'

'Good to hear,' Kitty said, as two officers walked past them and climbed into a car. 'It looks like they're going to start getting statements. I'd better leave and make sure Annabel doesn't say anything ridiculous. I love my sister-in-law but there's no denying she can be a stuck-up ninny at times, and if I hear one more mention of the curse—'

Kitty broke off, as if thinking better of it.

'You don't believe in it then?' Ginny said, pleased to find at least one person who didn't.

'Of course not. I'm on several charitable boards and go into Little Shaw all the time, as do many other people from Walton-on-Marsh, and none of us have managed to get struck down with lightning or turned to stone.'

'That's reassuring.' A bemused smile tugged at Ginny's lips. If only more of Theo's family could be like the down-to-earth Kitty. Then she stiffened as the penny dropped. If Kitty was married to Theo's uncle, Sir Spencer Faulkner, then she must also have a title. Heat stung Ginny's cheeks. 'I'm sorry, I'm quite new to the area. I didn't realise who you were.'

'Oh dear. Is it bad of me that I prefer that?' The other woman let out a rueful sigh. 'Truth is that Annabel would have made a much better lady of the manor that I ever could. But part of falling in love with my beloved Spenny was also taking up the mantle of the role.'

'What should I call you?'

'I prefer Kitty, but most people seem to be in the habit of Lady Kitty,' she admitted, as the police car pulled away. She frowned and looked at her watch. 'I'd better go. But it was nice to meet you, Ginny. And tell Grace not to fret over anything. As soon as this business is settled, the wedding will be back on and it will be lovelier than ever.'

'I'll definitely let her know,' Ginny said, before saying goodbye and going back to her own car.

There were still no signs of onlookers, or any suggestion that the folks of Walton-on-Marsh even knew what had happened. Which hopefully meant Lady Kitty was right and that it would all blow over quickly, and the gorgeous young couple could finally get married.

THREE

'A skull? Goodness, you were lucky. Was there any flesh on it? An eyeball, maybe?' Tuppence tugged at a clump of weeds growing along the side of a cracked headstone. She was dressed in a pair of denim jeans rolled up above her ankles, along with a white linen shirt and a pair of gold gumboots. It was a warm day, and her cheeks were pink from the heat.

'Stop being gruesome.' JM looked up from the rosemary bush she was cutting back. At seventy, she was the oldest of the four friends but the most stylish in black, wide-legged trousers and a striped T-shirt.

'Skulls aren't gruesome. They're fascinating, and a wonderful way to learn how to sketch faces. I've studied plenty over the years,' Tuppence informed her. 'Not to mention all the life drawing classes I've attended.'

'I've always wanted to go to one of those.' Hen appeared beside them, shoving along a wheelbarrow full of litter that she'd been collecting. Her floral skirt brushed her knees, while her hair was hidden below a floppy hat. Then she frowned.

'How did we go from finding a skull at a wedding to naked modelling? Poor Ginny, what must she think of us?'

'After all of yesterday's fighting, it's nice to hear friendly chatter,' Ginny assured her friends. Like her, they were widows, and they all had their own reasons for volunteering at the local cemetery. The garden and grounds were no longer overgrown, but there was still a lot of maintenance to do, especially in the older section where there were no longer relatives alive to pay regular visits.

'It sounds dreadful.' Hen let go of the wheelbarrow and joined Ginny at the headstone she'd been cleaning. 'Connor came by last night to pick up some clothing, and he said poor Grace hasn't come out of her room and doesn't want to talk to anyone, not even him.'

Connor had moved into Hen's spare bedroom a few months ago and the arrangement had worked very well.

'It's a bad business.' JM made a tutting noise. 'I take it Connor is going to stay with his mother?'

'Donna was devastated, and Jake has been trying to pick a fight with anyone who looks at him,' Hen explained. 'I can appreciate why he needs to be with his family.'

They all nodded in understanding.

'I hope Grace and Theo can get through this.' Ginny sighed. 'All the talk of the curse doesn't help. I still don't understand where it came from.'

'It started the moment Walton-on-Marsh killed Old Jack.' Tuppence narrowed her eyes.

'What?' JM and Ginny chorused as one. While Hen and Tuppence had grown up in Little Shaw, JM and Ginny were newer arrivals.

'Who was Old Jack?' Ginny asked.

'And how could a village kill him?' JM wanted to know.

'Old Jack wasn't a *who*.' Hen shook her head and toyed with the damp cloth in her hands. 'It was a small cluster of farms called Jackson Fold. They weren't very prosperous and, according to rumours, when one of the mill owners offered to buy them out, they took the money. But the new owner only wanted it to redirect a small river tributary.'

'What do you mean by redirect?' JM's brow furrowed.

'She means that they flooded the area and created the Walton-on-Marsh canal, so that their mills could have better water access. It was in the 1830s,' Tuppence said. 'It was like a human sacrifice. I'm surprised they didn't do it on Beltane.'

Hen sighed. 'Not only did it kill the agriculture in the area, but it meant the mills in Little Shaw couldn't compete and a lot of the workers and industry moved to Walton-on-Marsh. And guess who owned the largest mill of them all. Joseph Faulkner.'

A cold shiver ran through Ginny as she thought of the regal expression on Annabel Faulkner's face and of the best man's horror at Theo's choice of bride. It explained so much of the animosity between the two villages. Because while Little Shaw was lovely – these days it was very much a picture-postcard village – the old mill buildings were run down; not to mention the deep pockets of poverty in some of the estates that spread out around them. And all the while Walton-on-Marsh had a history that gleamed like a newly minted pound coin. It also explained where the baronetcy came from.

JM made a snorting noise and straightened. 'I have no patience for snobbery. What did the police say? Was there anyone there you recognised?'

Ginny shook her head. 'No. The detective was called Sterling, and I didn't know any of the officers. I did see the new pathologist, Imogen Smith. Sterling said someone would be in contact to get a statement. But I presume that since it's a cold case, it might take a few days, depending on how busy they are.'

'That's if you believe it *is* a cold case,' JM said. 'Seems odd to me that a dog could dig up a skull. What if someone planted it on purpose to stop the wedding?'

'Like the wailing ex-girlfriend?' Tuppence let go of the weed she'd been tugging at, eyes wide. 'I didn't think of that, but it makes sense.'

'That's dreadful.' Hen's eyebrows pushed together. 'Surely she wouldn't want to ruin Grace's big day like that.'

'Then why did she wear a red dress and a black veil? The only thing worse would've been if she turned up in white lace,' JM retorted. 'Though from what Ginny said, just about everyone on the groom's side could have done it.'

'They weren't all like that. When I was leaving, I met Kitty – I mean, Lady Kitty – and she was lovely.' Ginny explained about the rescued food and the baroness's involvement in making sure it was redistributed.

Hen nodded her head. 'I've seen her at numerous charity events over the years, including ones in Little Shaw, and she's very down to earth.'

'Pity Theo's mother couldn't take a leaf out of the same book.' JM stripped off her gardening gloves so she could rub her chin. 'Wallace says there are no such thing as coincidences.'

Wallace also said civilians should leave investigating to the police. And judging by Sterling's glacial mask, Ginny suspected the Walton-on-Marsh detective agreed with him.

Which was why she'd been doing her best *not* to think about it. Though it had probably been too much to hope that her friends might feel the same way.

She was saved from answering by the beeping of Hen's phone alarm, signalling it was time to finish, and there was no more mention of it as they made their goodbyes and promised to see each other at the weekly exercise class Ginny had signed them up for.

It was called Senior Shake and Shuffle, and the first session last Thursday had been as uninspiring as the name suggested, but she'd promised herself to get in shape. JM, who was a regular swimmer, and Tuppence, who played social rounders, were the fittest of the group, but had agreed to go along, as had Hen. Besides, there was always the chance the next class would be better.

It was only a short drive to Middle Cottage, the semi-detached house that was now her home. Ginny and Eric had bought it as the place where they would retire to, once they left Bristol, but his devastating death had meant that she'd moved there alone.

As Ginny climbed out of her car, a sharp meow came from Wallace's house, which was the mirror of her own, with dull yellow bricks and just enough space for a small garden and a driveway.

The white electric vehicle parked there had become a sleeping place for Edgar, the small cat she'd adopted almost a year ago. His black fur shone in the afternoon sun and his amber eyes had a blank expression as if he'd never met her before.

It pretty much summed up their relationship, but she loved him all the same.

'You wouldn't dare sleep there if Wallace was at home,' she said, as he slowly padded across the bonnet of the car and gracefully jumped over the fence. He then nudged her ankle with the side of his head, as if wondering why she hadn't opened the door yet. 'What did your last servant die of?'

Edgar shot past her, no doubt straight to his food bowl. She didn't bother to remind him that he had a perfectly good cat flap at the back of the house as she stepped inside.

'Mrs Cole?' A voice with a Glasgow accent called out, and Ginny turned to see PC Anita Singh striding down the path, clutching her police notebook. She was petite with long dark hair, which were a tribute to her Indian heritage. Trailing close behind her was PC Bent. 'I hope this is a good time. We need to get a statement about yesterday.'

'Of course,' Ginny said, relieved it wasn't one of the poker-faced officers. It still didn't stop her pulse from flickering at the sight of the police car. 'Would you like a cup of tea?'

'I could murder one,' PC Bent said, before Anita gave him a quelling glare. The young officer coughed. 'Er, I mean, yes, please. If you're making one for yourself.'

'I am.' Ginny led them to the wooden table and chairs before returning to the kitchen. She turned on the kettle and stacked a tray with cups and saucers, milk and a plate of biscuits before scooping tea leaves into the pot while the water boiled.

'Ah, that's better.' PC Bent took a sip and rolled his shoulders. 'Sterling has us running around like headless chickens.'

'I can imagine. There were quite a few guests at the church. I suppose it's a lot to get through. Is that why she's asked for your help?'

Anita nodded. 'Yes, though it was obvious she didn't want to. She made it clear what she thinks of Little Shaw, which is why we're only allowed to get statements from Grace's family and friends, while her officers do everyone else. Maybe she's worried we won't hold a teacup the right way.'

'Oh dear.' Ginny didn't like to think badly of people, but the detective had certainly given her the impression she wasn't interested in Grace's side of the church. 'How is Grace holding up?'

The two officers exchanged a glance and Anita sighed. 'Not great. She's staying with her mother, but it's clear they've been fighting. Poor thing, I felt right sorry for her being stuck there.'

'Can't she go back to her own place? Surely it's not cordoned off?'

'No, nothing like that.' PC Bent shook his head. 'But she shares it with Theo Faulkner, and I got the distinct impression she hadn't spoken to him yet.'

Again, Ginny's heart pounded with sympathy. It seemed so unfair that what should have been such a special day had been ruined.

'Have they identified the skull yet? Do they know how it got there?' she asked now.

PC Bent opened his mouth, but Anita gave him another sharp look. 'Sorry, but we can't say anything about that.' Then with a conspiratorial grin she added, 'I've recently put in my application to train as a detective constable, so I need to keep on Sterling's good side. Especially while Wallace is away.'

'Of course. I shouldn't have asked. And you'll make a wonderful detective,' Ginny quickly assured her. Ever since she'd first met Anita, the young woman had been working towards becoming a DC, and Ginny would hate to do anything to get in the way of that.

'Thanks, Mrs Cole. Anyway, we'd better get your statement and then head off. We've still got a load of paperwork to get finished.' Anita flipped back the cover of her notebook. 'Can you walk us through what happened at the wedding?'

'Of course.' Ginny pushed away her teacup and did as she was asked. It didn't take long, and once Anita had finished writing everything down, she looked up.

'And you're sure you didn't touch the skull?'

'Absolutely. Even if I'd wanted to, I think I would've heard Wallace's outraged voice in my head.'

PC Bent let out a reluctant smile. 'You and me both. Don't tell him I said so.'

'Your secret's safe with me.' Anita nodded her thanks, and Ginny walked the two young officers to the door, before returning inside.

It didn't take her long to tidy up then send Connor a text message, hoping things weren't as bad at the house as PC Bent had implied.

He replied almost instantly.

Jake came home at four a.m. and got into a huge fight with my mum and now Grace is upstairs packing. She doesn't want to go back to her flat, and Hen doesn't have room at the cottage, so she's going to stay in an Airbnb just to clear her head.

Oh dear.

Ginny knew only too well how Grace must be feeling: the terrible shock of waking up to discover that the life you thought you were going to have suddenly not existing. And Connor was right – there was no room at Hen's cosy cottage.

If only there was something she could do.

Edgar chose that moment to walk through to the kitchen and nudge at her ankle again. She scooped him up and pressed her cheek into his soft, black fur. He'd been so thin when she'd first taken him in, and despite settling well, the suspicious shadows in his amber eyes were still there.

'We all carry our scars, don't we? But I like to think we helped each other,' she said to him. In response, he wriggled out of her arms and padded across to his food bowl. Ginny smiled. As far as roommates went, Edgar had proved to be easy to understand. All she had to do was give him exactly what he wanted, and he was happy. And in turn, that had given her more happiness than she had imagined possible without Eric by her side.

She glanced down at Connor's text message again. If Grace needed to clear her head, surely it would be better to do it in a place where she could relax?

Like here.

The thought caught her unawares and she looked over at the wall, half expecting to see Eric standing there, a gentle smile tugging at his lovely mouth. Tears caught in the corners of her eyes, and she gripped the kitchen counter to stop her knees from shaking.

Ginny had a spare bedroom, which doubled as a study. Not that she'd used it very often, preferring to use her laptop downstairs in the kitchen. She tried to tell herself that it was because it was closer to the internet modem, but the truth was that a year on and she still thought of it as 'Eric's study', despite him never living there.

Is that why I'm suggesting this? To help Grace... and me?

It was certainly the sort of thing Eric would have done. He hated to see anyone in distress, which was what had made him such a wonderful doctor.

Warmth flooded her and Ginny turned away from the wall. She'd stopped waiting for him to answer and instead took comfort in how she felt when she thought of him. A lump formed in her throat, but she swallowed it down and picked up her phone.

> I have a spare room if Grace would like to come and stay.

FOUR

Monday, 28th July

'I hope I didn't wake you,' Ginny said the following morning, as Grace stepped into the kitchen. Her hair was pulled up in a messy topknot, and purple shadows sat below her eyes, suggesting she hadn't slept well. She'd arrived late last night and had been so exhausted that Ginny hadn't done much more than show her around then let her get settled into the spare room.

'Not at all. I'm an early riser.' Grace stood on the threshold, clutching her fingers tightly together, as if trying to hide her nerves. She began to wring her left hand, and the dazzling sapphire engagement ring caught in the early morning light. Despite herself, Ginny looked down at her own fingers.

She and Eric had never bothered with an engagement ring, but she still had the plain gold band he'd given her so long ago, while his own band was in a drawer up in her bedroom. Pushing back the memories, Ginny forced herself to smile as she poured hot water into the teapot and gestured to the table.

'Then we'll get on splendidly together. Now, why don't you sit down, and I'll bring the tea over.'

'Please, you shouldn't put yourself out for me.'

'It's nothing of the sort. I have a cup of tea every morning and I always make too much.'

'Okay, well, thank you, Ginny. I'm used to being busy, you see.' Grace's gaze swept the room, as if hoping to find an errant child in need. 'If you have anything that needs doing, I'd love to help.'

'That's very kind of you.' Ginny finished loading the tea tray and walked it over to the table. She didn't want to admit that her house was almost spotless because she, too, liked staying busy. 'But it might be a good chance for you to relax. Which reminds me, I put some books out you might like, along with the internet code and some old movies. Though Connor assures me that no one watches DVDs anymore, so just ignore them if you think it's silly. And don't forget to try sitting in the garden. I think it's going to be a nice day.'

'I'm sorry.' Grace's face crumpled and she let out a soft sob. Ginny's heart lurched and she longed to give her a hug, but Grace's arms were wrapped protectively around her torso as if she didn't want to be touched.

'Oh, love, I didn't mean to upset you.' She led her to a chair.

'It's not that.' Grace fumbled for a tissue to mop up her tears. 'You must think I'm so rude. But you're being lovely, and I feel terrible that Connor talked you into letting me stay. It must be the last thing you want.'

'Nonsense. Connor didn't do anything of the sort, it was my idea. And' – Ginny paused and sucked in a breath – 'I'm pleased. Usually, it's just me and the cat.'

On cue Edgar joined them and, after studying Grace for several moments, decided it was safe to jump on her lap. A reluctant smile spread across Grace's face as the black cat settled himself down for a nap.

'Th-thank you. And I promise it will only be for a couple of weeks. The family I work for left for holiday yesterday, but when they're back, I can move in with them. I used to live there before Theo and I got the flat together—'

She broke off and pain rippled through her large, dark eyes. Ginny's heart ached, wishing there was something she could do. But short of inventing a time machine to stop Colin from digging up the skull, she couldn't think of anything useful, so she filled their cups.

'Here you go. Tea might not make everything better, but I'm sure it doesn't make things worse.'

Grace's dark lashes glistened with tears. 'Thank you.'

'Don't give up hope yet,' Ginny whispered, her own throat suddenly dry. 'Have you heard anything else from the police?'

'Anita's left a voice message, but I couldn't bring myself to listen to it. What's the point?'

'What do you mean?' Ginny leaned forward.

'I love Theo so much, and I know he loves me,' Grace added, shyly. 'But he also loves his family and though he doesn't admit it, he finds it hard that they don't like me. And now this has happened... it's not just a warning to them. It's for me as well. I don't fit in there, I never did, and I never will.'

'I'm sure that's not true. Lady Kitty told me that she was very happy about the wedding, as was her husband.'

'Lady Kitty and Sir Spencer have always been so welcoming. But it's all useless because Annabel will never change her mind. Especially after what happened.' Grace leaned back, despair etched across her face.

Ginny wished there was something she could say. To promise Grace it would all be fine. But no matter how much she wanted it to be true, she really didn't know.

Getting to her feet, Ginny gave Grace an encouraging smile. 'I have to go to work but try not to fret. It's easy to think the worst when you're tired and stressed, but maybe once the shock has worn off, things won't seem so bad.'

'Maybe,' Grace agreed, though there was no strength to her

words. Still, Ginny knew better than most that even the deepest pain could be lessened with enough time.

She tidied up her breakfast dishes and finished getting ready before wishing Grace a good day. The young nanny had already discovered the broom and was sweeping the kitchen floor when Ginny retrieved her handbag and stepped outside, almost crashing into Connor.

He'd graduated from the all-black look he'd favoured when they first met and was wearing a white T-shirt and denim jeans. But the large cake tin in his hands was new.

'Hey, Mrs C. I hope it's okay. I wanted to check on Grace before work.'

'Of course. She's in the kitchen. Why don't you stay with her for an hour or two and I'll open up the library?' Ginny suggested, her gaze drifting down to the tin. 'That was nice of you to bake. I'm sure she'll love it.'

'That's what you think. Grace still remembers the time I used salt instead of sugar in the pancakes. Plus, I doubt she'd believe I made this.' Connor wrinkled his nose and lowered the tin so he could ease the lid off to show Ginny the contents.

'What do you mean? Did you buy it?' She peered at a delicious-looking fruit loaf with glistening icing that was nestled in the tin. The warm smells of cinnamon, sugar and butter danced in her nostrils.

'Nah. It was sitting on your doorstep when I arrived. Someone must've left it for her.'

'Left it for her? But why?' Ginny asked, cautiously. She'd recently become entangled with the complicated hierarchy of Little Shaw amateur bakers, and she knew better than to take any cake at face value. No matter how wholesome it smelt.

'I don't know. I suppose someone just wants to make sure she's okay. It's one of those dumb Little Shaw traditions. People have been dropping stuff at my mum's house since Saturday night. Jake's been loving it.'

Ginny had no problem believing that Little Shaw residents were keen to help Grace. Nor did she think it was a 'dumb' tradition. But she wasn't sure how the cake had ended up on her doorstep.

'How do people know she's here?'

'How does anyone know anything in this place?' Connor shrugged, before giving her a cautious look. 'Is it really okay if I come in a little later? I thought it would be good to hang with her. Between Mum, Jake and Nan giving her a hard time, she's pretty down.'

'Of course.' Ginny held the door open so he could get past. 'Take as much time as you need.'

He nodded and went inside, leaving Ginny to make the short walk to the library, wondering what Edgar would make of the extra company.

FIVE

'I've got it.' William, one of the Little Shaw library regulars, burst through the doors, waving a newspaper in the air. He was in his eighties with a round face that was currently sheened in a layer of sweat from the summer heat.

Ginny got to her feet, worried about his heightened colour, but was elbowed out of the way by Cleo, one of the usual volunteers.

'What does it say?' Cleo demanded, eyes bright with curiosity.

'Is there any news?' Andrea, another volunteer, chimed in.

'They've identified the skull,' William announced with a flourish of the paper, and the entire library went silent as the sparse collection of patrons drew closer.

Ginny couldn't blame them. It had been five days since Grace's wedding was called off and there hadn't been any news. Which explained why, along with the sunny weather, the library had been so quiet. Usually when anything happened in the village, residents would flock inside to exchange gossip, updates and theories. It had been like that on Monday, but after people had realised that Ginny and Connor didn't have any news, they'd thinned out. Though various people had continued to leave offerings on Ginny's doorstep. For the most part it was delicious cakes that Grace had insisted on sharing.

There was no hope for it – Ginny would need to continue shaking and shuffling to keep trim.

There had also been several vouchers for haircuts, manicures and massages, as well as numerous bunches of flowers.

Grace had been grateful, but nothing had lessened the terrified expression in her large eyes, and she'd spent most of her time up in the spare room, constantly worried she was taking up too much space in Ginny's house. And all Ginny had been able to do was make cups of tea and bring home Grace's favourite fantasy books.

'For goodness' sake, William. Tell us what you know.' Cleo tried to snatch the paper from his hands, but he held it out of reach as he came to a puffing halt at the issues counter.

Ginny dragged over a chair so he could sit down.

'Alright, but let me get my breath back first.' He lowered himself down and fanned his face.

'Here you go, buddy. We don't want you pushing up daisies before the big reveal.' Slim, Ginny's newest library volunteer, appeared from the back of the library holding a glass of water. He passed it over then shot Cleo a wide smile, revealing three missing teeth. 'I think we need to get everyone to move back, so he has some breathing room, but I'm not sure they'll listen to me.'

'Here, let me do it. It's all in the execution. Watch this.' Cleo stopped her attempts at getting the newspaper and turned to the small crowd. 'You all need to take two steps back so poor William can have some space.' Her tone would have put a sergeant major's to shame.

'Yes, give him some space,' Andrea echoed, as both women

looked fondly over to Slim, who was now rubbing his hands on his jeans.

Ginny wasn't sure how Slim had managed to befriend the prickly Cleo, and all the other volunteers and patrons, in such a short time. He was somewhere in his late fifties with scraggly hair, and a large belly that sat atop his skinny legs. His knuckles were covered in faded tattoos, most of which had been done in prison.

She'd first met him while trying to solve the murder of the local haberdashery shop owner, and despite his chequered past as a career criminal, he'd become one of her most reliable volunteers.

The other thing she wasn't sure about was where William's paper had come from. The Little Shaw weekly edition didn't have any mention of the skull, just a front-page headline announcing the opening of a new hairdressing salon, and a sale on curse-busting aromatherapy candles. There had been nothing in the national papers either.

She tried to get closer to see the name of it, but it was crushed under William's protective grip.

'It's the *Walton-on-Marsh Gazette*,' Cleo said, her voice almost reverent. A murmur went up around the library as the small crowd tried to edge forward again.

'They refuse to deliver their papers to Little Shaw,' Andrea explained, then gave William a piercing glare. 'How did you get it?'

'Never mind that, let the old boy tell us what it says about the skull. There might be something I can use for my book.' Slim extracted a notepad from his back pocket along with a pencil stub, which he licked with his tongue. He was the first to admit he wasn't much of a reader but after entertaining the patrons with antics from his past life, they'd encouraged him to write them down. Though it wasn't entirely clear if it was going to be a memoir, fiction... or a how-to book.

'Well, you're in luck there, Slim. Because the skull belonged to Lesley Charlton, and you know what that means…'

Another collective gasp went up from the crowd and William waved his fingers in the air, as if at a chorus line.

'This is outrageous. Why is the *Walton-on-Marsh Gazette* first to print it?' Cleo huffed. 'I was speaking to our editor yesterday and she said the police are refusing to even answer her calls. Yet here they are giving an exclusive to their own newspaper.'

'Talk about rubbing salt into the wound,' Andrea muttered, while several regular patrons began to discuss the failure of the system that meant they were the last to hear the news.

Only Slim seemed calm as he extracted the paper from William's hands and spread it out on the counter. 'Let's see what it says.' He angled it towards Ginny.

Unlike the local paper, which was addicted to puns and exclamation marks for their front-page stories, the *Walton-on-Marsh Gazette* took a more serious tone.

The Final Piece in the Murder of Lesley Charlton Has Been Found.

The twenty-year mystery of what happened to Lesley Charlton is at last solved after a skull was discovered at St Luke's Church six days ago. Detective Inspector Angela Sterling confirmed dental records were used to make the identification and that soil samples proved it had only been moved there recently. An initial inspection confirms evidence of blunt force trauma.

'Charlton's murder has long been a blot on our wonderful history, so despite the grimness of this discovery, we're delighted to finally close the chapter,' Sterling said.

The history teacher was first reported missing on 5 April 2005 and, three days later, Lesley's husband, Terrence Charlton, was found dead by suicide in their house. Next to him was a hammer smeared with Lesley's blood, along with a confession to the crime.

The shocking discovery caused ripples in the community at the idea that a beloved church member, Terrence, could be capable of such a heinous crime. And with no body to prove her death, many locals were convinced Lesley Charlton killed her husband and staged her own disappearance. This was certainly what Terrence's late sister, Jill, believed right up to her own death.

'We tried to welcome Lesley into our family, but there was always something I didn't like about her. Unfortunately, my brother found that out for himself and paid the ultimate price.'

But this theory was put to rest five years after Lesley's disappearance when human bones were discovered. Forensic reports confirmed they belonged to Lesley, though despite a thorough search of the area, the skull was never recovered.

Sterling wouldn't give any further comments, apart from to say the coroner's office is happy with the evidence and that the case is closed. Now is the time for the healing to begin. Our community has been through a lot, and we must come together and cleanse ourselves from the ongoing effects of the local curse.

'Surely they're not really blaming the curse?' Ginny turned to Slim, who was busy jotting something down in his notebook.

'Oh, aren't they?' Cleo broke off from her conversation with Andrea, eyes angry. 'It's victim shaming. And totally despicable.'

'Lesley was from Little Shaw.' Slim jotted down more notes

before finally looking up. 'Real nice lady. Too smart for the likes of me, but she was friendly.'

'That was until she married Terrence Charlton and moved to Walton-on-Marsh,' William chimed in, clearly eager to reclaim his spot as news bearer. 'We never saw her after that. Only child, you see, and she taught history at *their* high school. When she went missing and the husband was found dead, the inhabitants of Walton-on-Marsh all tried to make out Lesley had done it, just because she came from Little Shaw. Cleo's right. Victim shamming.'

'It's shaming, not shamming,' Andrea corrected him.

'That's what I said.' William shot her a mulish frown.

Ginny had numerous questions floating in her mind, but before she could ask them, the library doors opened and Harold Rowe walked in.

He was in his seventies, and despite the heat was wearing a pair of meticulously ironed navy trousers and a deep blue shirt and tie. He'd been Ginny's temporary manager at the library, before taking over as Little Shaw Parish's chairperson. Which still made him her boss, even if they didn't interact daily anymore. But Ginny had stayed friends with both Harold and his suave husband, Myles, who walked in a step behind.

Their arrival had the immediate effect of breaking up the small crowd.

William snatched up his precious newspaper and eased himself out of the chair. 'Is that the time? I need to visit Esme and Elsie to show them the news. Oh, and Rose. Goodness, it's going to be a busy day. Don't worry about my library book reservations. I'll collect them tomorrow.' He waved his hand and hurried out into the heat of the day.

He was closely followed by the other patrons, while Cleo and Andrea disappeared to the back of the library, dragging Slim along with them.

'I take it you've heard the news about Lesley Charlton.' Harold looked around the now empty library.

'Yes, there was no mention of it in our local paper, but William had a copy of the *Walton-on-Marsh Gazette*,' Ginny explained. 'It sounds terribly sad. Did you know Lesley very well?'

'Our paths crossed several times, but despite inviting her to join our historical society, she refused. Still, probably best that she didn't bring the curse back with her.' Harold folded his arms, face tight.

'Not you, too.' Ginny raised an eyebrow. She could usually rely on Harold to avoid local bickering. Or believe in village curses. This must have shown on her face, and Myles, who still had the trace of a French accent, gave her a bemused smile.

'*Oui*... I'm afraid my usually sensible life partner has a superstitious streak when it comes to our neighbouring village.'

'With good reason,' Harold retorted. 'The fact the police refused to issue a statement to our newspaper speaks volumes. Nor did their council chairwoman even do me the honour of a courtesy call. And did you see there was no mention of a memorial service for poor Lesley? No doubt they'd leave the body on Boundary Road, with their council claiming that it's not their responsibility.'

'I'm sure they won't do anything of the sort.' Myles put a comforting arm around his husband's square shoulders. 'Even though Lesley doesn't have any family left, it's still a relief for both villages that they can draw a line under the terrible death. It might help Grace West start replanning her wedding day now that there isn't any speculation hanging over her head.'

'Humph.' Harold frowned and looked around at the almost empty library. It seemed to jolt him out of his mood and he cleared his throat. 'But that's not why we're here. I got your email about Connor's leave of absence tomorrow. Myles reminded me that lately you've been having Fridays off, so I'll stand in for you.'

'That's very kind,' Ginny said, holding back a smile as she took in the pained expression on Harold's face. He was a brilliant archivist and historian but wasn't much of a people person, so it was clear whose idea it had been. 'But I don't mind coming in tomorrow to work.'

And it was true. Connor, who was currently out in the stacks sorting out reference books, had asked for tomorrow off so he could drive Grace to her flat and get some of her belongings. Ginny had immediately said yes, hoping the visit might give his sister a chance to speak with her fiancé.

'Well, we do,' Myles said. 'The last thing Little Shaw needs is for their library manager to get burnt out. Besides, I suspect Harold will get more work done here than at the council office.'

'Myles is right. So that's settled.' Harold gave a definitive nod of his head before he produced a duck-egg blue envelope from his pocket and passed it to Ginny. 'The other reason we're here is to give you this.'

'It's nothing formal. Just a meal for the three of us next Tuesday,' Myles added.

'Thank you. I would be honoured.' Ginny smiled at the two men who had become her friends, knowing that their 'nothing formal' meals were more like a gourmet feast thanks to Myles's wonderful cooking and Harold's love of wines. She gratefully tucked the lovely invitation away, already looking forward to it.

'Excellent.' Harold glanced at his watch and smoothed down his already smooth trousers. 'Now, I'd better go. There's a sub-committee meeting about the increase in graffiti at the village swimming pool.'

Ginny walked them to the door and then spent the rest of the afternoon listening to Cleo and Andrea dissect the discovery of Lesley Charlton's skull with anyone who would listen. The story had since been picked up by other media outlets, all quoting DI Sterling saying that she was relieved to finally be able to close the chapter on the twenty-year mystery.

Ginny wasn't sure if it was from the ongoing gossip or from being stuck inside the stuffy library, but by the time she and Connor finished locking up, all she wanted to do was go home and read a book in the shady part of her garden. However, she still had her exercise class. If left to her own devices, she would have skipped it, which was why she'd been grateful when her friends had agreed to go, since there was safety in numbers. Or at least accountability.

As she and Connor began walking, she tightened her grip on Eric's old cricket bag which now held her pale green leggings and a long T-shirt that covered her lumps and bumps. Sun heated the back of her neck and there was no hint of a breeze, which meant the old church hall where the class was being held would be like an oven.

Next to her, Connor scuffed his sneakers as he read a text message. He came to an abrupt halt and swore under his breath.

'Is everything okay?'

'Not exactly.' He raked a hand through his dark hair, expression grim. 'Nan's just sent a message. Turns out the reason Grace wants me to take her to her old flat tomorrow is because she just called off her engagement with Theo.'

Oh. No.

Ginny hated that one event could destroy the happiness of two young people who were so obviously very much in love. Another stab of pain went through her as she thought of Eric, but she pushed it away. At least she'd had thirty-five years with him, unlike poor Grace and Theo, who were just at the start of their journey.

'I'm sorry to hear that. Is there anything I can do to help?'

'Actually, yes—' He broke off, and Ginny's skin prickled. She'd worked with Connor long enough to know that he didn't ask for favours. Finally, he looked up. 'Nan wants to see you.'

'See me?' Ginny parroted as she peered around, suddenly concerned that Maureen West might be parked in a long, black, tinted-windowed car somewhere close, waiting for her. But apart from the children playing in the park next door there was no sign of anyone. Least of all the notorious Maureen West. Ginny had only met the matriarch a handful of times, and it had never been for long.

Connor seemed to pick up on her thoughts. 'She's at home but wants me to drive you over. I've been borrowing her car this week.'

'B-but I've got my exercise class. JM, Tuppence and Hen will be waiting at the church hall,' Ginny tried feebly.

'Nah, they're already at the house. Nan wants the whole detective club together.'

'We're not a detective club,' she reminded him. It was an ongoing joke, but for the first time Connor didn't smile. *Oh dear.* Ginny shifted her grip on the old cricket bag and ignored the tightness in her chest.

Unlike the politely crafted invitation she'd received from Harold and Myles, she had the feeling that Maureen's offer wasn't so much a request as a summons. And if Connor was worried, then whatever this was, it couldn't be good.

SIX

Maureen West lived on a new estate on the outskirts of Little Shaw in a large, detached house half hidden behind an imposing fence, complete with security cameras. Across the road, a For Sale sign sat outside the property that had belonged to the previous library manager, Louisa Farnsworth, before her murder last year.

Ginny shuddered and turned away as Connor clicked a remote control and waited for the heavy security gates to slide open before driving the late model Ford into the compound. It seemed an unlikely car for his grandmother, and Ginny wondered if it belonged to his Uncle Joey. Connor had been quiet on the drive over, so she hadn't wanted to ask.

He brought the car to a stop outside a double garage and they both got out. The front garden was lovely with large, raised vegetable beds, two apple trees and even a long strip of wildflowers where the grass would once have been.

'Is your grandmother a gardener?'

'Yeah, she started during Covid when she couldn't go to

bingo,' Conner replied as he opened the front door and ushered her into a wide entrance. Its glossy white floor tiles and orange floral wallpaper made Ginny gasp. It was broken up by a large chrome-framed mirror and a matching sideboard.

Voices drifted through from the back of the house and Connor led the way into a wide, open-plan kitchen. The wallpaper was covered in a riot of colourful birds that clashed with the pink fridge and dishwasher, and large bifold doors led out to the garden, where Ginny's friends were sitting, all dressed in a variety of exercise gear. JM was jotting away in a notebook while Tuppence fiddled with the stem of a cocktail glass. It was filled with a luminous pink drink, complete with a small cocktail umbrella. Next to her Hen was sipping a dark blue drink through a straw, with a large flower hanging out one side.

Grace was also seated at the table, absently toying with the rim of her glass, her large engagement ring visibly absent. Again, Ginny's heart lurched for her and how much everything had changed in under a week.

'Are your mother and brother coming?' she whispered to Conner.

'No. Ever since their last argument, Mum refuses to cross the threshold. As for Jake, he's still shouting at anyone who walks in front of him. But I'm guessing we'll go and visit them tomorrow. Can't wait.' Connor sighed as a nearby phone rang. He ignored it. 'We'd better go outside.'

The phone continued to ring, and Ginny resisted the urge to snatch it up. As a doctor's wife she was used to answering every call, never knowing when it might be an emergency. But this wasn't her house, so she resolutely followed Connor to the large patio area.

Her friends immediately looked over and smiled.

'Ginny, you're here. I must say this is better than Senior Shake and Shuffle.' Hen chuckled and JM nodded in agreement.

'Wait until you try these drinks. Maureen makes a mean cocktail.' Tuppence held up her half-empty glass.

'Everyone needs a hobby.' A wiry woman appeared from a garden shed, holding a tray of more brightly coloured cocktails.

Maureen West was five foot two with hot-pink hair, matching lipstick and a possible Botox habit that made it difficult to pick her age. She was wearing a bright green velour tracksuit with silver trainers that clashed with the orange drinks on her tray. Ginny guessed Maureen was behind the colourful interior design.

'Absolutely correct. You're never too old to learn,' Tuppence said.

'Or to get drunk,' Maureen retorted with a grin, and placed an orange drink in front of Ginny. Tiny bubbles danced along the surface and sugar granules covered the rim of the glass. 'Here you go.'

'Thank you,' Ginny said, as the fumes made her eyes water.

The sharp shrill of the phone started up again. Maureen either didn't hear it or had no interest in talking to the caller.

'You're welcome, Ginny. I'm fond of an afternoon tipple. It's what keeps me young. Now, drink up and don't worry about how you'll get home. Connor will play taxi.' Maureen handed out the rest of the cocktails then settled herself at the head of the table, with Connor to her left.

Ginny cautiously picked up the drink and took a taste. It was light and summery with the bitter aftertaste of champagne, and helped take the corners off the strange setting. Her sip seemed to act as a trigger and her three friends also picked up the new drinks and followed suit.

'Very nice, Maureen,' JM commended. 'Do I pick up a hint of Grand Marnier?'

'Yes. I find it gives it an extra kick.' Maureen's own drink was a milky concoction that had lines of chocolate running across the surface. She took a long gulp and turned to Ginny and her three friends. 'Now, let's get down to business.'

'Business?' Grace spoke for the first time, her dark eyes wide in alarm. 'Nan, what's this about? I told you that I don't want you to do anything.'

'And I'm not... well, not *directly*. But if you think I'm going to sit around and let *that* family disrespect you, then you have another think coming, my girl,' Maureen retorted, and turned to Ginny. 'Did you know she's called the engagement off?'

'Nan.' Grace's face turned red, and she stumbled to her feet before rushing into the kitchen.

Connor gave his grandmother a telling stare, as if he'd warned her this might happen. 'I'll go and check on her,' he said.

'You do that, lad. And don't pull a face at me. I'm not going to make her marry someone she doesn't want to, but you know as well as I do that she only called it off because she didn't want to embarrass his family... which is outside of enough,' Maureen growled.

Connor sighed and followed his sister into the house.

Ginny closed her eyes. There hadn't been time to tell her friends about the broken engagement and it was clear by their faces that they were all shocked. And yet she couldn't fault Maureen's staunch insistence of her granddaughter's worth.

It was JM who spoke first. 'I'm very sorry to hear Grace's news, but it doesn't explain why you wanted to speak to us.'

'Then let me elaborate.' Maureen took a sip of her drink. 'You lot seem to have a knack for solving things, which is why you're here. I want to know who buried that bloody skull in the church garden and ruined my girl's special day.'

Hen frowned and retrieved a copy of the local paper from her handbag. 'But we do know. They've identified the skull. It is Lesley Charlton, which means Terrence buried it before he killed himself.'

'Bollocks.' Maureen waved her hand dismissively. Hen gulped and quickly put the paper away. 'There are *many* excellent places to bury a skull and a bleeding church in Walton-on-Marsh ain't one of them. Besides, it said in the paper that the soil sample didn't match. Someone moved it there.'

'That doesn't mean it was because of the wedding.' Tuppence held up her fingers. 'There could be any number of reasons for someone to bury a skull. Maybe someone found it and wanted to give it a better resting place? Or a bird picked it up and dropped it by accident. Some birds are quite remarkable like that. Or... it could be the ghost of Lesley Charlton, trying to save Grace from making the same mistakes she did. There's a name for it... some kind of tale. Oh dear, what's the thing I'm thinking of, Ginny?'

'I think you're referring to a cautionary tale.' Ginny winced, not liking where this conversation was going. She peered into the house to where Connor and Grace were having a whispered conversation. It was clear this meeting hadn't been their idea.

'Yes, that's it. A cautionary tale. A reminder of what would happen if another bride from Little Shaw married someone from Walton-on-Marsh. Not that I'm implying Theo Faulkner is a killer, because from what Ginny's told me, he's quite lovely. And, of course, Grace is an angel. But you can't argue with the fact that the curse is alive and well.'

'I don't believe in curses,' Maureen broke in as her steely gaze swept across the table in a way that seemed to make the temperature drop. Even the sun, which had been bright in the sky, suddenly disappeared behind a bank of clouds. 'Or cautionary tales.'

'Exactly.' JM gave her an approving nod. 'If you want my legal opinion, you should always ask questions and read the fine print. Or, in this case... the fine points. It makes no sense for a skull to suddenly turn up twenty years later, on the same day your granddaughter is due to get married.'

'Thank you, JM. I can see we are as one on the matter. There is something about this whole situation that stinks,' Maureen said, as the phone rang again. 'Someone has done this on purpose. My money's on the mother.'

'Annabel Faulkner?' Ginny said, before she could stop herself, which earned her a sharp glare from Maureen. But still, despite Annabel's cutting remarks inside the church, it was hard to imagine the perfectly groomed woman sneaking into a garden and digging around to hide a skull for Colin to find.

Especially when that skull was already part of a murder case.

Ginny swallowed, the alcohol sitting heavy in her stomach. Since moving to Little Shaw less than a year ago, she'd ended up in the middle of two murder investigations and she had no intention of getting involved in a third.

Not even for someone as imposing as Maureen West.

'You might be on to something.' JM stood and walked the length of the patio area, as if she were in a courtroom. Although the effect was slightly marred by a garish blue swizzle stick tucked behind her short silvery grey bob. 'Didn't the dog belong to her?'

'You're right.' Tuppence also stood. 'And Annabel Faulkner insisted the dog had to be part of the ceremony. Plus, I heard she was friendly with Theo's ex, Jacinta Theakston.'

'Oh dear.' Hen reached for her knitting bag, as if unsure how else to deal with the information. She retrieved her needles and soon there was the soft click, click, click as she got to work. 'It's terrible to think she might have purposely ruined her son's wedding. Maybe we should leave it to the police.'

'The police couldn't find their way out of a paper bag. It's taken them twenty years to find all of Lesley Charlton's remains, and that was by accident. I doubt they'll be in a hurry to follow this up, either.' Maureen slammed down her cocktail so hard that the milky contents splashed onto the table, and she gave Ginny a fierce stare. 'Which is why I want you to find out who did it. Or *I* will.' Maureen's words echoed around the patio.

The answer had to be no. But, with her people-pleasing bent, Ginny had always found it difficult to deliver news that might upset anyone. In fact, she would prefer to go bikini shopping, followed up by trying on skinny jeans in a brightly lit changing room. But she had to say something.

'If it's a police case then we can't get involved.'

There was silence as the small matriarch's face hardened into a tight mask.

Oh yes, bikini shopping would be preferable to this. Even without the aid of any exercise classes.

'Fine. I'll do it myself. We have a roomful of wedding gifts to return. I can question the guests while I drop them off.' Maureen drained her drink, leaving a faint milk moustache on her upper lip.

The phone rang for what seemed like the hundredth time.

Connor stalked out of the kitchen clutching an old mobile phone about the size of a brick. He was closely followed by Grace, who was holding on to his arm.

'Speak to him before he does something stupid.' Connor stared at his grandmother as he held out the phone to her. If they had been in a movie, Ginny would have expected a thunderclap at that moment, or at least some kind of dramatic music to start playing.

Time stretched as Maureen's mouth tightened, but at last she took the phone from him with a sigh. Putting the phone to her ear, she listened for a moment and then said, 'Alright, Joey. Keep your hair on. I told you we've got it under control.'

Ginny and her friends stiffened.

Joey West had been on the run from the police for years and from the little Connor had said, the man wasn't the kind of person you wanted to have on your bad side.

'Is that really your uncle?' Hen whispered to Connor, who gave a grim nod of his head.

Maureen began to pace the patio. 'If you think you can give me an ultimatum, we'll see how far that gets you. Now, pull your head in and stop acting like a ninny. I have it under control, so you just stay where you are and don't do anything stupid. Give my love to Carla and the kids and tell them that Nanny West will talk to them soon.'

Once the call was finished, she casually slid the battery out of the phone and passed it to Connor, who disappeared into the house, returning several moments later empty-handed.

Ginny's eyes widened and Tuppence leaned over and picked up the old handset. 'Is this a burner phone? I was watching a YouTube video on them the other day. Do you have an older model because it's better than a smart phone?'

Maureen nodded. 'That's right. I replace the SIM card regularly and keep it powered off most of the time, with the battery separate. It's a pain, but family's important.' She turned to her grandchildren. 'Your uncle is giving us one week to get this sorted before he comes over.'

Connor turned to Grace and they exchanged a silent nod, before she got to her feet and held her hand out to their grandmother. 'Come on, Nan. Let's go and make some coffee while Connor talks to the detective club.'

'Why? What can he say to them that his old nan can't hear?' Maureen challenged.

But Grace, despite her quiet personality, returned the older woman's stare. 'Plenty. Now, let's go and get that coffee and give them a minute,' she said, making Ginny appreciate what an excellent nanny she must be.

Once they were gone, Connor let out a long groan. 'Sorry you got dragged into this,' he said.

'Yes, but *what* is it that they're trying to drag us into?' Hen put down her knitting, eyebrows pushed together. 'Do your uncle and grandmother really believe someone put that skull there on purpose to break off the engagement?'

'They do.' He sighed. 'The thing is that everyone loves Grace, including Joey. He went ballistic when he heard about what happened and is threatening to come home and rip the place to pieces.'

'Come back to England? But how is that possible? As soon as he steps into the country, his passport would be scanned and he'd be arrested,' Tuppence said with a frown.

Connor closed his eyes and sighed again. 'Probably best if you don't know too much... but let's just say it's not outside the realm of possibility.'

'Even if he could get back unseen, surely he wouldn't risk trying to investigate the wedding. What if someone recognises him?' Hen clutched at her knitting needles, concern etched in her eyes.

'*I* know that, and *you* know that. But my uncle and brother have a lot in common.'

Ginny blinked. An hour spent in Jake's company had left her in no doubt as to what a hot head he was, and it was hard to imagine that same, hair-trigger temper on a man who had controlled a drug empire before going on the run. Then she thought of Connor and Grace – both had been working hard to make different choices. And even Jake and Donna, from all Ginny knew, had never had serious run-ins with the law.

But if Joey West came back, what would that mean for the family?

And for the two villages?

'What does Grace want?' Tuppence asked Connor.

'She wants everyone to stop fighting while she figures things out. And she doesn't want Joey turning up and making more of a mess of her life.'

'What a muddle.' Hen's needles continued to click away. 'But Ginny's right about the police. We've learnt a lot recently, and they really don't like civilians getting involved in murder cases.'

Connor sighed. 'It's my fault for calling you a detective club. It must've stuck in Nan's mind. I did try to talk her out of it, but she's not easily swayed.'

Guilt caught in Ginny's throat. She hated letting people down. Especially Connor, who never asked for anything and who, despite his gruff manner, was always ready to help anyone who walked through the library doors.

But if they agreed to do it, how would Wallace take the news? Or DI Sterling?

Oh, wait.

Ginny sat up straight and turned to Hen. 'Can we look at the newspaper again?'

'Of course.' Hen put down her knitting needles and fumbled around in her bag for it.

'Look, Ginny's doing that thing with her mouth.' Tuppence pointed, and Ginny winced.

What thing? Her hand flew up to her mouth, hoping for a clue, but it seemed as mouth-like as ever.

Before she could ask for more information, Hen spread out the newspaper. 'Does that mean we're going to take the case?'

'Of course we are. It's our civic duty to help those who need it.' JM joined them and peered over Hen's shoulder, before frowning and glancing over to Ginny. 'So... what exactly are we looking at?'

Even Connor appeared uncertain as Ginny forgot about her mouth and scanned the article until she came to the part at the end. She read it out loud. '"*Sterling wouldn't give any further comments, apart from to say the coroner's office is happy with the evidence and that the case is closed. Which means now is time for the healing to begin.*" How could I have been so silly? The police won't care less that we're looking into it, because it's not an active case.'

'So, what did you decide? Will you help?' Maureen West materialised beside them, holding a cafetiere, closely followed by Grace who was carrying a tray of mugs, a milk jug and a large cake.

Ginny swallowed and her hand drifted to the roll around her stomach. Playing detective seemed to involve an awful lot of cake. But then some of her tension eased as her friends started to laugh and chat.

And so, Ginny fixed Maureen with a cautious smile. 'Yes. We can't promise anything, but we'll do our best.'

SEVEN

Friday, 1st August

'You'd think we have the plague,' JM announced the following day, as they marched down Walton-on-Marsh's cobbled high street. It had been pedestrianised, but despite the space, people steered across to the other side, as if there was an unseen electric fence between them.

'It's because we're from Little Shaw,' Tuppence whispered, as they passed several vintage shops, an antiquarian bookseller, and a delicatessen with a front window display that made Ginny's mouth water. Further along was a bespoke hat maker, a perfumery and several lifestyle stores, which looked too expensive to step inside. The pavement was dotted with huge planter boxes overflowing with cobalt-blue hydrangeas.

'How can they tell?' Ginny asked, as an oncoming man darted sideways, which almost sent him careening into a sandwich board. He steadied himself and hurried away, wiping his forehead, as if escaping a dreadful fate.

'Probably because we're not wearing designer clothing like those women over there.' JM eyed the man's hasty retreat, before turning her attention to four well-groomed women standing outside an apothecary. They were all wearing what looked like Chanel suits, complete with stockings and high-heeled shoes.

It seemed like a lot of work for a Friday morning in a small village.

'Goodness, I don't think they'd even make a skirt in my size.' Hen self-consciously patted the loose-fitting pink linen dress she was wearing.

'And if they did, I can't imagine wearing it would be comfortable. Especially not in this weather.' Tuppence adjusted her denim apron dress.

'Very impractical. Still, if they live here, they might be able to help us. I'll go and speak to them,' JM said, and went striding over.

It had an alarming effect on the four women, who scuttled away at an impressive pace considering they were all wearing heels.

Ginny watched them go. Before she and Eric had offered to buy Middle Cottage, they'd looked at several properties in both villages and she'd never picked up a hint of animosity. Instead, all she'd seen were the pristine clean streets, the thriving shops and the beautifully refurbished brick mill buildings that clung to the side of the canal. Though after a morning spent under Walton-on-Marsh's watchful glare, she was pleased with the decision to settle in the more welcoming Little Shaw. It had also been a lot more affordable, which had been the other factor in their decision making.

'So much for that idea.' JM rejoined them.

'I thought that we'd at least find one person who wanted to talk to us.' Tuppence frowned. 'In Little Shaw, people fall over themselves to share their thoughts. But here they're falling over each other to run away.'

'Maybe I should have left Brandon at home?' Hen was

clutching a lead in her hand and bent now to pat the chocolate-coloured labrador at her side. He didn't usually go with them on shorter trips, but Hen had worried that without her or Connor at the cottage, he might start to bark.

'Nonsense. He can help. After all, Edgar likes getting involved in our cases,' Tuppence said.

Ginny wouldn't go as far as saying her cat *liked* getting involved. But whether it had been intentional or accidental, he had managed to help solve a murder case. Though, as she kept reminding her friends, they weren't looking into a murder case. Their job was simply to find out if someone had purposely tried to ruin Grace's wedding.

And if Brandon could help them solve this quickly, she would be grateful.

As if knowing they were discussing him, Brandon came to a halt and helpfully barked at a neatly weeded bed of sweet-smelling pink and cream stocks, the spires of tiny petals swaying in the warm breeze. Rising above them was a bronze statue of Sir Joseph Faulkner, the first baronet, as well as a plaque detailing the long history of his dazzling success as an industrialist, through to his mighty feats in Parliament.

'Is this the chap responsible for the village's inflated sense of self-importance?' JM studied the statue.

'That's him. I'm surprised they didn't include his school report card.' Tuppence finished reading the shopping list of achievements and turned away.

'Makes me pleased we only have a statue of a magpie and a sheep,' Hen said, as they continued to walk along the picturesque street, which had started to resemble a ghost town. Ginny half expected to see a tumbleweed rolling down the middle or have a sheriff ride up on a horse and tell them that they weren't welcome. Or, worse, the first baronet himself stepping down from the plinth and shooing them away with a brass hand.

Finally, they reached a two-storey stone building with an arch that led through to a courtyard. The wide windows above made Ginny think it had been a storage yard, back when the town had thrived due to all the mills there. However, like the rest of the high street, it had been turned into a series of upmarket stores and businesses, and on the stone wall was a brass plaque, that read:

MILL CORNER *WAS RESTORED THANKS TO THE GENEROUS*
SUPPORT OF THE
FAULKNER CHARITABLE TRUST
2008

JM craned her neck. 'Is there anywhere in this village that the Faulkners haven't touched?'

'They do seem to be very generous,' Ginny admitted, as they beelined to the far end of the courtyard where eight wrought-iron tables were set up in front of a sign saying 'Weaver's Tearoom'.

They selected their table: a beautiful vintage tablecloth had been laid on it, along with a collection of porcelain teacups and heavy silver cutlery. A cut glass vase filled with soft pastel peonies and greenery stood in the centre, and there were even carefully ironed linen napkins placed on the antique china. A large umbrella hung over the table to protect them from the warm morning sun, and a dog bowl of water sat by one table leg.

Brandon gave a bark of delight, either from the water or the sight of a small terrier peering out from underneath a chair. The terrier took one look at Brandon and turned away.

'Did that dog just stick its nose up at Brandon?' Tuppence spluttered.

'And I swear there was an eye roll.' JM frowned.

'Oh, well, that's just rude.' Hen bent to rub Brandon's neck. 'Maybe coming here wasn't such a good idea.'

'Speak for yourself. I need a cup of tea.' JM's regal voice floated across the courtyard. 'Maureen West can sure mix a cocktail.'

'That she can. And besides, it's important that we regain our strength so we can come up with a plan.' Tuppence's eyes had widened with pleasure as a waitress appeared in the doorway holding a three-tier cake stand filled with small sandwiches and cakes and pastries.

'I wouldn't mind a cup of tea as well,' Hen admitted.

Ginny reluctantly nodded. Like JM, she was feeling the effects of Maureen's concoctions from the previous evening. It also explained why they hadn't come up with a plan when Connor had delivered them all home. Instead, they'd decided to walk around Walton-on-Marsh the next day and see what they could find out.

It hadn't been successful, unless cold shoulders counted as a clue.

The lovely setting was slightly spoiled by a middle-aged woman who appeared at the end of the table, holding an order pad and a whole lot of disdain. Her frown seemed to be one she reserved for Little Shaw residents.

'Will that be to take away?' the woman asked, once they'd given their order.

'Do people usually sit down at a table if they're going to take things away?' JM raised an eyebrow, before an innocent smile spread across her face. 'Besides, we're not in a hurry.'

The woman scowled and turned on her heel.

'Oh dear. I hope they don't do anything dreadful like drop our food on the floor.' Hen hooked Brandon's lead around her chair leg and then fumbled for the knitting bag that was never far from her.

'I'll be leaving them a negative review online if they do. Bad reviews are a thing, you know,' Tuppence said, before opening her pink backpack and withdrawing a small book covered in Laura Ashley fabric print, and a pink ribbon to tie it shut.

'What a lovely notepad.' Hen cast on her wool as Tuppence untied the ribbon and spread it open.

'It's not a notepad, it's an address book.'

'I am pleased you still use one. Someone tried to tell me it was "old school" the other day,' JM said, withdrawing a slim black book out of the tiny leather bag she had at her side.

'Everything old is new again,' Hen piped up, and produced a green book with gold figures embossed on it.

Ginny smiled and brought out her own, which was battered with age.

'Excellent. Great minds think alike.' Tuppence grinned.

'And fools seldom differ,' JM retorted, before putting her address book away. 'Now, what is this about? I don't think the waitress will be giving you her details anytime soon.'

'No, she did seem very grumpy.' Tuppence flipped the book open to a blank page. 'When Taron's mother died, I found boxes and boxes of stationery – I haven't had to buy anything in years thanks to my mother-in-law. I thought this would make a good murder board, because no one would think to look in it. It even has a few old addresses, which will give it an air of legitimacy.'

They were all silent for a moment. Tuppence didn't often speak about her husband who had died over ten years ago.

'That's a jolly good idea.' Hen finally broke the silence, her knitting needles clicking together. 'Given we've had to hand over our last two, it's important we have something that the police won't notice.'

'But we're not looking into a murder,' Ginny reminded them. 'We know who did it.'

'Oh yes, that's right,' Tuppence agreed, with a smile that left Ginny feeling distinctly uneasy.

'I don't think we can make any assumptions here. Just because the police said Terrence killed her, that doesn't mean he did. What if the *real* killer is still alive and they're the one who put the skull there?' JM announced, and Ginny's stomach dropped. But before she could say anything, the waitress stepped out into the courtyard carrying the tea tray, which she put down with a clatter.

Their budget hadn't extended to the three-tier cake stand, but they had ordered a plate of scones, which came out with bowls of bright raspberry jam and fresh cream, as well as two Bakewell tarts to be shared. Once the waitress had dashed away, the next few minutes were spent pouring the tea and passing around the plates.

Ginny's knife slid through the still-warm scone, and she covered it with jam and then cream before taking a bite. It was light and soft, and the full richness of the raspberries danced on her tongue.

'This is marvellous.' Hen let out a happy sigh before her eyes filled with worry. 'I feel like I'm cheating on Little Shaw. We have some good tearooms, but nothing this nice. Is it wrong that I like it?'

'I have no time for rivalries,' JM announced, as she spread a layer of jam on her scone.

'That's because you weren't born here and haven't had to put up with this village lording it over you for *everything*. Plus, we all know they cheated in the great cricket match of 1984.' Tuppence picked up her pencil and tapped her book. 'I still think we should consider that this is Lesley Charlton's attempt to warn Grace about what happens to Little Shaw brides who get married in Walton-on-Marsh.'

'A message from beyond the grave does make sense,' Hen agreed.

'We are not putting ghosts into the address book. Or curses.' JM gave them a stern look and took a bite of her scone, which left a layer of cream above her lip. 'I have a reputation to uphold. Though it would stop the police from thinking we were investigating the murder.'

'Except there's no murder to investigate,' Ginny reminded them yet again. 'And I do agree with JM that we keep the supernatural out. At least for now. That means either Maureen's right that someone wanted to stop the wedding, or it's a coincidence it was found on that day, and there's some other reason it turned up.'

'And we need to figure that reason out before Maureen tries to do it herself. Or Joey West,' Tuppence added, in an ominous voice. 'So, how do we want to do this?'

'We should start with the facts.' Hen put down her knitting and reached into her bag for a folded copy of the Little Shaw newspaper, which she spread out on the table. 'We know the skull belonged to Lesley Charlton, and that someone moved it to St Luke's church.'

'Hang on, let me get that down.' Tuppence turned towards the back of the address book and jotted down some notes. Then she looked up. 'I put it under "R" for research.'

'Clever. We should make a list at the start of the book so we don't lose track of what the different pages are for. Like "A" for alibi and "T" for theories.' Ginny leaned forward. Despite her current job, she hadn't trained as a librarian, but she did have a natural love of systems and processes.

'And "M" for murder. Like the Hitchcock movie.' Hen grinned.

'Oh, that's excellent.' Tuppence wrote it in then looked up expectantly. 'Right, what else do we have?'

The table was silent as everyone turned to look at Ginny, so she took a deep breath and organised her thoughts. At least the fog from last night was finally leaving her mind. 'Maureen thinks Annabel Faulkner is behind it. But no matter how opposed she was to the marriage, it's hard to imagine her sneaking into a churchyard and burying a skull.'

'True, but we once tried to dig up a body and remember how surprised Wallace was to see us there,' Hen pointed out.

'His reaction was purely based on bad stereotypes concerning what a menopausal woman is capable of,' JM growled. 'I hope that he now knows better.'

'I think he does,' Ginny said. While Wallace hadn't always appreciated their help, he did respect their abilities. More importantly, he didn't treat them as invisible women who no longer had a role to play in society.

'Don't forget that Colin is Annabel's dog. She could have trained him to deliver the skull to Grace,' JM pointed out.

'That's true. According to Connor, she insisted it was a family tradition for a dog to be a ringbearer,' Ginny told them.

'As lovely as Jack Russells are, there's no denying they're very excitable. A lab would've been a better choice for something involving training.' Hen leaned down and patted Brandon.

'I might put this under "S" for suspects. What do we know about Annabel Faulkner?'

'She's married to Randal, who is a well-known polo player from back in the day, and she owns Faulkner Antiques and Curios. It's that lovely shop we just passed. Not that I've been inside,' Hen quickly added, as her cheeks went red. Clearly, she was once again feeling guilty for liking anything about the rival village.

'She owns a shop?' Tuppence raised an eyebrow. 'From the picture you painted, she struck me as a lady who lunched – like those women we just saw.'

'Everyone needs to earn a living,' JM reminded her, before reaching for her phone. 'Besides, despite the fancy name, her husband is the younger son, and Annabel married into the family. Let's see what I can find on the genealogy site.' There was silence for several minutes as JM bent over her phone, before finally looking up. 'Annabel May Faulkner nee Gladstone was born in Chester and married the Honourable Randal Charles Faulkner in 1992, and Theo is her only child.' She looked down at her screen again. 'Sir Spencer and Lady Katherine don't have any children, which means the inheritance could be a possible motive.'

'You're right.' Ginny sat up and told her friends about the conversation with Lady Kitty. 'They both consider Theo more like a son than a nephew.'

'So, maybe Annabel was worried that the rich relations would disinherit him if he married someone like Grace?' Tuppence scowled with annoyance. 'That's very shabby.'

'Lady Kitty didn't seem like that. In fact, she was the opposite. She arranged for the food to be delivered to a night shelter... and comes into Little Shaw all the time. Plus, she felt the same way we do about the curse,' Ginny said.

'Yes, but if Annabel Faulkner's as stuck up as she sounds, she might not like the idea of her son becoming the next baronet with Grace by his side,' JM said, in a grim voice. 'I've just done a quick internet check on her parents and her father is an electrician and her mother is a hairdresser. Sounds like she's trying to climb the social ladder, so maybe she doesn't want her son to slide back down it.'

'And we have Theo's ex-girlfriend, Jacinta Theakston,' Hen added. 'From what Ginny said, she put on quite a performance.'

'She seemed very overcome with emotion.' Ginny sighed. 'Her brother had to lead her away, though afterwards, when we were sitting in the church, waiting for the police, she was almost smiling. As was Digby, who told me Theo was throwing himself away on Grace.'

'Clearly he'd have preferred Theo to be marrying Jacinta,' Tuppence said. 'Which means both Digby *and* his sister could have planted the skull. Or done it together. Wait a moment.' She tapped her cheek with her finger. 'Maureen thought that

Annabel preferred Jacinta as well. What if they were all in it together?'

'A conspiracy of Faulkner–Theakstons?' Hen's hand flew to her mouth. 'How terrible. If it is true, how will we prove it?'

'Let's see what we can find out about the Theakstons.' JM opened up her phone again, but this time simply did a search for the family. She let the phone sit flat so they could all see as newspaper articles flashed up, along with numerous photos of the family at formal weddings and events.

Ginny recognised a younger Digby and Jacinta standing next to their glamorous parents.

JM pressed onto a Wikipedia entry and Ginny scanned it with a sinking stomach. Digby's cut-glass accent and conde-scending attitude had been forged from generational wealth that had come from the same mills that made the Faulkners so well-known. There had even been a partnership at one stage before the two mill owners had gone their separate ways, though apparently remaining close friends.

There was silence as the four of them digested the informa-tion. Then JM turned her phone over and steepled her fingers. 'I think it's time we went and had a chat with Annabel, Digby and Jacinta.'

'Therein lies the rub.' Tuppence put down her pencil. 'We don't know where any of them will be, and considering the reception we've had this morning, I doubt they'd want to talk to us.'

'That's where the wedding presents come in. We have everyone's addresses from the invitation list Maureen gave us,' Hen reminded her.

Ginny had been unsure about adopting Maureen's plan to give back all the wedding gifts, but now she could appreciate it might be the only way to get a conversation with anyone from this village. She scanned the list of addresses and frowned.

'Digby and Jacinta aren't on here, and we don't have phone numbers for our suspects.'

'What about Theo? Would he tell us?' Tuppence turned to Ginny. 'Do you have his number?'

'Yes. Connor gave it to me on the day in case there was a problem.' Ginny retrieved her phone and scrolled through it. In day-to-day life she wasn't fond of putting herself forward, but after years of running the surgery, she'd learnt to embrace outbound calls.

She pressed the call icon, but it went straight through to voicemail. It wasn't really a surprise. Connor had said that Theo was taking the break-up badly, and she couldn't imagine him wanting to talk to a virtual stranger. Still, she left a message.

'I don't think we should wait for him to ring back. We do know that Annabel owns the antique shop, though I'm not sure what Digby and Jacinta do, or where they might be on a Friday morning.'

'Leave that to me.' JM gave them a wide smile, clearly feeling more like her old self. 'And once I find out where they are, we can split up, to make sure we're not wasting time.'

'Divide and conquer.' Tuppence nodded in approval as they all stood, much to the relief of the grumpy waitress monitoring their progress from the door.

JM regally swept past her as they went inside to pay the bill, and then the four of them walked out onto the bustling high street of Walton-on-Marsh.

Here goes nothing.

EIGHT

Ginny stood outside one of the upmarket boutiques they'd passed earlier. True to her word, JM had no problems in discovering that Digby Theakston had a flat in an exclusive refurbished mill building further along the river, and that his sister Jacinta owned a clothing store called Coco.

Hen and Tuppence had elected to drive out to the mill building and give Brandon a quick walk at the same time, and JM was eager to tackle Annabel, which left Ginny to venture into Coco. She stared at the gold decals on the front window and a single mannequin wearing a stunning wraparound dress and a heavy gold necklace.

Ginny clutched at the carrier bag containing the beautifully wrapped box that Jacinta had left on the gift table last Saturday and stepped into the boutique.

Like the window display, the space was minimalist, with white walls, dark wood floorboards and carefully curated racks lining the walls. In the middle was a display of large red leather tote bags and matching heeled sandals, none of which had price tags. It reminded Ginny of the JP Morgan quote: *If you have to ask how much it costs, you can't afford it.*

Not that Ginny was in the market for large red leather tote bags or strappy sandals. All the same, it was hard not to be intimidated as she peered down at her white trainers, simple denim skirt and favourite linen blouse. No wonder she and her friends had all stood out in the immaculately dressed village.

There were no other customers, and a soft murmur coming from out back suggested Jacinta must be on a phone call. There was a bell on the glass-topped counter and Ginny was contemplating using it, when an all-too-familiar tan and white dog appeared and began to bark.

'Colin? What are you doing here?' she said, remembering too late that not everyone spoke to their animals and dead husbands.

Like them, Colin didn't bother to answer. Instead, he continued to bark, until a tall, slim woman with straight hair and an aggressive centre parting appeared. Her angular face was highlighted by thick, dark eyebrows that were combed into submission. According to JM's genealogy research, Jacinta Theakston was twenty-five but the world-weary energy that surrounded her deconstructed navy dress made her seem older.

'Colin, hush. You promised to be on your best behaviour if I let you visit me.' Jacinta scooped him into her arms, before her gaze swept across Ginny's face. 'Oh, it's you.'

As far as customer service went, it wasn't great, but after spending the morning in Walton-on-Marsh, Ginny's bar was set quite low, so she gamely replied, 'Yes. We didn't get to meet properly at the wedding last week. I'm Ginny Cole.'

'What are you doing here?' Jacinta asked bluntly, her eyes not losing any of their intensity.

It was a good question, since it was obvious from Ginny's outfit that she probably wasn't there to shop. Not to mention that she was from Little Shaw, and therefore clearly not a desirable Coco customer.

'Grace's family has asked me to return this to you.'

'Return what?' Jacinta scowled as Ginny fumbled with the carrier bag and retrieved the gift. Jacinta's eyes lost their animosity and clouded with confusion as she registered it was her own wedding present.

Colin, seeming to sense the shift, began to wriggle his small body, demanding to be lowered to the ground. She did as he wished and then did a model-esque walk back behind the counter to retrieve a small dog snack, which she dropped on the ground.

Colin snuffled it up and then trotted around her ankles looking for another one.

'Goodness, he's well trained,' Ginny said, as Colin dropped on his back and added a belly roll into the routine.

'I wish I could take all the credit, but the truth is that he's a snack monster, aren't you, boy?' Jacinta said then flushed, as if regretting letting herself get distracted.

Colin barked in reply and Ginny stiffened as she realised what this meant. If someone had wanted Colin to find the skull and bring it out during the wedding, all they'd need to do was lay a dog treat trail to where it had been buried. The question was, had Jacinta been the one to do it? And how could Ginny lead the conversation in that direction?

'Still, he seems to like you a lot. I can't imagine he'd let me give him anything.'

'Clearly,' Jacinta snapped, but her gaze was still fixed on the gift in Ginny's outstretched hand. 'Why are they returning the gifts? I... well, I thought they would just reschedule for another date. Not that they'd get St Luke's again. It's booked up a year in advance.'

Oh. Ginny had assumed it was common knowledge that Grace had called off the engagement. A pang of guilt went through her at the idea of discussing it with the very person who might have been the cause. But it was either that, or risk Jacinta returning to her frosty persona.

'After what happened last Saturday, I believe they've broken up,' she admitted.

There was silence as Jacinta's pale face flushed with colour. *She really hadn't known.* Ginny put the gift down on the counter and licked her lips. 'Grace was very distressed about having Colin drop a skull at her feet.'

'The curse works in mysterious ways,' Jacinta said, a broad smile spreading across her red lips. 'Clearly they weren't compatible.'

'How so?' Ginny asked lightly. She wanted to feel sorry for the young woman, but it was difficult when she knew what Grace was going through.

'If the wedding was meant to go ahead, it would have.' Jacinta shrugged, with what she seemed to believe was infallible logic. Then her eyes hardened. 'If that was me, I would never have left the church sobbing. I would have insisted the wedding go ahead. After all, that's what you do if you *truly* love someone.'

'They could hardly go ahead once the police were called,' Ginny pointed out, hoping her shock at Jacinta's black and white beliefs didn't show on her face. 'And I saw you at the wedding trying to convince Theo to call it off.'

A ripple of something crossed Jacinta's masklike face as silence spread between them. Ginny kept her lips firmly pressed together, determined not to be the next one to speak and the quiet continued, broken only by Colin's heavy breathing as he snoozed now, curled up in his basket.

Finally, Jacinta coughed. 'That was wrong of me, and I will apologise to him when I see him next. The emotions of the day got the better of me. But it's what happens when you're in love.'

Is it? In Ginny's experience that kind of excessive emotion was from passion rather than enduring love. But everyone was different, and who was she to tell someone what they felt? 'When did you first start dating?'

Jacinta's mask suddenly dropped and she seemed to be experiencing an internal battle – torn between wanting to talk about Theo and not wanting to give ammunition to anyone from Little Shaw. Theo obviously won out, and she sighed. 'The day I turned twenty. It was on my birthday and it was just perfect, just like I'd always known it would be.'

'So, what happened? Why did you break up?'

Jacinta bowed her head. 'Because I made one stupid mistake. Theo had gone away for the summer, and I worried that he might be getting sick of me. I guess I was trying to make him jealous by hooking up with this guy. But it backfired and he dumped me. Then he met bloody Grace West two months later and refused to even consider giving me a second chance.'

'That must have been difficult for you,' Ginny said.

'Difficult? It's been more than that. It's been torture.' Jacinta's voice was rough as a tear rolled down her angular face. She angrily brushed it away. 'Do you have any idea what it feels like when you meet *the* person you're meant to spend the rest of your life with? And then you're forced to watch them get married.'

'So why did you go to the wedding?' Ginny asked in a soft voice, not because she was trying to solve something, but because she couldn't imagine how painful it would be to watch the love of your life with someone else.

'I went because—'

'Sorry I'm late to pick up Colin,' a voice said as the glass door swung open and Annabel Faulkner appeared. 'I got back from my aromatherapy appointment and stopped at the shop to make sure that girl I hired wasn't spending all her time on her phone, and when I was leaving, I got trapped by the most dreadful woman. But... I do have wonderful news.'

Startled awake, Colin looked up and barked.

'Yes, my darling, here I am. Did you think that I'd forgotten you?'

Colin barked again, and whatever Jacinta had been about to say was gone as she pushed past Ginny and over to where Annabel was scooping up the small dog.

'He's been fine,' Jacinta assured her, before guiding Annabel back towards the counter, where Ginny was standing.

The sight of her had a sobering effect on Theo's mother, who tightened her grip on the small dog. 'What are you doing here?' Annabel asked in a sharp voice that would usually have Ginny cowering, but she was too angry at hearing JM described as a 'dreadful woman'.

'The same thing my lovely friend, JM, is doing – returning the wedding gifts to all the guests.' Ginny pushed her shoulders back, hoping for confidence. And then without another word she left the shop.

It wasn't a moral victory. Or even a real one. She just hoped that her friends had fared better than she had.

'You're back.' The same waitress from earlier in the morning didn't try to hide her disgust as Ginny and her friends sat down at the wrought-iron table a second time.

Part of Ginny longed to go home to the welcoming Little Shaw, but there were still too many unanswered questions.

'After receiving such a warm welcome this morning, how could we refuse?' JM said in a cool voice. 'Could we have tea for four, please?'

'I don't suppose you know where Digby Theakston works, do you?' Hen asked in a hopeful voice, which earned a sharp glare from the waitress.

'I take it that's a no,' JM interpreted, as the woman stomped away.

Ginny smoothed the linen napkin into her lap and tried to sift through the puzzle pieces. Hen and Tuppence had sent a text message to let them know Digby hadn't been at his flat, and they hadn't been able to find him anywhere.

'What a nuisance that none of his neighbours would talk to us. I'm going to write them all down under "S" for suspects because it's very suspicious.' Tuppence made a tutting noise with her tongue and retrieved the Laura Ashley address book from her backpack.

'You call it suspicious, I call it rude,' JM retorted.

'These people are so tight-lipped. It's unnatural.' Hen continued with the sleeve she'd started earlier.

'Everything about this place is unnatural. Maybe that's why we're having so much trouble working this one out,' Tuppence grumbled. 'I hope you two had better luck than we did.'

'It's hard to say,' Ginny admitted, and then gave them an update on what she'd learned, from the dog snacks and how close Jacinta was to both Annabel and Colin, to – more importantly – that as well as still having strong feelings for Theo, she had no idea about the break-up.

'I can confirm that Annabel didn't know about it, either. Not that I got much out of her. I think I'm losing my touch.'

'It's part of the curse. It drains us of our superpowers.' Tuppence gave JM a supportive pat on the arm. 'We should have set a timer to make sure we don't stay here for too long.'

JM opened her mouth as if to remind them that she didn't believe in curses but then closed it again and steepled her fingers before finally looking up. 'Whatever the cause, I don't like it. The only thing I got from Annabel is that Theo has been away for the last few days and isn't answering his phone. Which explains why you haven't heard back from him. The only other thing I discovered was that she's not happy with Lady Kitty about some project. She was on the phone when I walked in.'

'Jacinta was also on a call. I wonder if they were talking to each other?' Ginny pondered.

'They could've been plotting.' Tuppence looked up so quickly that Brandon woke from his nap. 'What if step one was to stop the wedding, and step two is to knock off Sir Spencer and Lady Kitty so that Theo inherits, and step three is for Jacinta to become his new wife.'

'Oh, that's "D" for dastardly.' Hen shuddered. 'If only we had more information. We might find there is a perfectly logical explanation for everything. What a pity that Walton-on-Marsh's library was no help.'

'You mean they were downright rude, too,' Tuppence added. 'We went there on the way back from Digby's flat to see what else we could find out about Lesley's murder.'

'I didn't even know they had a library here,' Ginny admitted. 'Where is it?'

'It's in a lovely old cottage just past that statue we saw. But it's not a patch on yours. Can you believe they don't let the public into their local history section?'

'William wouldn't like that.' Ginny frowned, thinking of how often the library regular read and reread all the books in their small collection, not to mention all the trips she made to the stacks to get old newspaper articles for him. 'Though that reminds me – I can check for information on Monday. See what the local newspaper said at the time about Lesley's murder.'

'It's a sad state of affairs that we have to go back to Little Shaw to find out what goes on in Walton-on-Marsh,' JM said. 'But it's a good idea. I'd like to know more about the murder. Like where was the rest of Lesley's body found?'

Ginny picked up her phone and did an internet search, as if she was the kind of person who always casually looked things up on her phone, rather than waiting until she was at a proper desk with a pen and paper next to her. Then she let out an inward groan as the blank screen stared back at her. She'd forgotten to turn on her data so that she could connect to the internet.

She tried it again and this time, when she tapped in Lesley Charlton's name along with 'Where her remains were found', a page of answers came up. She scanned through them, but they were all vague on details. 'Sorry, I can't find it, but hopefully between Connor and William we'll be able to get more information.'

'What about asking PC Anita Singh?' Hen suggested. 'You said she's working on the case.'

'She is, but I don't want her to get in any trouble,' Ginny said, as the waitress returned with the tea tray and a large *Reserved* sign that she plonked on the table.

'You'll need to be quick with these because we have a party of people arriving in fifteen minutes.' The waitress unloaded the tray, along with the bill, and then marched away.

'This time I really will leave them a bad review.' Tuppence picked up the teapot and poured the fragrant amber liquid into the four cups. 'And it makes me jolly pleased I didn't get a second Bakewell tart.'

'So, what should we do now?' Hen put down her knitting and took a cup. 'We need to figure this out before Joey West does something silly. But I don't have a clue what it should be. Maybe we need a different murder board.'

'It's not the murder board's fault,' Tuppence defended.

'Oh, I didn't mean it was a bad idea.' Hen's face coloured. 'I just meant it's not very visual, so it's hard to see how everything fits together.'

'Hopefully we'll have better luck this afternoon. We still have most of the presents to return. I started tracking a route last night.' JM pulled out a carefully folded map from her small bag, which appeared to have the internal dimensions of the Tardis.

Ginny looked at it enviously. Her own handbag was a

nondescript black leather affair, so large that Eric had always dreaded whenever he had to try and find something in it.

'Goodness, I've not seen one of those in ages. I use my phone most of the time,' Tuppence admitted.

'I stopped using my phone last year after the stupid thing took me on a three-mile detour.' JM huffed. 'Then, a week later, when I wanted to visit a friend, it had the audacity to tell me the street didn't exist. Turns out it was too new to be on there. It's very irritating trying to argue with AI. At least with a paper map I'm only arguing with myself.'

'That's true,' Ginny agreed, feeling the tea give her renewed energy. 'I think it's a great idea, and while you do that, I could go back to the church. After all, that's where the skull was found.'

'Oh yes,' Hen agreed, then turned to Tuppence. 'Maybe we should put this all down under "N" for new plan.'

'I told you it was a good idea,' Tuppence said, her good humour returning. 'It's helping give us a different perspective on things. Whereas the police only do things one way with their big boards and their rules. Maybe that's why they never solved this murder?'

Ginny opened her mouth to remind them that the murder *had* been solved, but before she could speak Hen let out a little squeak.

'I know what I can do. I remember reading that Lesley lived around the corner from the college where she taught. Brandon and I could walk over and talk to the neighbours. What about you, Tuppence? Would you like to come for a walk with us?'

'Er, actually, I might tag along to the church.' Tuppence gave a quick shake of her head and looked away.

Ginny blinked. Tuppence was the most energetic of the four of them and walks usually suited her best. But it was clear by the way she was folding and refolding the linen napkin in her lap that she didn't want to talk about it.

Ginny didn't want to push her friend but hated that something had upset her. Unsure what to do, she reached out to pat Tuppence's arm but was distracted by the sudden appearance of a tall woman with broad shoulders that were squeezed into a grey trouser suit.

DI Sterling.

Next to her was an older man with a similar jaw and matching shoulders. Was that her father? The observation didn't calm Ginny's thumping heart rate.

Her nerves must have shown because Hen's brow creased. 'Is everything okay?'

Ginny swallowed the lump in her throat and leaned forward, keeping her voice low. 'It's the lead detective, Angela Sterling.'

'Oh dear. What do you think she's doing here?' Hen quickly stuffed her knitting away.

'Maybe she wants a lovely scone?' Tuppence said, looking over at the woman. 'Do you think that's her father?'

'Whoever it is, they've clearly been here before. Look at that.' Hen glanced to the waitress, whose previous air of disdain had been replaced with a Uriah Heep style subservience as she led them to a recently cleared table at the far end of the courtyard.

'I for one am not in the mood to find out. I think it's time to go.' JM effortlessly folded her map back into its original shape.

'I concur.' Hen unwound Brandon's lead from around her chair leg.

'Yes,' Tuppence agreed in a loud voice, as she scrambled to her feet. 'I'll just put my *very* harmless address book away in my bag.'

Ginny followed her friends inside to pay. When they returned, Sterling and the older man were deep in conversation, for which Ginny was heartily pleased.

It might not be a murder case, but she had no desire to get tangled up with the police ever again.

NINE

The old sandstone church was exactly where Ginny had left it, still nestled along a tree-lined street, filled with lovely cottages. And, thankfully, there was no sign of any police tape. Or, for that matter, any police.

That's a relief.

Connor had looked online last night and found an article mentioning that SOCO had finished their investigation, and while she trusted his internet skills better than her own, it was still good to see it was true. Especially after their earlier sighting of the formidable DI Sterling.

'It doesn't look like much of a crime scene.' Tuppence frowned as they stood in front of the lychgate.

'The garden where the skull was found is down the side. But Colin brought it over to where we're standing,' Ginny explained, though her friend was right. The perfect green grass didn't look like it had been trampled on, let alone scuffed by numerous boots walking over it. Either the police had been very careful, or St Luke's had an excellent caretaker. Or... just like the delicious scones and meticulous table settings at the Weaver's Tearoom... the church was part of Walton-on-Marsh's evolved perfection.

'Hmmm, let's see what we have here.' Tuppence dropped to her knees and touched the ground with the tip of her finger, before holding it to her nose and inhaling. Then she wrinkled her brow and stood. 'We should have brought Brandon with us. He might've been able to sniff something out.'

Ginny wasn't so sure about that. And more to the point, she would hate if Brandon started digging up the garden the same way Colin had. 'Maybe we should start by talking with someone, and see if we can look around the gardens,' she suggested, pleased the heavy oak doors of the church were slightly ajar.

'Roger that,' Tuppence agreed, and they walked along the path. It was another warm day, and it was nice to step into the coolness of the church. There was no sign of the white flowers that had been draped along the pews or the large urns that had flanked the altar.

She came to a halt at a noticeboard. Just above it was a small brass plaque.

ST LUKE'S BELOVED LADY CHAPEL WAS RESTORED THANKS TO
THE GENEROUS SUPPORT OF THE
FAULKNER CHARITABLE TRUST

2010

Connor had mentioned that Annabel Faulkner insisted the ceremony was held at this church. Clearly there was a close family connection. She and Tuppence began walking towards the Lady chapel but stopped as faint voices came from the back. With a silent nod at one another, they headed towards a door in the panelling.

It led through to a spacious kitchen. Unlike other church kitchens that Ginny had seen, this was modern with small white tiles running up the walls, and wide marble-topped benches. The fragrant scent of fresh lavender filled the air and Ginny breathed it in, feeling the tension in her shoulders loosening.

Around one of those benches were the same four women from the high street, their Chanel suits hidden beneath heavy canvas aprons complete with leather straps over the shoulders. They were gathered around a huge wicker basket of flowers and either hadn't heard them enter or were too engrossed in their work to break off.

Ginny paused, but Tuppence boldly walked towards the group, her Crocs squeaking on the floor.

They finally looked up, like meerkats surveying the tundra, before one woman stepped forward. She seemed impossibly delicate, with light wrinkles around her dark eyes, but no silver or grey in her black hair, which had been styled into a rigid beehive.

Ginny now recognised her. She'd been at the wedding and had been standing with the rector and the photographer. And it was clear by her sharp glare that the woman recognised Ginny as well. She gulped, not liking their chances of finding much out. However, Tuppence didn't seem to notice the frosty reception and just held out her hand.

'Hello there. I'm Tuppence and this is my friend, Ginny.'

'I see,' the woman replied, her accent sounding like she'd stepped out from behind a 1950s BBC news desk. When Tuppence continued to smile, the woman let out a reluctant sigh. 'I'm Cynthia Eagle-Edwards. If you're here to join the flower team, I'm afraid that we're not currently taking volunteers.'

'That's okay, we're far too busy for that,' Tuppence explained, in a sunny voice. 'We volunteer at Little Shaw cemetery, though it's mainly weeding and litter patrol.'

'Little Shaw?' The second woman grimaced.

'Litter?' The third one coughed, as if it was a foreign concept that she'd never heard of before. Maybe no one littered in Walton-on-Marsh. It would explain why it was so chocolate-boxy.

Cynthia gave the other two women a quelling look and then stepped forward, arms wide as if trying to herd Ginny and Tuppence back towards the door. 'If you don't want to volunteer, then why are you here? If it's to see Rector Hedley, then I'm afraid he won't be back until four o'clock. It's been a... trying... week for us all.' Cynthia let out a pained sniff.

'That's exactly why we're here,' Tuppence ploughed on. 'To ask you all about the skull.'

'The—' Cynthia choked and turned away. The three other women immediately comforted her.

Oh dear. This isn't going well.

'We do understand how stressful it must have been for everyone at the church,' Ginny added, hoping it would smooth things over.

'Stressful?' the fourth woman shot back. 'Do you realise we had to cancel last Sunday's service, and our poor organist hasn't stopped crying? She's played at over two hundred weddings and isn't used to such carrying-on. And the rector has hardly slept, because he's been so worried about the congregation. And it's all because of *that* dreadful family.'

'Dreadful?' Tuppence interjected. 'I think you need to take that back. It's one thing to blame the curse, but to say this has anything to do with the Wests is just cruel.'

To Ginny's surprise Cynthia flushed and bowed her head. 'I'm sorry, that was uncalled for. But like I said, it's been a trying week. We're not used to anything like this.'

'I think it's safe to say that none of us are,' Ginny said.

'Except you, Ginny,' Tuppence helpfully pointed out. 'After all, you did study archaeology and have been on several digs. Which is what got us wondering how Lesley... er... I mean, the skull might have got there.'

'How it got there?' Woman two let out a distressed wail, her eyes going wide.

'Exactly.' Tuppence bobbed her head, her grey curls spiralling out around her. 'Do you think someone put it there on purpose?'

'What are you trying to say?' woman three demanded.

'I'm not *trying* to say anything. I just want to know if the skull was there to break up the wedding,' Tuppence explained in a patient voice. 'Of course, it could be the curse... but for now we're putting that theory on hold. However, if you do have any thoughts on that aspect, please feel free to share them.'

A series of emotions flickered across Cynthia's face, as if she wasn't sure where to start. Ginny swallowed and gave Tuppence an apologetic smile. Despite the bluntness, it had been a good attempt at starting the conversation, but it seemed the women of Walton-on-Marsh disagreed.

Ginny's own attempts at interviewing witnesses for information had given her mixed results. Some people had been happy to share what they knew, but others had been less so. She pressed her lips together and studied the flowers on the bench, suddenly recognising some of the white dahlias and eucalyptus leaves from Saturday.

'Oh, what a clever idea to reuse them. I was thinking how beautiful they were and what a pity that—' She broke off, not wanting to steer the conversation the wrong way again. 'I mean, it's nice they aren't getting thrown out.'

Cynthia's frosty expression melted slightly. 'Thank you. Part of our mission at the Walton Marshigolds is to advocate for sustainable floral arrangements.'

'That's commendable.' Ginny nodded, trying not to think about all the hairspray that was holding Cynthia's elaborate style in place. After all, everyone was on their own journey.

Then she remembered her encounter with Lady Kitty and how much she supported local charities, and their donation to the church. 'I imagine that Sir Spencer must approve of what you're doing.'

'Oh yes. Sir Spencer and Lady Kitty are huge supporters of our work.'

'And what about Annabel Faulkner?' Ginny tentatively asked, thinking of the conversation JM had overheard. If Annabel had been talking about Lady Kitty, did that mean other people were as well? 'Do you know her?'

At the mention of Annabel's name Cynthia's face completely closed, her haughty expression slipping smoothly back on. 'I think it's time you leave.'

Ginny sighed. Maybe they should have gone with JM and returned the gifts. They might have had more luck. She turned to Tuppence so they could take their leave, but her friend was staring at a small surveillance camera perched above a very modern-looking fridge. There was a second camera by the exterior door and a third one trained directly out of the window and onto the side garden, where the skull had been buried.

Ginny let out a gasp at what her friend had discovered. Then she turned to Cynthia, who was still glaring at them, looking as if she'd swallowed a lemon.

'How often does the CCTV footage get checked? Is it possible that whoever was responsible for the skull was caught on camera?'

'Do the police know about it?' Tuppence added, as she joined Ginny.

'There's nothing to know. The cameras don't work,' the second woman snapped, before clamping her mouth shut under Cynthia's withering glare.

'What do you mean, they don't work?' Tuppence frowned.

A tiny muscle in Cynthia's jaw began to tick, as if she was a bomb about to go off, but then she sighed and walked over to five large glass jars filled with an array of home-baked slices and biscuits that made Ginny's jar of Hobnobs seem rather average. She patted them then glanced back at the cameras.

'We only have the cameras there to stop Sam Griffen from helping himself to the Sunday School snacks.'

'He doesn't even bother to take his work boots off,' the third woman chimed in, before also receiving one of Cynthia's icy glares.

Cynthia then turned and firmly shepherded Ginny and Tuppence towards the door that led out to the grounds. 'Now, I really do need you to leave. And if you don't, I'll be calling Detective Inspector Sterling, who is not just a member of our congregation but a close personal friend.'

Ginny peered over to Tuppence and gave her a quick nod before they both made their way out of the church kitchen and to the side garden.

The CCTV cameras might not have been working, but Cynthia and the three other women were all crowded in the doorway, watching them, which meant there was no chance to inspect the area where the skull had been found.

Not that Ginny had been very hopeful, since she couldn't imagine SOCO missing much.

'Well, that was a bust.' Tuppence wrinkled her nose as they reached the lychgate. 'Maybe I should have let you do all the talking?'

'Don't be silly. Sometimes the direct approach is the way to go. Though, I don't think they would've told us anything no matter how we asked them. What we really needed was someone from Walton-on-Marsh to ask on our behalf.'

'Goodness, that would be an even more impossible task.' Tuppence snorted.

'I agree.' Ginny sighed as a man in his seventies appeared from behind a tree. His white hair was smoothed down and his face was weathered from years outside.

He carefully peered around then, to Ginny's amazement, suddenly gestured for them to join him. She blinked. There was something familiar about him, then she remembered where she'd seen him.

He'd been at the wedding, pushing a wheelbarrow and muttering to himself.

And he hadn't looked happy.

'What do you want?' Tuppence asked, but Ginny touched her friend's arm to stop her from charging over. If the man worked in the garden, he could very well have been the one to lead Colin to the skull. Or, had Colin interrupted the man as he'd been digging? Then she frowned. It was hard to know how the criminal mind worked, but trying to bury a skull in the middle of a society wedding seemed far-fetched.

'Shhhh.' The man stepped closer to the tree and again gestured them over. 'Don't want them to know I'm talking to you.'

At the mention of 'them' Ginny raised an eyebrow. Did he mean Cynthia Eagle-Edwards and company? Some of her caution dissipated and she lowered her voice so only Tuppence could hear. 'I think we should find out what he wants.'

'Excellent,' Tuppence agreed, and they made their way down the immaculate gravel path.

The tree trunk was wide and kept the man hidden from the church entrance. He was wearing navy trousers and a white T-shirt, and his work boots were covered in dry grass.

'You must be Sam Griffen. I saw you at the wedding on Saturday.' Ginny held out her hand and made the introductions.

'That's right,' he said in a gruff voice, as he thrust out his hand first to Ginny and then to Tuppence. 'Nice to meet you both.'

'You too,' Ginny automatically replied, before remembering

they were hiding behind a large tree with a man they didn't know. She straightened her spine. 'What's this about, Sam?'

He swallowed, his Adam's apple bobbing in his throat. 'It's 'bout what happened on Saturday. Been looking after this garden for forty years and never had anything like it.'

'And from the look in your eyes, you have something to tell us. Do you know how the skull got there?' Tuppence asked, with an encouraging nod.

'Aye,' he replied, before peering around the tree trunk one last time. 'I have a good idea of *who* put it there. And when.'

'What?' Tuppence squealed, and then put a hand over her mouth, as if worried she'd been overheard.

'Who was it?' Ginny asked in a quieter voice.

'It's Colleen Murphy's girl, Gemma. Calls herself an "influencer".' This last word was accompanied by air quotes.

Tuppence straightened up, eyes bright. 'Oh, that's exciting. I've always wanted to meet one in real life. What's her area of expertise? I'm partial to one called Flying Bolts. It's this chap from Bradford who buys second-hand cars and blows them up. I wonder if that's what she does?'

Sam blinked and rubbed his brow and even Ginny was confused. Why would someone try to blow up a second-hand car, and how could that influence people? Then she caught herself. *Now isn't the time.*

'What was Gemma doing here?' she asked instead.

'She often came at night looking for ghosts and talking about the history of Walton-on-Marsh.'

'Ah. A paranormal investigator.' Tuppence nodded in understanding. 'Not my usual interest but I will have to look her up. So, what happened? Did you see this Gemma burying the skull? I wonder if it was on a full moon. Could have been a ritual.'

'No idea. She was often filming at night, but I never paid much attention. Unlike *that* lot.' He nodded towards the kitchen. 'They didn't like it. Neither did the rector, but not much they could do about it. And she seemed harmless enough.'

'Why do you think she was involved?'

'Two weeks ago, I was walking back from the pub and saw her leaving. But as well as having her tripod and camera gear, she also had a shovel.'

Ginny let out a soft gasp. 'Have you told the police?'

Sam nodded, but didn't look happy. 'I told one of the PCs, and that they might find something on that camera in the kitchen window.'

'And what did they say?'

He frowned. 'Nothing. They didn't seem interested.'

Ginny and Tuppence exchanged a look. Did the police know that the camera didn't work, or was it because the Faulkners had made it clear that they were happy the wedding had been cancelled?

'Could someone have paid Gemma to put the skull there?' Ginny said.

'Someone like Annabel Faulkner?' Tuppence added. 'Or Digby Theakston?'

Sam sighed. 'Let's just say I don't think anyone in Walton-on-Marsh is upset that it happened—'

He was cut off by the sound of voices drifting over from the church doors as Cynthia Eagle-Edwards and her three companions stepped out. Sam immediately stiffened.

'We won't keep you any longer. But thank you for letting us know.'

'Seemed only right,' he said, as he stepped further away from them. 'Tell the little bride I'm sorry.'

'We will,' Tuppence assured him, and then grinned. 'And by the way, Sam, none of those cameras in the kitchen work. Which means if you ever feel peckish after all the work you do... you should help yourself to something to eat. Like a biscuit.'

'Or two,' Ginny added.

His eyes widened and then a slow grin spread across his face. 'You know what? I think I'll do just that.' And then he was gone, slowly ambling back down the side of the church, no doubt to where those five glass jars were waiting.

Ginny and Tuppence grimly exchanged a smile. It was the least they could do to repay him for their first lead.

TEN

'Ain't you two a sight for sore eyes.' Slim walked up to the issues counter and grinned at Ginny and Connor, who were in the process of turning on the computers and setting up for the day. 'I was starting to think my volunteering days were at an end. Which would've been a pity because my case worker is a lot happier now that I'm what she calls "gainfully distracted" from the temptations of my previous life.'

'You mean she's happy you're no longer nicking stuff,' Connor retorted, and Slim grinned.

'Your words, my friend. Your words. But in a nutshell, yes.'

'Was there a problem? Did something happen while I wasn't here?' Ginny did a quick scan of the library for clues, while trying not to think of all the disasters that might have taken place in a single day. There was no visible damage, but what if the petty cash had been lost? Or someone locked in the toilets? Or—

'I don't see how.' Connor gave him a sceptical look. 'Yesterday was hot, which means it should've been dead in here.'

'Yeah, it was... and that Harold was the one to deliver the final blow.' Slim sat down on the edge of the counter and peered over to see what they were doing. 'Remind me not to put my name down to work on any day that he's in here.'

Oh dear.

It hadn't occurred to Ginny that Harold and her newest volunteer might have clashed, but now it was too easy to see how different the men were. She wasn't sure she wanted to know. But Connor clearly did.

'Mr Rowe's an acquired taste, but he's okay. What happened? He didn't give you a quiz on cross-referencing, did he? I got one of them when he first came back to the library.'

'No, but it just proves he can kill the fun in any room.' Slim shook his head in disgust before jumping back off the counter. 'He refused to let me eat my sardines in the staffroom. Said it stunk the place out because I put them in the microwave. Then he complained about me and William just because I was having a laugh with the old fella.'

Ginny sighed. Slim's idea of having a laugh could be anything from drawing a moustache on William's face when he was sleeping, through to pretending to be a flat earther, and she made a mental note to check in with William and Harold. *Oh, and to clean the microwave.*

She bit back a yawn and tried to focus. She usually spent her day off pottering around her house, tending the garden and curling up with a book and cup of tea. But yesterday had been non-stop, and after a quick meal, she'd spent the evening going through the influencer's channel.

It was called 'Gemma M Gets Real' and according to the bio, she was a twenty-something truth seeker who 'just knew' there was more out there than science could explain. She made heavy use of the skull and heart emojis in her writing; somewhat randomly, she was also a yoga teacher and ran classes three times a week.

The videos consisted of Gemma talking about the numerous ghosts of Walton-on-Marsh while she did things like walk her dog, go out for a cup of tea and open parcels containing clothing, perfume and make-up. She was lovely-looking, with large dark eyes and thick auburn hair and a lean figure that suited all the outfits she received.

Then there were also videos of Gemma at night. Most of them involved walking through open fields, inspecting gravestones and standing outside crumbling ruins talking to the camera in a hushed voice.

There had been no mention of her physical address, which Ginny knew was quite common, for safety reasons. The only details she could find was the address of the yoga studio, which wasn't open on a Saturday, leaving her at a standstill.

Various messages throughout the evening revealed that her friends hadn't fared much better in their endeavours from yesterday, either. Not even JM, with her powerful personality, could get anything from the wedding guests as she returned the gifts. It was the same story with Lesley and Terrence Charlton's old neighbours, too.

Ginny pushed away her fatigue and smiled at Slim. 'I'll make sure you're not on the rota if he has to stand in for one of us again,' she promised, as Cleo and Andrea walked through the front door. 'Why don't you have a cup of tea while we finish getting set up?'

'Don't mind if I do... hey, wait up, you two.' Slim joined Cleo and Andrea as they headed towards the staffroom in a cloud of chatter.

'Poor Mr Rowe.' Connor pressed his lips tight, as if to stop from laughing. 'We should've warned him about Slim.'

'I'm not sure who I feel the sorriest for, Slim or Harold,' Ginny admitted, as she typed in the computer password. Then her smile slipped as she took in Connor's tired face. 'How did it go yesterday at Grace's flat? I was hoping to see her this morning, but she'd already left the house for a jog when I came downstairs.'

'She does that when she's stressed. I think it went okay. She was worried about seeing Theo, but it turns out he's gone away for a couple of nights to clear his head.'

'Yes, that's what we discovered yesterday when we went to Walton-on-Marsh.' Ginny told him what happened, including their accidental admission. 'He hadn't told his family about Grace calling off the wedding, so I'm afraid we put our foot in it. Jacinta was very surprised, and Annabel was—' She broke off, not wanting to tell Connor how thrilled Theo's mother had looked.

'Let me guess. She was dancing a jig,' Connor said in a dry voice. 'I hoped Nan and Joey were looking for demons when there were none, but if the old guy from the church is right about seeing someone leaving the garden with a spade, it doesn't bode well.'

'I agree. But I don't think we should say anything to your grandmother until we've spoken to Gemma. I'd hate to cause trouble without all the facts.'

'Yeah, I wouldn't put it past Nan to do something crazy. And it would only stress Grace out more. What's the plan? Are you going to talk with Gemma?'

'I want to, but we haven't been able to find her address. As well as doing her influencing, she works in a yoga studio. It seems an odd combination.'

'Having multiple income streams and side hustles seems to be the thing these days.'

It was? Ginny often found having one job exhausting so was pleased it wasn't something she had to do. Then she realised that in a way she *did* have a side hustle. Just not one that paid.

'Do you want me to see what I can find out?'

Ginny nodded. 'Yes, please. The yoga studio isn't open until Monday, so JM, Hen and Tuppence will go along, but

I'd rather speak to her sooner. Unless you know her, of course.'

'Never heard of her. Though it's not the kind of thing I'm into,' Connor admitted, as he typed her name into the computer and brought up her channel. He shuddered at an image of Gemma standing next to a gravestone wearing a long black veil and holding a candle. 'Yeah, not my vibe. Anyway, leave it with me.'

He began to type as Andrea returned from the staff room. It was time to open the doors for the day.

Once things had settled into the usual morning routine, Ginny headed out to the stacks at the back of the library. They were only accessed down a small lane, and it's where they kept some of the older books as well as the newspapers and other reference material that couldn't fit on the floor.

She unlocked the security door and stepped inside. The storage space had been almost destroyed by a fire, but after months of repair work it was once again usable. Unfortunately, parts of the collection had been smoke-damaged and disposed of, but the newspaper archives had survived.

Not that they had any copies of the *Walton-on-Marsh Gazette*, which she hadn't realised even existed until William brought in a copy. But hopefully the local papers might have information about Lesley Charlton, Annabel Faulkner and Digby and Jacinta Theakston.

Ginny stacked up as many copies as she could fit on the trolley and went back to the library proper.

By lunchtime, however, she was ready to admit defeat. Not that she knew what she was looking for; just any article with the headlines: *Please Read for Some Very Useful Information.* Strangely enough, nothing had materialised, and she sent a text to her friends, who had decided to ask their neighbours what they remembered about Lesley's murder.

JM immediately replied.

Nothing from us. Time for Plan B

Ginny swallowed, hating that there wasn't a Plan B.

Next to her, Connor tapped his foot as he worked. His mouth was tight with concentration and he was frowning. Despite the frustration of not having any contact information for Gemma Murphy, Ginny felt better that it hadn't just been her.

Slim, who had been entertaining a group of young mothers who met every Saturday to play Dungeons and Dragons, returned to the counter with the handbooks and dice. He peered over Connor's shoulder. 'Still no luck?'

'Not yet, but I'm determined to find it.' Connor frowned again and tapped something else into the keyboard.

'Looks complicated to me.'

'If you've got an easier way, I'd love to know,' Connor said, sounding unusually gruff, but Slim just grinned and patted him on the shoulder.

'Computers are your thing, not mine. But there's always an easier way. You wouldn't believe the number of times I've seen some fool trying to squeeze through a top-floor window because they didn't think to check under the doormat for the key.'

Connor raised an eyebrow. 'Not on my estate they don't.'

'Yeah, but no one's going to nick anything from the Hilton now, are they?' Slim said, using the nickname for Connor's estate. 'We don't play in our own backyard, if you know what I mean.' Then he gave an apologetic wave of his hand. 'Er, I mean in my past life, obviously. Though now I think about it, I should write all that down. For my book. Mind if I finish a few minutes early, boss?'

'Of course not. And thanks for doing the Dungeons and Dragons.' Ginny smiled, wondering if he knew that once upon a time the library key had been underneath a rock by the door, in one of the worst-kept secrets of Little Shaw.

He coloured. 'It's nothing. Turns out I have a knack for table-top role-playing games, thanks to my out-of-the-box thinking.' He wandered away, jotting things down in his notebook.

'I don't believe it,' Connor muttered, looking up from the computer and glancing over at Slim's retreating figure.

Ginny peered at the screen. 'Did you find something?'

'I think so. Which means Slim is a genius. I'm just not sure if it's for good or evil.'

'Good,' Ginny assured him, though took a cautious breath in case whatever Connor found involved house-breaking. 'What have you got?'

'I've been going through Gemma's videos and realised that every Saturday afternoon she has a segment called "Spill the Tea with Gemma" where she sits in a pub and talks about... well, I'm not really sure what. And why talk about tea when she's in a pub?'

'It does seem like a missed opportunity,' Ginny admitted. 'I don't suppose you know what pub she films in?'

He flashed a rare smile. 'Actually, I do. I zoomed in and caught the name on the menu. And there is a big clock in the background with the time. It's called the Fresh Fields and is in Walton-on-Marsh. She seems to be there from three in the afternoon until at least six in the evening.'

'Connor, that's brilliant.' Ginny checked the time. It was almost two o'clock, which meant it was closing time. And after that, she and her friends could find out just what the young influencer had been doing at the church.

ELEVEN

Saturday, 2nd August

Fresh Fields pub was an airy building with huge windows overlooking the Walton-on-Marsh canal. It was filled with summer tourists enthusiastically admiring the view. And there, in the corner, checking her make-up by using a mirror app on her phone, was a girl in her mid-twenties with a swishy auburn ponytail and full lips.

Gemma Murphy.

'Connor was right,' Hen whispered as they stepped inside. 'It almost seems too easy.'

'I'm okay with easy,' Ginny said, as they both made their way across the busy pub. JM, feeling that her interrogation powers hadn't fully returned since yesterday's visit to the rival village, had opted to do more genealogy research, while Tuppence had volunteered to keep watching Gemma's YouTube clips, looking for hidden messages. It was a task that none of them envied.

'Good point. I didn't mean to jinx us,' Hen said, as they reached Gemma's table.

'These chairs are taken. Go somewhere else.' Gemma didn't look up from what she was doing, and her voice didn't sound nearly as bright and chirpy as it did in her videos. It was hard to tell if she was being rude because they were from Little Shaw, or because she was having a bad day. Either way, it wasn't a promising start.

'Of course. We just have a few questions to ask you.' Hen gave her a motherly smile and put down her knitting bag. Then she wrinkled her nose and fanned her face. 'Gosh, I need a cool drink. What about you, Gemma? Can I get you anything?'

'What the hell? How do you know my name?' Gemma put down her phone and gave them a flinty stare. One eye was coated in thick black mascara-ed lashes and eyeliner, while the other was much smaller, but a lot more natural-looking.

'Sorry, we didn't mean to scare you,' Ginny apologised, and quickly sat down as heads turned in their direction. They'd attracted quite enough attention yesterday and she didn't want a repeat of that. 'We know you record your show today, so we'll make this short. But if you would like a drink, we'd be happy to get you one.'

'It's not bribery, you understand, because that's morally a grey area, so we try not to go there. I'm Hen, by the way, and this is Ginny.'

Gemma's jaw went slack as she gave them both a piercing glare before finally shrugging. 'Fine. Tell them you want a Gemma Special. They know me here. I didn't think I had any fans in your demographic,' she added, before returning to her make-up.

Ginny, who didn't manage much more than sunscreen and lipstick every day, watched in fascination as Gemma expertly applied the second lot of lashes and then set about adding a huge amount of mascara. She tried several times to make small talk, but Gemma didn't give any indication she'd heard, and it was a relief when Hen returned with a table number and two lemon, lime and soda waters.

'Whatever the Gemma Special is, it needs to be delivered separately,' Hen explained, before slipping into the spare chair. 'So, what did I miss?'

'I have *no* idea,' Gemma retorted, as she glared again at Ginny. Clearly the attempt at small talk had not been successful. 'What's this about? Because if you want to discuss a sponsorship deal then you need to go through the proper channels. And, no offense, but I don't think any of your products would suit me.'

'We're not here about that,' Ginny said. 'It's about what happened last week at St Luke's church.'

Gemma's eyes flickered with interest. 'You mean Lesley Charlton's skull.'

'So you've heard about it.' Hen fixed Gemma with a piercing look as she retrieved her knitting and got to work on the blanket she was halfway through.

'Of course I've heard about it. I'm the fifth biggest paranormal influencer in Lancashire, so it's my business to know. It's one of my open cases that I've been reporting on for the last two years, and my fans have been clamouring for more information. This is a very important moment for me.' Gemma narrowed her eyes. 'I hope you don't want to come onto my podcast to discuss it. You're both way too old.'

'No, I'd be far too nervous to do anything like that,' Hen admitted. 'Though our friend Tuppence would probably love it. She adores YouTube.'

Gemma's eyes filled with horror but before she could reply the waitress brought over a cocktail glass with Gemma's name written along the side in gold lettering. The drink was pale yellow with a layer of froth covering the surface. The influencer paused to take a photo of it then put down her phone.

'Thanks, babes. I'll post it tonight,' Gemma promised the

waitress and then turned back to Ginny and Tuppence impatiently. 'You have five minutes to tell me what this is about. I need to do my pre-recording routine. It's very important that I'm feeling calm and balanced. That's the secret to how I connect with my viewers. But between you and the fact my videographer is late, my vibration levels are a mess.'

Ginny didn't feel up to asking about vibration levels or videographers so just smiled and took a deep breath. 'Two weeks ago, the caretaker at St Luke's church saw you leaving there at night with a shovel.'

'That guy is dead old. He probably got muddled up.' Gemma shrugged, though some of the colour left her face.

'He's not that old,' Hen protested. 'Well, I don't think he is.'

'Everyone over thirty looks old to me,' Gemma retorted. 'Why are you asking about this?'

'We're trying to discover *how* the skull got there,' Ginny admitted, starting to feel exhausted by the conversation before they'd even begun. 'Do you know Theo Faulkner or Grace West?'

'Do I look like I know them?'

'That's not really an answer.' Hen's brow furrowed and Ginny sighed. Was Gemma purposely trying to evade the questions, or was she just naturally obtuse?

As Gemma smirked and took a sip of her cocktail, despite herself, Ginny wondered if the young woman would still be smiling if Maureen West was the one asking the questions. *No.* Ginny shuddered. It was far better that they kept going than risk letting the terrifying matriarch loose.

'You grew up in Walton-on-Marsh, so you must have at least met Theo,' Ginny tried again.

'Must I?' Gemma gave her a hard smile.

'It does stand to reason,' Hen encouraged, her needles clacking faster and faster.

'If you say so.' Gemma shrugged.

Hen and Ginny exchanged a perplexed look. This was not going well.

'How do you think Lesley's skull got there?' Ginny asked instead, and almost cheered when Gemma's eyes brightened with interest.

'Could be the curse. We all know it works in mysterious ways, and since the bride was from Little Shaw, maybe Lesley Charlton's ghost was trying to warn her off?'

'We did consider that,' Hen agreed. 'Did you hear about the person who went to buy a cabbage?'

'OMG, yes. They totally disappeared. So freaky. I've been telling my viewers for *years* that the curse is really a dark power out for vengeance.' Gemma's eyes sparkled with drama.

'Vengeance?' Ginny said in surprise. 'Against who?'

'Against anyone who dares to cross it. There's so much we don't know about what happens on the other side of the veil. That is why what I do is *so* important,' Gemma said, before her mask of indifference suddenly reappeared. 'Now, your five minutes are up. I have to finish getting ready. I'm doing a live Q and A today.' She picked up a large red leather tote bag and rummaged around in it before withdrawing a set of headphones.

The bag was familiar, and Ginny's skin prickled with recognition. Then she peered down to Gemma's feet, where perfectly manicured toenails were peeping out from a pair of red heeled sandals that matched the bag.

They were identical to the ones from the upmarket boutique that Jacinta Theakston owned.

The hairs on her arms stood up and her mind whirled. Gemma and Jacinta were roughly the same age and while they seemed unlikely friends, that didn't mean they weren't.

Is this a connection?

'How long have you known Jacinta for?' Ginny asked

abruptly, hoping the change in tack might surprise Gemma into giving them a straight answer.

It did not.

'Jacinta who?' Gemma blinked, though her mouth puckered in a way that suggested she was hiding something. 'I have no idea who that is.'

'She owns Coco, which is the shop where your sandals and handbag came from.'

'Oh. How extraordinary.' Hen squeaked then turned to Gemma. 'Ginny's ever so clever at piecing things together. Are you sure you don't know her?'

'One hundred per cent,' Gemma growled, her face turning into a hard mask as she dropped the red bag back onto the floor. 'Now, I'm very busy. With all the extra interest in Lesley Charlton it's important that I don't lose any traction. Do you know that three of my videos are going viral because of it? Speaking of which, there is the videographer.'

Ginny watched as a harassed, middle-aged man made his way across the pub, his shoulder straining under a bag of equipment. He didn't look delighted to be there.

'He doesn't seem happy,' Hen commented. 'That can't be good for your vibration levels.'

'God, no. Ted is. The. Worst. And costs an absolute fortune just because he once worked for the BBC. He needs to get over his inflated sense of self and accept that his best days are behind him.'

Ginny pressed her lips together to stop herself from saying something rude. But really, Gemma did not seem like a nice person. She got to her feet. 'Thank you for speaking to us.'

'I'm used to the public wanting to spend time with me.' Gemma's sharp gaze raked over them, then she produced a business card with a photograph of herself wearing skintight workout gear, her auburn hair gleaming like a new penny. 'Take this. If you book six classes, you can get a ten per cent discount. And... no offence, but you could use some core strengthening.'

'I'm not sure that's necessary,' Hen protested. 'We do Senior Shake and Shuffle. Well... we keep missing the classes, but we'll be there on Thursday.'

'What a stupid name.' Gemma pulled a face and got to her feet. 'Now, I really need to prepare. Ted... get your arse over here.'

It was a clear dismissal, so Ginny slipped the card into her handbag and hoped that Tuppence or JM had had a more successful afternoon.

It was after six by the time Ginny finally arrived home. She'd dropped Hen at her cottage, and they'd all arranged to meet at Tuppence's house the next day to see what else they could find out about Gemma, but right then she just wanted a bath and a cup of tea.

She opened the door to the scent of onions frying and the soft hum of classical music.

In the kitchen she found Edgar curled up in his basket as Grace stood over the hob, an apron covering her summer dress. Despite the smudges under her large eyes, she managed a wan smile.

'I hope you don't mind. Everyone has been so lovely dropping off cakes and sandwiches, but it feels like I haven't eaten a vegetable in years.'

'Of course not. It smells divine.' Ginny put her workbag on the floor, since the counter was filled with bunches of flowers and yet more cake tins. 'How are you?'

'Apart from being mortified that Nan has dragged you into this?' Grace said, some of her reserve seeming to fall away. Then she sighed and looked at the spot on her finger where her engagement ring had once been. 'I'm still lousy – second-guessing myself every moment of the day. Which is the other reason I wanted to cook something. I need to keep busy and my go-to is tidying up, but your house is so very neat.'

Ginny gave her a reluctant smile. 'I'm afraid you're not the only one who likes keeping busy.'

'Does it ever get easier?' Grace's voice was scratchy, like it was being dragged out of her across rocks.

Ginny swallowed, not sure she was the best person to answer that question. 'Yes,' she forced herself to say, then glanced over at the hob. 'And I'm pleased you're cooking. I want you to feel at home while you're here.'

'Thank you for everything.' Grace sniffed and turned down the heat on the onions. 'Connor told me you went to talk to a YouTuber.'

'That's right,' Ginny said, cautiously. So far, she hadn't dared ask Grace any questions, not wanting to cause her more pain than she was already experiencing. But after an hour in Gemma Murphy's company, it was clear they needed to try other avenues for information. 'Have you ever met Gemma? Or know if she's a friend of Theo's?'

'No, I'd never even heard of her until Connor sent me some of her videos. And if Theo knows her, he's never let on.' Anguish filled her eyes. 'Unless he was hiding it from me.'

'I'm sure that's not the case. But would you mind if I spoke to Theo about it? We're finding it very hard to get anyone in Walton-on-Marsh to tell us anything.'

Grace was silent, before finally nodding. 'If you think it will help.'

'I do. But I won't tell him anything about you... unless you want me to.'

'It's okay, I know you wouldn't.' Grace swallowed, her face still pale. It went paler still when the doorbell buzzed.

'That's probably someone else dropping off a care package for you. Would you like me to answer it?'

'Yes, please. Everyone's been so kind but it's quite draining to go over it again and again. Th-thank you.'

'Don't be silly. Why don't you pop upstairs while I see who it is?' Ginny waited until Grace had disappeared into the spare room before opening the front door to see a familiar figure with long purple hair holding a small glass bottle.

'Heather, how lovely to see you.' Ginny smiled. She'd always got on well with the lovely Irish woman who worked at the Lost Goat and who made the best Eccles cakes in the area. 'Sorry I haven't been into the pub in a while.'

'You're not alone.' Heather's mouth flattened out. 'The latest manager has some funny ideas on personal hygiene. I swear if things don't change soon, Mitch and I might have to start rethinking our career choices. Anyway, I heard Grace was staying here and brought her over a little something to help keep her spirits up.'

'That's very kind,' Ginny said, taking the outstretched bottle. The thick glass was warm in her hands and was filled with pale liquid that had tiny rose petals floating up the neck of the bottle. It was lovely but she had no idea what it was. Not to mention that Heather was famous for her baking. Her confusion must have shown on her face and Heather let out a soft laugh.

'Don't worry, it's not poison. It's mainly essential oils and some natural ingredients. And, of course, magic.'

'Magic?' Ginny's fingers slackened and she almost dropped the small vial.

'Yes, magic. My coven and I have been working on it for several days. It's a curse buster.'

'Oh,' Ginny managed to say. Living so close to Pendle where the witch trials had taken place, it wasn't uncommon to come across modern witches, but she hadn't realised Heather was one. Was that why her baking always tasted so marvellous? 'I didn't know there was such a thing.'

'Oh yes. We make a lot of them. Especially when Walton-on-Marsh has the strawberry festival. Quite a few of our locals love going, but of course can't go unprepared, so they'll order a few vials to keep them safe.'

'I see.' Ginny tightened her grip on the small bottle that was getting warmer in her hand. She liked to think of herself as open-minded, but she wasn't quite clear on how it could possibly work. Then again, since she didn't believe in the curse in the first place, it was likely a moot point. 'What did your coven say about the curse? How do they think it works?'

'Asher said it's because Walton-on-Marsh polluted the waterways and it's brought a darkness down on them, that they still try to project onto us.' Heather's smile faded and her silvery eyeshadow glittered. Then she shrugged. 'As for me, I think it's because they're entitled. Every now and then they'll come into the pub and act like they own the place. Though not Theo... he's lovely, and I hope things work out for them both.'

'I do as well.' Ginny tilted the bottle, admiring its contents. 'And if we could find out more about what Asher knows of the rivalry, I'd like to hear it.'

Heather's mouth twitched with a smile. 'I told Mitch you and the others would be trying to get to the bottom of this. He now owes me a week of foot massages.'

'*Trying* is the operative word,' Ginny admitted. 'We're not getting very far. Have you ever met someone called Gemma Murphy?'

At the mention of the name, Heather did an eye-roll. 'No, but I've heard of her. She tried to do a segment on our work, but we refused. What we do is important to us, not something to be mocked or monetised by anyone. Anyway, I'd better go – but give Grace my love.'

'I will,' Ginny promised and shut the door, not sure she should tell her friends about the visit. After all, things were frustrating enough already without adding magic to the equation.

TWELVE

Sunday, 3rd August

'Edgar, look how well the sweet peas are coming along.' Ginny stepped back from her vegetable patch the following morning. Edgar, who was lazily swiping a piece of grass with his paw, didn't bother to respond. In the last few months, Ginny had purposely curtailed the number of times she spoke out loud to her cat and her husband. Especially while Wallace's father, Ted, had been staying next door, since the man seemed to spend his entire visit doing DIY tasks in the back garden.

But with them both safely away in New Zealand and Grace out on a morning jog, Ginny felt free to chat to her heart's content.

'Besides, it's not like it's hurting anyone,' she added, before stripping off her gardening gloves and stepping into the coolness of the kitchen.

She'd been up for several hours doing housework and gardening, but needed to get ready for going to Tuppence's house.

It didn't take long to have a shower and throw on a pale blue linen dress with a loose shirt to protect her arms from the sun, and find her car keys. The small vial of oil that Heather had delivered last night still sat on the bench, nestled between the bouquets of flowers. To Ginny's relief Grace hadn't scoffed at it, instead sending the barmaid a text to say thank you and that she'd use it soon.

Ginny supposed there were worse things she could be trying to help with the grief. Then she checked her hair and headed for the front door, only to be stopped by Edgar, who let out an annoyed meow and nudged her back towards his full food bowl. Up until three days ago it had been his favourite brand of food, but he'd suddenly taken exception to it, and had no issues about letting her know.

'I'm not sure you fully understand the concept of food insecurity.' She topped up his water and stepped outside.

Edgar followed her and defiantly jumped up onto her neighbour's white car again.

Ginny decided that Wallace could fight his own battles and said goodbye to her non-responsive cat. She drove to the lovely slate-roofed cottage that had been in Tuppence's family for many years. Outside were three other silver cars, and Ginny pulled up next to them, hurrying to the open door that led into a short hallway.

As usual, it took her breath away. Large trees had been painted onto both the walls, with the bird-filled canopy spreading out across the ceiling, making Ginny feel like she was stepping into a jungle. Woven through the giant roots near the floor were discarded pieces of plastic, drink bottles and chocolate wrappers that twisted up the tree trunks like barbed wire. It was one of the many murals that Tuppence's late husband, Taron, had done, both in the house and around Lancashire.

'Oh, you're here. Excellent, we've just made a pot of tea.' Tuppence appeared in the doorway that led through to the lounge area. Her feet were bare, and Brandon was at her heels, looking very at home in the small cottage.

Ginny followed her friend through to a sun-drenched room with a large television on the wall and two brightly coloured sofas facing each other. Her friend had spent the last few months re-upholstering them and Ginny admired the stunning print and the careful piping along the arms. She doubted she'd have the patience to do anything like that.

Hen and JM were on one sofa looking glum as the sound of Gemma's YouTube channel played in the background.

'Is everything okay?' She sat across from them, her brow already furrowing.

'You mean apart from having to sit inside to watch rubbish, when we could be at the cemetery, gardening?' JM scowled. 'Makes me pleased I don't own a television.'

'It's not my cup of tea, either,' Hen admitted, before brightening. 'Speaking of which, I'll play mother. Maybe we just need some caffeine for it all to make sense.'

'I think it's going to take more than a cup of tea,' Tuppence admitted, turning back towards the screen. 'I'm going to suggest she watch a few of Flying Bolt's episodes. Might give her some pointers.'

'And I might suggest she stops indulging in so much fast fashion, or endless plugging of products,' JM grumbled, before taking the cup of tea that Hen held out. 'If she's so interested in the supernatural, she could at least mention it more.'

'Her speciality subject seems to be talking about nothing,' Hen admitted. 'By the time we left her yesterday I had no idea if she'd told us anything useful. Ginny couldn't get anything from her... and we all know how good she is at interviewing.'

'I wouldn't say that,' Ginny protested. They'd already filled their friends in on the disastrous interview, and Tuppence had put the details into the address book. Not that they had many details. Just an expensive red bag and sandals that might have come from Jacinta's store. 'We couldn't get a straight answer out of her.'

'Sounds like she's a politician in the making.' JM huffed. 'Which means what is coming next is going to be painful.'

'Very. I watched over two hours of videos yesterday and I like to think I'm very liberal in my tastes. Still, I suppose we need to finish watching the rest of them.' Tuppence sighed, and Ginny settled into the sofa as they all focused on Gemma Murphy.

Her thick hair was pulled back from her face as she leaned over a neglected headstone and pointed at a well-weathered stone skull with chiselled wings coming out from each side. The camera zoomed in as Gemma chatted in an excited voice.

'How cool is this winged skull? Below you can see the Latin phrase, *Memento mori*, and regular viewers to my channel will know how much this resonates with me. I mean, come on – it is just so powerful. *Remember you must die*. I get goosebumps every time.' On cue, she peeled up her well-fitting crop top to reveal a tattoo of a skull, along with the Latin phrase. The camera hovered for several beats before panning back to Gemma's smiling face.

'This was done by my favourite tattoo artist, DoctorInkGuy-Guru, and for this week only, you can get a ten per cent discount there. The links and code are below in the comments section. But now... let's get back to business...'

'I'm tempted to get my own tattoo. I think it will say: *Please, kill me now*,' JM grumbled as Gemma chatted away in the background about the symbolism of Death's head. 'How many more of these are left to watch?'

'Four hundred and twenty-three.' Tuppence grimaced.

'Then I suppose we'd better get our sugar levels up.' Hen passed around a plate of biscuits then squared her shoulders, as if preparing to go into battle. 'Let's get this over and done with.'

The next half hour passed in a strange blur as they watched

Gemma drape herself over different gravestones, all with skulls carved into them. But occasionally she would discuss serial killers and unsolved mysteries in the same cheery sing-song voice she used for everything. There were several shots of her walking along paths at night and one of her standing on a giant boulder, holding her arms up to the starless sky.

Ginny reached for another biscuit as the next video came up. In it, Gemma stood outside an old cottage surrounded by fields. For some reason the clip was in black and white, which only added to the feeling of neglect. The whispering didn't help, nor did the way she crouched down, as if trying to stay safe.

'Now, fans, today I have a treat for you. Twenty years ago, Lesley Charlton went missing. Three days later her husband, Terrence, committed suicide and left behind his confession. *But*' – she broke off for a painfully long dramatic pause – 'her skull has never been found, and many of the Walton-on-Marsh locals, myself included, don't believe Terrence was guilty. Later in the episode I'll be talking to his neighbour, but because I'm a serious investigator I wanted to give you a balanced view. So, we're about to talk with Lesley's close friend, Ross Mitchell. Now, there's a noise coming from the back of the cottage, so I think we're going to be in luck. And remember, *memento mori*, so let's make it count.' This was accompanied by a thumbs-up as Gemma crept closer to the back of the house, following a sign that said: *Bespoke Furniture... this way.*

Her progress was stopped by Tuppence, who hit pause. 'I can't believe that Gemma Murphy has given us a lead.'

'Yes, it's a lot more useful than a discount code for body piercing,' JM retorted in an exasperated voice, before gesturing with her hand for Tuppence to play the clip.

After knocking three times with no luck, Gemma turned and dramatically whispered to the camera that Ross must be hiding something. 'It just proves I'm on the right track.' She then let out a soft giggle, before the video cut to her interviewing a young woman of about her own age. Most of the discussion involved make-up tips and a convoluted explanation of what might have really happened to Lesley, and when it finished five minutes later, Tuppence switched off the television.

Hen picked up her phone and typed something in. 'Let's see, his name was Ross Mitchell, and the business is called Bespoke Furniture, and... bingo. Here we go. The address is fifty-eight Boundary Road, Little Shaw. Hmmm, that's interesting. If he's from here, then why haven't I heard of him before?'

'I don't know him either, but it does explain why he wouldn't answer the door to Gemma. He must've known she was from Walton-on-Marsh.' Tuppence got to her feet and slipped on her Crocs. 'Let's just hope he's happier to talk to us. Who wants to drive?'

THIRTEEN

Ross Mitchell's cottage wasn't nearly as rundown as Gemma's black and white gloomy video had tried to imply. The stonework was clean and tidy, and the pitched roof gleamed in the hazy afternoon sunshine. A large For Sale sign hung from the fence, which might have accounted for the tidy appearance, and next to it was a second sign announcing he was open for business.

The faint hum of the radio and the fresh scent of sawdust was coming from behind the cottage, so one by one they stepped along a flagstone pathway that wove between flowerbeds and through to a workshop.

Roses climbed up each side of the workshop's doorway and a handmade wooden bench was positioned under the window. It was a charming scene and Hen let out a small gasp of admiration. The radio immediately stopped playing and several moments later, a man in his mid-sixties appeared in the doorway of the shed, wearing a leather work apron.

His dark skin glistened with sweat and his hair was in thick cornrows that hung down his back. He greeted them with a smile and peeled off the apron before joining them, hand outstretched.

'Hi, I'm Ross. Would you like to come in and have a look around?'

'Oh yes,' Hen said, before wincing as JM gave her a sharp glare. 'Er, I mean hello, I'm Hen, and this is JM, Ginny and Tuppence. We were hoping to talk to you about Lesley Charlton.'

'Tuppence?' His attention turned to Ginny's friend and recognition bloomed in his gaze. 'You were married to Taron Wilde.'

'You knew Taron?' Tuppence went stiff.

'I wouldn't go that far.' Ross gave her a rueful smile. 'I met him a few times while he was working on the mural for Walton-on-Marsh College, where I used to teach. I often stopped to chat with him while he was there. I was sorry to hear about his passing.'

'Oh.' Tuppence swallowed, as if trying to push down her rising emotions. 'Th-thank you. It's been almost eleven years.'

'If it's any consolation, his work lives on. I was driving past the school last week and the mural looked as vibrant as the day it was painted. And in the ultimate compliment from our industrious youth, there's no graffiti on it.'

Tuppence managed a smile and Hen reached over and squeezed her hand, while JM stepped forward.

'You mentioned Walton-on-Marsh College. Is that where you met Lesley Charlton?'

'That's right,' he said, voice cautious. 'Are you journalists? I've had a few approaches in the last week.'

'No, we're not here in any official capacity,' Ginny assured him, trying to ignore Wallace's voice in her head wondering why they were there at all. 'We're friends of Grace West. It was her wedding that was cancelled.'

His face softened, and he gestured to the door that led through to the back of the cottage. 'I was sorry to hear about that. It must have been quite distressing. Let's get out of the heat.'

'Thank you.' Hen fanned her red face and followed him through to a large farmyard kitchen, with Ginny close behind.

The interior was light and sparsely furnished, with a stone floor and a long, reclaimed-wood table surrounded by a collection of antique chairs.

'Oh, this is lovely,' Ginny said, admiring the copper cooking pans and the gleaming Aga.

'It would be more lovely if it was a mile down the road. A house on the Walton-on-Marsh side sold for almost double what I'm likely to get.' He lifted a large jug of water out of the fridge and carried it to the table. Thin slices of lemon and pieces of mint floated at the top. He put it down and returned with glasses.

'Yes, but if you lived on that end, you might lose all your manners,' JM retorted. It was clear she hadn't recovered from the trip to the small village.

'Touché.' Ross let out a rueful bark of laughter. 'I taught there for twenty years, and heard every crude joke and reference you can imagine. "You know what they say, sir. Little Shaw equals little—"' He broke off from mimicking the students, as if suddenly remembering where he was. 'Well, never mind that. Point is, I'm Little Shaw born and bred but there's no denying it has its drawbacks.'

'I'm sure you'll find a buyer soon,' Hen told him with an encouraging nod. 'So, are you happy if we ask you a few questions?'

He poured five glasses of water and nodded. 'I take it you don't believe it's part of the curse.'

'Absolutely not,' JM said in a stern voice as Tuppence

pulled out the small address book and opened it to "I" for interview.

'But we do want to find out how Lesley's skull ended up at the church, and whether someone did it on purpose to stop the wedding,' Ginny admitted. 'Do you know an influencer called Gemma Murphy?'

He sighed. 'She was one of my students a few years ago before she started her videos. When she first approached me about the murder, I agreed to look at her questions, but they were so ridiculous that I refused. What is it with twenty-somethings and their obsession with internet fame?'

Ginny had no answers. She knew they weren't all the same – Connor, for a start – but she'd definitely come across a few in the library, obsessed with likes and clicks.

'I don't suppose you know where Gemma lives, or have a contact number for her?'

He shook his head. 'Her mother died a few years ago and she doesn't have any other family in the area, but since I retired from teaching, I don't have much to do with Walton-on-Marsh anymore.'

Tuppence gave him an approving nod. 'That's probably wise. Do you know someone called Jacinta Theakston? She's about Gemma's age.'

'The name doesn't sound familiar.'

'So, she didn't go to the college?' Ginny confirmed.

'Not that I know of. But there's a lot of well-off families who send their children to boarding school. Perhaps she was one of them?'

'That makes sense.' Hen nodded. 'My own daughter went to our local school, but half a dozen of her friends headed off at the end of every summer to their fancy schools that cost more per term than what I earned in a year.'

'What about the Faulkners? Did Lesley have any connection to them?'

He frowned. 'Apart from walking through some of their fields, I don't think she knew them.'

Ginny tried not to show her disappointment. It had been a long shot that he might be able to help them find a connection, and it didn't lessen the niggle that kept reminding her that the appearance of Lesley's skull at the church may not have had anything to do with the wedding.

It could all just be a cruel coincidence.

She thought of all Gemma Murphy's confirmation-biased reasoning, and unsupported logic. Was that all that Ginny and her friends were doing? An association fallacy, where they were pushing two ideas together and assuming they were connected? Or, as Gemma had a habit of saying: were they following the clues because 'it just *feels* right'?

Giving a small shudder, Ginny forced herself to be more robust in how she looked at the problem. If there was a connection, then where did it start? With the skull, a small voice whispered, and she sat up straight.

Oh.

She turned to Ross. 'Do you know where Lesley's remains were discovered? We haven't been able to find anything.'

'Tell me about it. Usually, these things get turned into a shrine of corner-shop flowers and teddy bears, but for whatever reason the police decided not to release the information publicly.'

'Whyever not? I hope it's not because she was from Little Shaw,' Hen said.

'I have had about enough of this damn rivalry.' JM bristled in outrage.

'Which means we still don't know where her bones were found.' Tuppence tapped her pencil against the table.

But the gloom around Ross seemed to fade as he grinned. 'I never said that *I* didn't know.' He abruptly stood and disappeared into another room, returning with a framed antique map, which he placed on the table. It was stunning – while there was no hand colouring, it was covered in tiny triangular slopes, curving lines for waterways, and church crosses, and the name of all the villages and towns had been painstakingly written in a beautiful cursive. Some she recognised but others had changed over the years.

'You have the location?' Hen gasped.

'Like I said, Lesley was a friend of mine, and she liked to go rambling. So, after the news came out that her remains had been found, I did one of her favourite walks. Like a pilgrimage, I suppose.' Then he gave them a self-deprecating smile. 'Well... if you can call three miles a pilgrimage – I'd set off to do the Harris Hill walk, but three miles in, I stumbled across a load of police tape around an area just off the path, and when an officer found me standing there, they moved me on, saying it was still a crime scene and not a tourist spot.'

'Sounds like that was before sensitivity training existed.' Hen gave him a sympathetic look before glancing over to the map. 'Where was it?'

'It's here. Just under halfway along the Harris Hill walk.' He pointed to a tiny skull that was barely visible, next to a pile of rocks.

At the sight of the skull, Ginny's heart rate increased and her friends all stiffened.

Ross, on noticing the reaction, let out a bitter sigh. 'I know. The irony isn't lost on me. A lot of these old maps have the original trig markers the surveyors would've used. They also include things like hills and church spires. But this is to mark the limestone caves that used to be there.'

'Used to be there?'

He nodded. 'Historically, they were probably used by the lime burners, but the cave system collapsed sometime in the seventeen hundreds and at least twenty miners were killed. You can't see any evidence of the mine, but there's a large boulder marking the spot. And it's probably why a skull symbol was used on the map.'

'And that's where Terrence chose to bury her body?' Tuppence shuddered. 'That's gruesome.'

'Indeed. Lesley knew the area well and used to often take classes there on field trips. I suppose she told Terrence about it.'

'Do you remember who found the bones?'

'No, the information was never released but I heard that it was someone out on a run. There'd been a lot of storms the previous month, which might have eroded the ground and exposed the—' He broke off, pain etched across his face at the loss of his friend.

Ginny closed her eyes, suddenly wishing she hadn't tried to be so robust. Just thinking of the history teacher being buried in the spot where so many others had died seemed cruel. And then to be buried all over again by a police department who seemed to want to pretend it hadn't happened was almost worse.

Hen reached over and patted Ross's hand. 'That was very kind of you to make the pilgrimage. I never met Lesley when she was alive, but I'm pleased she had a friend like you.'

'Thank you,' he said, gruffly. 'I just wanted her to know that someone remembered her for the right reasons, and not just because she was an article in the newspaper... or the topic of the week for an influencer.'

Silence fell as they all retreated into their thoughts. Ginny still wasn't sure if there was a connection between Lesley and the wedding. And if there was, how would they find out what it was without knowing where the skull had been for the last twenty years?

Ginny sighed. It seemed unlikely the police had overlooked the skull when they'd found the rest of the remains, which suggested Terrence had concealed it somewhere else. But why? And if someone else had found it more recently, why hadn't they informed the police? Still, this was the only clue they had right now.

'Do you mind if I take a photo of your map, in case we want to find the spot and have a look around?' Ginny asked.

Ross composed himself and nodded. 'Of course. It seems fitting you use this, since Lesley loved this map and often studied it when she came over.'

'Was that because she liked to visit historic spots?' Ginny asked, as she slipped her phone away.

'Yes, she had an old map of her own by some chap called Malcolm Lawson, and she was always talking about it. In the map world he doesn't seem to have been well known, but Terrence was convinced it could be worth money and wanted her to sell it. However, she refused to even get it appraised because it was a family heirloom.'

'It was worth money?'

He shrugged. 'She never showed it to me, so it's hard to say. I did try researching Malcolm Lawson but couldn't find any information on him.'

'Did Lesley and Terrence argue about it?' JM narrowed her gaze.

Hen's hand flew to her mouth. 'You don't think he murdered Lesley over a map?'

'People have killed for less.' JM shrugged. 'Is there a demand for old maps?'

'Oh yes. These old prints are extraordinary. Once the cartographer created them, they were engraved onto copper plates for printing. This map' – he nodded to the one on the table – 'was done by Henry Stanley in 1745. He surveyed all over England. This is from a first edition atlas,' Ross explained, and turned it over to show a typeset providence. 'I bought it from a place in London many years ago.'

'Even if Terrence *did* kill Lesley for the map, why would he then commit suicide?' Hen's eyes filled with worry.

'Maybe he had killer's remorse?' Tuppence wondered aloud.

It was a depressing thought, and the room was silent until the crunch of tyres came from outside.

A middle-aged couple climbed out of a late model car and Ross stood. 'I'd better go and greet them. Things have been tight lately.'

'Of course.' Ginny thanked him and they followed him out.

'I'm sorry I couldn't be of more help. I liked Lesley a lot and if there is something sinister about her death, I hope you or the police can find the answers.'

So did Ginny, and she shielded her eyes from the sun as another thought occurred to her. 'What happened to Lesley's map after her death? Who inherited her estate? Is there a chance they'd still have it?'

'I don't know. Neither of them had any relatives, so the house and the possessions were sold off. Which means it could've ended up on the auction block, at the bottom of land-fill, or in a charity shop if it was lucky,' he said, before giving them a final nod and then cutting a line towards the potential customers.

Ginny turned to her friends. 'What do you think?'

'I think that Gemma Murphy certainly liked doing a lot of late-night jaunts into the marshes and woodlands. Maybe that's how she stumbled across the skull?' JM suggested.

'Except to find out, we need to speak with her again.' Hen frowned as they climbed back into the car. 'And she might refuse. Which means we need another plan.'

'What are you suggesting?' Tuppence turned to her. 'I don't have much room left under "P" for plan.'

'Then use "W" for walk. We're halfway to Walton-on-Marsh – we could see where Lesley was buried. It might give us a clue as to who found her skull there,' Hen said.

'I've been thinking about that,' Ginny admitted. 'It doesn't seem likely someone discovered the skull there recently, because the police would have thoroughly searched the place at the time. But, if this is connected to Lesley's murder, then whoever is behind this might have visited the spot again.'

'Or there's another clue there that we're missing,' JM piped up.

'And who knows, there might even be some CCTV close by, or a local shop we could talk to,' Tuppence added, as Hen started the engine and headed in the direction of the long-forgotten lime caves.

Ginny wasn't sure if it was a good idea or a bad one, but at least it would let them pay tribute to the dead woman that no one seemed to care about.

FOURTEEN

Sunday, 3rd August

'I'll say this for Ross, he knows how to give directions.' JM climbed out of Hen's car and fixed the laces on her walking boots. In the end they'd decided to go back to Little Shaw and change their footwear and get small backpacks with water and trail snacks. The Harris Hill trail was a round trip of six miles, though the spot where Lesley's body had been discovered was only a three-mile walk. Still, they'd all been around long enough to not take chances.

There were several other cars already parked there but no sign of the owners. As they walked along the dirt path, the heat of the sun made Ginny pleased she was wearing a hat. Tree roots jutted out and the small creek that ran alongside the path was almost dried out from the warm summer. The fields gave way to a woodland as the terrain started to slope, and Ginny soon had a layer of sweat on her brow as her heart pounded from the exercise. Was this a reminder of how many Senior Shake and Shuffle classes she'd missed?

They didn't speak much as they followed the trail, until JM, who had a small compass in her hands, came to a halt. 'Right, this is the place. Can you see the boulder?'

'No, but everything is so overgrown I'm not surprised.' Tuppence peered around.

It was indeed very dense. The tree canopy shaded the trail, while ivy clung to small bushes and shrubs that had been trying to survive in the undergrowth.

There was nothing to indicate that any caves had once been there, let alone the marker Ross had told them about.

'I think we should have a look around,' JM announced, disappearing further into the thicket of branches, while Tuppence went in the other direction and Hen walked straight ahead. Ginny spied what might be a disused trail. It was barely visible, but some of the grass had been flattened down so she pushed back a few branches and stepped forward.

The path widened and the dry dirt had the faint imprint of shoes, which indicated it had been used recently. She arrived at a clearing and stared at a weathered boulder. Her skin prickled.

So, this is where Lesley Charlton was buried.

She glanced around, trying to picture the soil eroding away to expose some of those bones fifteen years ago. But whatever the SOCO team had done to recover the remains had long ago been reclaimed by nature.

The silence was broken by the scuffle of feet as a young girl darted into the clearing.

'Mama, look at me.' The girl scrambled onto the boulder and held her arms up to the sky. But her unimpressed mother, following on behind, simply pulled a face and lifted her down, scolding her to be careful.

As they disappeared back down the path Ginny stared at the boulder as a flash of Gemma Murphy making the same pose crashed into her mind.

She had filmed here.

It wasn't necessarily a surprise, since the influencer hadn't hidden her interest in Lesley Charlton's murder… but still, it did suggest she might indeed have a connection to the skull.

Branches crackled behind her and footsteps sounded as Ginny turned around, expecting to see the familiar faces of her friends. Instead, she came face to face with a man in his late twenties with dark hair and angular features.

Digby Theakston.

Ginny stiffened and took a step back, her mouth suddenly dry. 'Digby, what are you doing here?'

'I could ask you that,' he snapped, in the same sullen accent as when they'd first met last week. 'Unless you're simply taking a break from harassing my sister?'

'Harassing?' Ginny protested, not sure her conversation with Jacinta could be described that way. 'I was returning her wedding gift on behalf of Grace.'

At the mention of Grace's name, his lip curled with disdain. 'That's not what she said—'

'Digby, I think I've got it,' a second voice said, and the wedding photographer appeared in the clearing. The black dress had been replaced by denim overalls and a white T-shirt underneath. She was wearing stout walking boots, and her hair was pulled back from her face. At the sight of Ginny, she came to an abrupt halt, her brow wrinkling. 'Oh, I know you. You were at the wedding, right?'

'That's right. I'm Ginny Cole,' she answered and automatically held out her hand, as her mind tried to make sense of finding them both at the same spot where Lesley's skeleton had been discovered.

'Vanessa,' the other woman replied and, much to Ginny's surprise, she shook hands and smiled. 'We never got properly introduced the other day.'

'That's because it was a farce,' Digby retorted, his jaw tight. Then he shot Vanessa an annoyed glare, as if displeased by her basic courtesy. 'And if you've got the shot, let's get out of here. I'm suddenly finding the air less than refreshing.'

'Digby, stop being such a prick,' she scolded him with a shake of her head. 'Ginny must already think I'm a rude cow, without you making it worse.'

'Of course I don't,' Ginny said, though even to her ears it didn't sound convincing.

'You should. I was in an absolutely beastly mood.' Vanessa unhooked the camera equipment that had been slung over her shoulder and lowered it to the ground. 'How is Grace? Have you seen her? I heard she called off the wedding, which is heartbreaking.'

'Please, enough with the platitudes, V. Let's get out of here. I'm tired and hungry and sick of this,' Digby growled.

'You were the one who wanted to tag along.' Vanessa didn't seem moved by his theatrics as she looked around the clearing, eyes alight with interest. 'Besides, I need to get a few more shots.'

'Yeah, well, you can do it on your own. I'll wait at the car,' he snapped, and then picked up a shovel that Ginny hadn't spotted and disappeared back down the narrow path.

Vanessa's mouth dropped open, as if she wanted to protest but didn't have the words.

Ginny swallowed, still not sure how this all fitted together. Were Digby and Vanessa a couple? And why were they here?

More importantly, why did Digby have a spade with him?

'I'm sorry, I didn't mean to interrupt your photo shoot,' Ginny said.

'You're not at all. I was working further along. There's a stunning oak tree that is glorious at this time of year, but trying to get the light right is really tricky. What Digby doesn't seem to understand is that it's not as simple as pointing my camera at it and snapping.'

Ginny, who was very much part of the "snap and hope"

school of photography, nodded her head. Though she still wasn't sure what Vanessa was doing there. 'Are you thinking of using it as a backdrop for another wedding?'

Vanessa let out a shuddering groan. 'Definitely not. Theo and Grace's wedding was my first... and my last.'

'Oh, so you don't usually work as a wedding photographer?'

'No, I specialise in landscapes and mainly do work for film and advertising agencies. My approach is quite specialised... and time-consuming. But Lady Kitty, who is a friend of my mother's, begged me. My immediate response was "Hell, no" because I can't stand all that society bullshit. I'm much better out in nature than cooped up somewhere formal. I've worked hard for what I have and hate the idea of bowing down to anyone. But my mother was worried what would happen if I refused. So, I stupidly said yes.'

'You were worried it might affect your business if you said no?'

Vanessa let out a rueful laugh. 'Not quite as bad as that, and to be fair, even if it had gone smoothly, I still wasn't in the right frame of mind, as you might have noticed. My studio was broken into the week before and I haven't been sleeping well.'

'A break-in?' Ginny's eyes widened, both curious about what had happened, and pleased to have a bit more under-standing about Vanessa's bad temper on the day.

'It was terrible. I've got a solo exhibition coming up, and not only did they ruin several of my canvases, but they started a small fire and destroyed some of my equipment.'

Despite herself Ginny leaned in. 'What was the motive? Did the police find any clues?'

'No. They promised to follow up, but I haven't heard anything. I have no idea what the motive was except to cause me a big headache. Some of the images had been taken on my trusty old Minolta, and the negatives were destroyed, which is why I'm out here, trying to recapture them.'

Ginny's skin prickled again as she twisted back around to the weathered boulder that marked the spot where Lesley had been buried. 'Was it only the shots of the oak tree that were destroyed? Or were some of the shots from this clearing?'

'Hell, no. This place gives me the creeps. It was mainly the tree, and there's also a tiny inlet that runs into the creek, which I'm obsessed with. But I need an angrier sky for that one. It's meant to rain this afternoon, which would be perfect.'

'I see,' Ginny said, but something niggled at the back of her mind. Okay, at the front of her mind. Why *had* Digby been there, and what had he been using the spade for? 'Well, it's nice of Digby to accompany you. Are you an item?'

'No, I'm not into younger men. And between you and me, I don't have much time for people like him and his sister, who trade on their last name as if it's a currency.' Then she sighed. 'I suppose it is, in a way.'

'So why was he here?' Ginny ventured.

'Because I'm terrible at saying no. We have loads of friends in common, and a couple of months ago he came into the studio to look for an anniversary present for his parents. He got very excited when he found out where most of the shots had come from. He told me some story about looking for a time capsule that he and his friends had buried when they came here for a school trip years ago.'

'That's why he had the spade?' Ginny raised an eyebrow as she peered around for any sign of digging, but none of the earth had been disturbed. 'Did he find it?'

'No. But then I wasn't sure I believed him anyway. He heard about the break-in at my studio, called and I mentioned I'd be coming out here. That's when he said he'd like to tag along. Equipment is heavy so I agreed... though a fat lot of help he's been.'

Ginny opened her mouth to probe further but was cut off by the sound of voices, and this time it was her friends who appeared in the clearing. She quickly made the introductions but, after a few minutes, Vanessa gave them all an apologetic smile.

'It's clouding over, which means I need to get back to my stream and get the shot. Fingers crossed that it rains. But it's nice to meet you all. And, if you're free in two weeks on Friday, I'd love it if you came along to the show.'

She pulled out a postcard with a photograph of a wind-blown tree clinging to the side of a rocky outcrop. The colours were startling as the sun pierced through a bank of grey clouds – it was so vivid that it jumped off the page.

Above the image was the name *Vanessa Eagle-Edwards*.

Ginny's mouth dropped open. Cynthia was Vanessa's mother? It was hard to imagine them together, Cynthia with her towering beehive and immaculate suits, and Vanessa, the photographer who seemed happiest in nature.

'What is it?' Hen whispered once Vanessa had disappeared.

'We met her mother, Cynthia, at the church on Friday, and she was not a fan of ours. Or of Little Shaw,' Tuppence added in her own whisper, as she pulled the address book out of her pocket and flipped it open.

'And did we just see Digby Theakston storming back towards the car park carrying a shovel?' JM added with a frown.

'Yes.' Ginny told them about the encounter before pointing to the boulder that Gemma Murphy had been standing on.

'How extraordinary,' Hen marvelled. 'It can't be a coincidence.'

'Which bit?' JM folded her arms. 'Because as far as I can tell, we have three different leads to follow, and they can't all be right.'

Ginny closed her eyes and nodded in agreement.

They had too many leads, and not enough facts.

FIFTEEN

Ginny sat in her office the following morning, carefully laminating new library books in a practised rhythm that never failed to soothe her. She'd hoped that doing something familiar would allow her mind to think, but so far it wasn't doing anything more than increasing the number of books she wanted to read.

She smoothed down the clear contact paper and pressed out the air bubbles before adding the latest Nora Roberts to the pile. The next book was *Clouds: What the Sky is Trying to Tell You*. She'd ordered it in for one of their young patrons in lieu of their other suggestion: *Body Piercing for Beginners*. She didn't like to judge, but cloud-watching seemed like a less painful hobby.

Slipping off the dust cover, she got to work, and her mind returned to the problem.

There were so many separate threads. First was Gemma Murphy. Now they'd connected her to the spot where Lesley's body had been found, it made Ginny sure the influencer hadn't been entirely truthful with them.

Digby Theakston was already on the list, but his appearance yesterday had just earned him a tiny gold star next to his name in Tuppence's address book. He certainly hadn't concealed his animosity, but was that because he had nothing to hide, or because his sense of entitlement made him think he was untouchable? It also didn't explain his interest in going to Harris Hill with Vanessa.

Then there was Jacinta, who was not only Theo's ex and Digby's sister, but might have a connection to Gemma Murphy via a red handbag and matching sandals.

Not to mention Annabel Faulkner.

And as everyone came from Walton-on-Marsh, they were woefully short on answers.

Ginny finished the last of the books and walked out to the main floor. She'd already gone through the stacks a second time, looking through old *Hello!* magazines, and while there were several shots of both Annabel and Lady Kitty at various charity events, there was nothing of substance. She had also left several more messages for Theo Faulkner, but was still waiting to hear back.

In short, it was proving to be a frustrating morning.

She nodded at Connor, who was in the children's corner dressed in a pirate costume as he entertained his audience with an energetic story time, and reached the issues counter as her friends appeared in the doorway, all staggering under stacks of old newspapers.

'What are you doing here? I thought you were going to Gemma's yoga class?' she asked, staring at the newspapers. Where had they come from? Had she left the stack door open? But after the fire, she'd always been so cautious about that.

'The morning class was cancelled so we're going to the three o'clock session,' JM explained as William shuffled in, a wide smile on his face as he clutched his own stack of newspapers.

'I'm on the research team,' he explained. 'I knew it would only be a matter of time before my help was enlisted.'

Ginny turned to Hen, who offered up an apologetic smile. 'William was waiting for a bus, so I offered him a lift in, and while we were driving, I told him about the lack of news in our local paper. That's when he mentioned that he has forty years' worth of the *Walton-on-Marsh Gazette* in his cottage and was happy for us to look at them.'

'Forty years?' Ginny choked, trying to imagine how so many newspapers could possibly fit into the small house where he lived.

'I felt it was important to keep them all, since none of the Little Shaw library managers would buy them in,' he explained, as he pulled out a box of disposable gloves. 'However, I will require everyone who touches them to make sure they're suitably attired.'

'In case you catch something from Walton-on-Marsh,' Slim retorted, taking the pile from Hen's arms and carrying them to the table. Returning, he did the same for Tuppence. However, the dark glare that JM gave him stopped him from taking her pile.

'Gloves. Did I not just tell you that you need to wear them? No wonder you're no longer working in your previous profession. You probably left fingerprints everywhere,' William scolded him, which only caused Slim to extract the notebook that was never far from him these days.

'You know, we would have made quite the team back in the day, William. With your brains and my talent of climbing up walls and jimmying open windows, we would've been unstoppable.'

'I like to think I know a bit about crime.' William smoothed down his crumpled anorak.

'Yes, you do. I've seen all the sugar sachets you've nicked from the café.' Slim patted his shoulder and grinned. 'Now, before you start researching, do you want to see what I came up with last night for the book?'

The two men then entered a conversation about an improbable heist involving diamonds, a penknife and some chewing gum.

Ginny left them to it and joined her friends at the table. 'Sorry, I don't have much to report. I've been trying to find out more about Digby, Jacinta and Annabel in the society magazines, but I didn't have any luck. I asked Grace this morning, but she couldn't tell me much more than the fact the siblings are close.'

'Even more reason for Digby to want to ruin the wedding so that Theo and his sister could marry,' JM said in a dark voice. 'Old families trying to keep old money.'

'Let me write that down and then we can start looking through some of these newspapers.' Tuppence brought out the address book and flipped it open. 'I wonder how William even has these papers. It's hard to get them across the border.'

'I'm not sure we want to know,' JM retorted, as she watched William scratch his armpit.

'Oh, but at least we don't worry about Digby. We've already eliminated him.' Hen took out her knitting.

'Digby's not a suspect?' Ginny's mouth dropped. 'Why not? What did you find?'

'He's a vet.' Hen pushed her knitting needle into the wool, and then, seeming to notice Ginny's surprise, she continued, 'It stands to reason that vets can't be evil.'

'Because they look after animals,' Tuppence added, unnecessarily.

'I'm not sure Edgar sees it that way.' Ginny thought of her cat's behaviour when she'd taken him for a recent check-up. 'Let's keep him on the list.'

'What? You can't suspect a vet. That's ridiculous.'

William reappeared and handed out the gloves. 'Now, let's get to work.'

Ginny took a pile of newspapers back to the issues counter and began working her way through them, between helping customers. There were several photographs of Lady Kitty and Annabel together, and one of Jacinta and Digby at a charity gala, but not much else of interest.

'Those kids were energetic.' Connor returned to the issue counter, still wearing his eye-patch and fake beard. Then he wrinkled his brow. 'And why is William wearing gloves?'

'Turns out he has a forty-year collection of *Walton-on-Marsh Gazettes*,' she explained, before filling him in on what they'd found yesterday, including their run-in with Digby and Vanessa.

'Posh birds of a feather flock together,' Connor retorted in his trademark gruff voice. 'Maybe he just fancies her and that was his idea of being smooth?'

'I would suggest in future if he wanted to be smooth, then he should do without the shovel,' Ginny said, though Connor had a point.

Digby hadn't bothered to hide what he thought of Nina, the maid of honour he'd been arguing with, and even Grace seemed to fall below his notice because of her background. Whereas Vanessa was smart, articulate and had a double-barrelled surname. So, maybe tagging along with her on a photo shoot *was* his way of getting to know her?

'Ouch. Burn.' Connor gave her an amused smile.

Ginny wasn't entirely sure what a 'burn' was, but she suspected it was because she'd been mean-spirited. She made a mental note to do better and tried to hide the heat in her cheeks. 'Ignore me. I shouldn't have said that.'

'Then you don't want to hear what I think of him,' Connor retorted, before signing into the computer. 'I'll see what

Gemma Murphy's posted recently. Hmmm... look at this.' He nudged the monitor around so Ginny could see.

It was a YouTube video of Gemma. Her hair was in a swishy ponytail, and she was wearing the same outfit she'd had on when Ginny and Hen spoke with her. The heading underneath said 'Spill the Tea' and had Saturday's date.

'This is what she filmed after we left?'

'Looks like it,' Connor agreed, before clicking on the comments and scrolling down for Ginny to see. 'But what's weird is that Gemma hasn't responded to any of these.'

'Maybe she's been too busy?'

'Yeah, but in nearly all her other clips she's forever in the comments talking to people. A few of her fans are even asking if everything's okay.'

Ginny leaned forward and scanned through the comments.

Gemma M, where are you, babe?

Shocker. Another pseudo influencer MIA. Boo hoo.

No negativity here. Gemma M is awesome. Girl deserves a day off.

You look hot. Call me.

Gems, answer your DMs.

'Has she posted anything since Saturday?' Ginny asked.

'Nothing here. But she has a few other platforms, so I'll see what else I can find. And you'd better go and check in with the detective club. Looks like they've had a breakthrough.'

Ginny turned in time to see Tuppence push back her chair and do some kind of celebration dance. Next to her Hen had put down the knitting and was clapping, while JM's eyes gleamed with satisfaction.

'If you're happy to cover the desk I'll see what it is.' Ginny joined her friends.

'Perfect timing,' JM said.

'An article about Lesley Charlton's murder, and guess who was the lead detective?' Tuppence blurted out, before wrinkling her nose. 'Er, sorry, JM. I didn't mean to steal your thunder.'

'I should think not. I had to kiss a lot of metaphorical frogs before I found this,' JM said in a stern voice, before holding the article up in the air. 'But Tuppence is correct. Listen to this: *"Forensic evidence had confirmed that the bones discovered at an undisclosed location belong to Little Shaw native, Lesley Charlton, who went missing almost five years ago. And while police long suspected Charlton had been the victim of foul play, thanks to the suicide confession of her late husband, Terrence Charlton, up until now they've only been able to speculate. According to Detective Stuart Sterling, it has been a case for the ages. 'But at least now we can finally close the chapter.' Police refuse to give any more information and ask that the public respect the family's need for privacy."'*

Ginny's mind began to whirl at the name 'Stuart Sterling'. Did that mean he was related to Angela Sterling? From what Wallace had told her, it wasn't uncommon for children to follow their family into the force, but was it just as common for them to work on cases that were connected by twenty years?

They'd even used the same wording. *Finally close the chapter.*

Ginny's head began to pound from trying to juggle all the different pieces.

'Look, she's already figured it out,' Hen said proudly as she nudged Slim, who had drifted over. 'Ginny's very clever. I think it's because of all the crosswords she does.'

'Helps the neural pathways,' JM interjected with a grim nod. 'So, now things are getting interesting. And here's a photo of him.'

The image was in black and white but there was no hiding the similarity between the father and daughter. 'So, when we saw them both in the café, they could have been discussing the case,' Ginny said, and JM made a clicking noise.

'Damn straight. What's the bet that Stuart covered up Lesley's death and was asking his daughter to do the same?'

'It's possible,' Ginny said cautiously, as she recalled her conversation with Lady Kitty. She'd mentioned being close friends with Angela Sterling's father and that he'd also been a detective. She told her friends about it. 'It still doesn't explain *what* they are covering up.'

'Oh.' Hen made a squeaking noise and got to her feet, in a very unHen-like manner. 'What if Terrence Charlton didn't murder Lesley? JM suggested it the other day, but we've been so focused on finding Gemma that I forgot all about it.'

They turned as one to look at Hen, who coloured under the attention. *Of course.* They'd been so busy trying to walk through the trees that they hadn't stepped back to look at the woods. Ginny sucked in her breath and Tuppence clapped her hands.

'Well done, Hen. Looks like your neural pathways are pretty snazzy.'

'*Very* snazzy.' JM gave her an approving nod. 'I must admit I'd forgotten about it as well.'

'Yes, but we know the skull was only recently moved to the church, so does that mean the killer is still alive?' Ginny frowned, feeling like she was trying to catch clouds but kept coming up with nothing but air. 'And it still doesn't explain why they moved it, or what it has to do with Grace's wedding.'

It also didn't explain how they'd somehow become involved in a murder investigation, despite her best efforts to avoid it.

Hen, Tuppence and JM left the library not long after to attend Gemma's yoga class and see what they could find out. Was it wrong that Ginny was pleased she had to work? Somehow, she couldn't imagine enjoying a yoga class given by the self-absorbed woman.

The rest of the afternoon was spent convincing Cleo and Andrea that it was too early to start organising Slim's national book tour, trying to discover how William and his forty years of newspapers fitted into his small cottage, and making sure there were enough biscuits for the mahjong club. And yet, compared to her weekend spent in Walton-on-Marsh, she was grateful to live in a village where people cared about each other.

The sun was still hanging bright in the sky as she made the short walk back to Middle Cottage when her phone rang. She'd been trying to get better at talking while she was outside, so she retrieved it from her handbag and studied the screen.

It was Theo Faulkner.

Thank goodness. Because if Hen's theory was correct, they really could be dealing with a killer.

SIXTEEN

Ginny stared up at the old dower house nestled into one corner of the expansive Faulkner estate. It was a two-storey Georgian building with three chimney stacks and at least twice as many full-length paned windows on each level, all framed by the ivy that climbed the sandstone. A stunning formal garden wrapped around it, with ornamental hedges, roses and topiary, and while Ginny didn't wish widowhood on anyone, it must have been a balm for the dowagers moving out of the impressive Oldfield Hall, which sat on the other side of an ornamental lake.

The main residence, where Sir Spencer and Lady Kitty lived, was built of pale red sandstone that glowed in the early evening sunshine, while a large glasshouse glimmered like a diamond. It was straight out of an Austen novel, though unlike the formal gardens of the dower house, the front lawn was a field of wildflowers and grasses.

A brass knocker hung on the white wooden door and she cautiously raised it and let it fall. Several moments later the door creaked open as a figure appeared. If they'd been dressed in the black suit and white starched shirt of a Regency footman, she wouldn't have been surprised. But instead, it was Theo.

Shadows hung under his eyes and his dark hair was a tangled mess, as if he'd run his hand through it too many times. Ginny's heart broke for him and Grace all over again. She hadn't expected he would want a visitor but after speaking on the phone, it was clear he was desperate for any news of Grace, and despite warning that she couldn't tell him anything, he'd been happy for the visit.

Resolve flooded through her. Ginny had originally only agreed to help because Maureen hadn't given them any other option, but after spending time with Grace, and seeing Theo's obvious despair, had made her more determined to find out who was behind this and help get the lovely young couple back together.

'Ginny, it's nice to see you.'

'You, too, I'm just sorry it's not under better circumstances.'

'That makes two of us.' Another wave of pain rippled across his handsome face and he rubbed his eyes. 'I haven't been able to face going back to the place we shared – it's too empty without Grace there. So, here I am, at the tender age of twenty-seven, living at home with my parents.'

'It won't be forever,' Ginny said, trying to sound positive as they crossed the wide entranceway through to a stunning room with moulded cornices, a huge green marble mantelpiece and a heavy walnut bookcase. A cream Persian rug covered the wide floorboards, and light came in through the floor-length windows. 'It's a beautiful house. No wonder your mother owns an antique shop. She has wonderful taste.'

'She does have a way with interiors.' Theo sat down and gestured to the opposite sofa. 'You said on the phone that you were looking into how the skull turned up at the church.'

'That's right,' she agreed. Before reaching the estate, Ginny had been unsure of how much to tell him, but seeing the despair rippling across his face, she didn't have the heart to hide the truth. 'Grace's grandmother has asked my friends and I to... er... look into what happened.'

'What's there to look into? Is this about the curse? Because I don't give two hoots. I just want to be with her. Please, you have to tell her that.'

'It's not the curse. Maureen's convinced someone might have put the skull there on purpose. To... to stop the wedding,' she said, trying not to compare the wealth and grandeur of the room with Maureen's own colourful house. Or the rundown terrace Grace had grown up in.

'You don't really believe that, do you?' His dark irises flickered with surprise.

'It's not what I believe. It's what they believe. *And*' – Ginny swallowed – 'what Joey West believes.'

'Oh, hell.' At the mention of Grace's notorious uncle, Theo got to his feet and raked a hand through his dark hair. 'He's not in the country, is he? I know how much he loves Grace.'

'He's not here yet,' Ginny admitted, as Theo paced the room. 'Do you really think he might try to come back?'

'Yes, I do. He's very family orientated and... trigger happy. What a mess.' Theo came to a halt and stared at her. 'But I'm still not sure where you fit in.'

Yet again, Ginny was pleased that Wallace was out of the country, since he would be asking her the exact same question. She wouldn't blame him either, since the more they dug, the more apparent it became that there was a mystery to untangle.

'I can understand your confusion.' Ginny told him about the recent murders in Little Shaw and her accidental involvement in both, including the nickname Connor had given her and her friends. 'I suspect that's what put the thought in her head. We agreed to help because Maureen threatened to look into it herself, and now that we've spent a couple of days in Walton-on-Marsh—'

She broke off, not wanting to offend him. But Theo just sighed.

'You've discovered what raging snobs live here.' He sank into the chair. 'You'd better tell me the worst of it. Who does she think tried to ruin the wedding? My mother? Digby? Jacinta? Colin?'

'Colin's not on the list.' Colour stung her cheeks at how easily he had guessed their suspects. She wouldn't be joining a poker game anytime soon. 'We tried to speak to people on Saturday but didn't get far, which is why I'd like your help. We're looking at an influencer called Gemma Murphy, who was seen leaving the church with a shovel. She does a lot of videos about ghosts and unsolved murders in the area. Do you know her?'

'No, but then I don't spend much time online,' he admitted.

'What about Jacinta or Digby? Have either of them mentioned her?'

'Not that I recall. I can ask, but surely you don't really think either of them are behind this?'

'The real question is, do *you* think they could be?' Ginny said, but when he didn't answer she let out a sigh. 'I don't mean to pry, but why was Jacinta invited to the wedding?'

The silence stretched before he rolled his shoulders. 'The Theakstons are family friends and we grew up together. My mother invited her without my knowledge.'

Ginny's hackles began to rise that Annabel Faulkner hadn't been more considerate about her future daughter-in-law's feelings. 'How did Grace take it?'

'Like the angel that she is. I was all for rescinding the invitation, no matter how uncivil it might have been, but Grace wouldn't let me. She didn't want to upset my mother. *God, I miss her.*' The last part came out muffled as he buried his head in his hands.

A lump formed in Ginny's throat under the weight of his

sadness, but she knew she had to go on. 'Jacinta seemed very upset at the wedding. Upset enough to beg you to call it off, and Digby didn't hide how he felt either. That's why we need to speak to Gemma – to see if there's a connection.'

Theo sighed. 'I know he acted like an obnoxious twat at the wedding, but he's really a good guy. And he's a vet.'

'So I've heard,' Ginny said, still not convinced it was the get-out-of-jail-free card people seemed to think it was.

Aware of this, Ginny then walked him through her encounter with Digby the day before. By the time she'd finished, his mouth was set into a frown.

'Vanessa mentioned a time capsule, but she didn't believe him.'

His eyes widened. 'Oh, hell. We did bury one when we were about ten. We'd gone camping over the summer and decided to put in Nerf bullets and two Lego sets. But it wasn't anywhere near Harris Hill, and he knows that. There's only one reason he would've gone there, and that's to spend time with Vanessa.'

'So, he has a crush on her?'

'Big time.' Theo nodded. 'Vanessa's a few years older but he's fancied her for as long as I can remember. Unfortunately, she's only ever seen him as a friend, which is probably why he reverted to something so cheesy.'

Oh. Ginny took a moment to consider this. Theo had no reason to lie about his friend, which meant Connor might have been right about Digby trying to impress the photographer.

'Is it possible Digby and Jacinta planted the skull together?'

For the first time, Theo laughed. 'Definitely not. He loves her, but thinks she's spoilt rotten, and was furious when their parents bankrolled Coco for her. And while he might not have been thrilled about Grace, he did respect her, and me. He'd never have done that to us.'

It was clear that Theo didn't suspect his friend. Which still left Jacinta... and his mother. Ginny wasn't up to asking the son if he thought his mother could ruin his happiness, and was about to take her leave when she remembered what they'd discovered about Stuart Sterling.

'Your aunt mentioned being good friends with DI Sterling's father, who was the lead detective on Lesley Charlton's murder and Terrence's suicide.'

'Was he?' Theo's dark eyes widened. 'I didn't know that. Then again, I don't remember much about it at all, other than it was talked about a lot. I was only seven at the time. Do you think it's related?'

'I'm not sure,' Ginny admitted. 'From what we've read, Stuart Sterling seemed happy to close the case quickly, and Angela seems equally keen now. It could be nothing.'

Or it could be something.

Ginny thought of Hen's idea that Terrence hadn't been the one to kill his wife. But before she could try to articulate it, she caught sight of an antique map of Lancashire up on the wall. It was different from the one Ross had shown them and was almost twice the size. It was nestled in an ornate gold frame that hung above a marble-topped table, as if to pronounce its importance.

Her skin prickled as she stood and walked towards it, unable to hide her interest. Up close it was clear to see the differences between it and the Stanley map. It was hand coloured but had fewer details of the smaller villages. She searched for the name of the cartographer but couldn't find it.

'Ah, you've discovered my mother's obsession. She is an avid map collector.' He gestured to an antique globe that sat on a sideboard as well as several huge bound atlases that lay next to it. 'This is one of her most recent acquisitions.'

'It's lovely,' Ginny managed to say as her mind whirled. When she'd asked Ross Mitchell about what happened to Lesley's Lawson map, she had simply accepted his answer that it was long gone. But was it possible there was more to it? 'I don't suppose you know the name of the cartographer?'

Theo's irises widened with curiosity. 'Yes, it's Alexander Gladwell. Are you interested in maps?'

'Not exactly,' Ginny admitted and told him about their conversation with Ross Mitchell. 'Do you know if your mother has a map by Malcolm Lawson in her collection?'

He frowned. 'Not that I've heard of, but I can always check for you.'

'Thank you,' Ginny said as tyres crunched along the gravel drive. She turned in time to see a white Mercedes slide to a stop outside the long window.

Moments later, Theo's handsome father climbed out from the driver's seat and assisted his wife before helping a frail man out of the backseat. It was Sir Spencer Faulkner. The baronet was no longer in a wheelchair, but his gaunt frame declared he was far from well. Ginny tucked the information of the map to one side.

'How is your uncle? I heard he had pneumonia.'

Pain crossed Theo's face, and he bowed his head. 'He had heart surgery last year and has never really bounced back. The pneumonia was the most recent thing. He'd only just got out of the hospital and shouldn't really have been at the wedding. The wheelchair was a compromise. He's had health issues his whole life, but hates being perceived as weak.'

'It must be hard for you all.' Ginny remembered the look of pain that had flashed across Lady Kitty's face, at the idea her beloved husband might not always be with her.

It was a feeling that Ginny knew all too well.

At the sound of the front door opening, she got to her feet. 'I'd better not keep you, but thanks for talking to me.'

'If you can find something that will convince Grace to speak to me, I'd be forever grateful. And... would you mind giving her this?' He crossed to the sideboard and picked up a lump of fabric. On closer inspection it was an old stuffed toy in the shape of a rabbit, though age and usage had taken its toll. 'It's Grace's childhood toy. She gave it to me the night before the wedding. To keep me company—' He broke off and swallowed.

Ginny's own throat tightened, and she took the well-loved rabbit, its long slim ears both bowing forward.

'I can do that.' Ginny tucked it into her handbag, then followed him through to the hallway as Annabel Faulkner's sharp voice rang out.

'I'm sorry, Spenny, I know Kitty's your wife, but you can't expect me to believe that the front lawn of Oldfield Hall should be rewilded. It looks atrocious and is virtually buried underneath burdock. I'm all for sustainability but this is ridiculous.'

'Spenny has other things to worry about besides the front lawn,' another voice said.

'Only because his bedroom window is facing south and he doesn't need to stare at it every day,' Annabel retorted, before closing her mouth as Theo and Ginny stepped into the large hallway.

'Hello, Mum, Dad.' Theo dutifully kissed his mother's cheek, nodded at his father and then reached his uncle's side, and held out his arm. 'How are you, sir? What did the doctor say?'

'She moaned about my blood pressure, told me to keep taking the damn tablets, and refused to let me drink red wine.' He sighed, but brightened at seeing Ginny. 'Ah... now, who is this?'

'This is Ginny Cole. She's a friend of Grace's and was passing by.'

'She's a librarian from Little Shaw, I believe,' Annabel cut in, giving Ginny a frosty glare. 'And for some reason she keeps popping up.'

'That's enough, darling,' Theo's father said in a firm voice. 'Now, I'm taking Spenny to sit down. But it's nice to see you again, Ginny.' This was accompanied by a dazzling smile that far outshone his older brother's more mild expression.

'Hopefully you can stay longer next time and we can all have a gin and tonic together,' Sir Spencer added, before he was led off by his younger brother.

'Sounds lovely,' Ginny said politely, not quite able to imagine it coming to pass.

'Over my dead body,' Annabel muttered and without another word, she disappeared, leaving Theo and Ginny alone.

'Sorry about that. She's been on edge ever since the wedding. Actually, ever since the engagement party. But she doesn't mean it.'

'It must be difficult for her,' Ginny said, more out of politeness than because she empathised with Theo's mother. Then again, she'd never had children, so it wasn't really her place to judge. 'I wondered about the field, when I drove in.'

'It's been twenty years in the making,' Theo explained, as they walked outside and he pointed past the great house. 'My aunt and uncle have donated part of the estate to a local conservation group, and they've done marvellous things for the biodiversity. They suggested we should do something similar around the houses. Aunt Kitty loved the idea... but as you heard, my mother isn't a fan.'

'Sounds wonderful, though I suppose it's quite different from the formality of the dowager house gardens. Is that why she's not happy?'

Theo sighed and ran a hand through his hair. 'She's not against the rewilding project per se. She's worried about the estate being cut up because I'm the heir and she sees it as my inheritance. Running this place is the last thing I want to do, plus I'd much rather have my aunt and uncle alive and well. But my mother doesn't see it like that. It's also why she's struggled with my decision to marry. However, she'd never—' He broke off, and pain filled his eyes.

'Don't give up hope,' Ginny said, wishing there was more she could do for him. 'We will try our best to find the truth.'

'I can see why they love you so much. You're very generous.' Theo gave her a rueful smile as an old Land Rover pulled up and Lady Kitty climbed out. Her stout figure was swathed in a faded, over-sized shirt that might have belonged to her husband, and she was wearing gumboots. Next to her was a tiny woman with dark hair piled up on her head. She was wearing a blue version of the Chanel suit and once again had heels on.

It was Cynthia Eagle-Edwards. Vanessa had mentioned that her mother was close to Theo's aunt, so it made sense to see them together, even if their personalities seemed to be at opposite ends of the scale.

The two women spoke for several moments before Cynthia walked back down the long drive, while Lady Kitty joined them.

'Ginny, what a lovely surprise.' Lady Kitty gave her a kiss on each cheek, as if they were old friends, before giving her nephew a tight hug. 'Theo, tell me the worst, how furious is Annabel about the lawn? They were breaking ground for the pond today, and she's left me a trail of text messages.'

'She's no worse than when you first suggested it,' Theo assured his aunt with a smile. 'Except I suppose she's had all that time to simmer. Probably good that Cynthia's done a runner.'

'Is it that obvious?' Lady Kitty sighed and turned to Ginny. 'Cynthia's my right hand, and helps manage the house, but Annabel refuses to be civil around her.'

'My mother can be a paradox,' Theo admitted.

'That she can. And I shouldn't gripe since she and Randal were kind enough to take Spenny to the doctor's while Cynthia and I were at a funding meeting.' She took off the large hat she'd been wearing and wiped her brow. 'I'd better go and face the music, then get Spenny home. Did they say how it went? Poor darling is going mad not being able to have his evening tipple.'

'Yes, he might have mentioned that.' Theo's lips twitched.

'I won't take up any more of your time,' Ginny broke in, 'but it was lovely to catch up, Theo. And Lady Kitty, it was nice to see you again.'

'You too. Next time you'll have to stay for drinks,' Kitty said, before she and Theo disappeared into the dower house.

Ginny reached her car and made the short drive back to Little Shaw while going through what she'd learnt.

It seemed her friends were right about Digby not being a suspect: he was just a bit rude and suffering from an unrequited crush. But it didn't take Jacinta out of the equation. Or Annabel Faulkner, who was clearly still against her son's marriage to Grace West and concerned about Theo's inheritance being cut up. Not to mention her obsession with antique maps.

The problem was that Ginny still couldn't see why that would tempt her to ruin the wedding like that. Which meant they were no further forward than when Maureen West had given them her ultimatum.

SEVENTEEN

The following morning Ginny yawned as Edgar nudged at her leg. 'Is this because I stayed out too late last night, or because you're plotting to trip me when I go down the stairs?'

The black cat's blank expression neither confirmed or denied his intentions, but all the same she picked him up and let the warmth of his body and his soft purr relax her.

'I'm sure it will make a lot more sense after I've had a pot of tea,' she told Edgar, who had gone boneless in her arms, as if figuring he might as well get a free lift before starting his morning ritual of nagging for food. 'Good idea to conserve your energy.'

He didn't answer and they went past Grace's room and down the stairs.

It didn't take long for her to put a new brand of cat food into his bowl, cross her fingers that he'd like it, and pour hot water into her teapot. Still feeling half asleep, she decided to skip breakfast and instead sat down to check her phone messages. There was one from Theo saying that his mother had never heard of anyone called Malcolm Lawson. She quickly replied and returned to her messages, where she found three from Nancy.

Ginny winced.

The only person more concerned than Wallace about Ginny's habit of getting involved in murder cases was her sister-in-law in Bristol. And while this time had hardly been Ginny's fault, she wasn't eager to discuss it, so she sent Nancy back a message saying she would call later in the day.

A moment later her phone rang and Nancy's name flashed up on the screen. *So much for that idea.* Sighing, Ginny answered and then spent the next twenty minutes assuring her sister-in-law that she was safe, and that no, she didn't think it was necessary to move back to Bristol, and yes, the whole thing was very odd indeed.

By the time Ginny ended the call, she was running late for work. Thankfully it was Connor's morning to open the library. The traffic was light, and Ginny was soon at work, doing a quick walk around the library, as was her habit to start the day, when she came across William sitting at the long reading table with a stack of newspapers.

'How did you get them here? You should have got one of us to collect you.' Ginny joined him at the table. She couldn't remember arranging for him to bring in more papers, but it seemed churlish to mention that. And there might be some information on the Faulkners and their relationship with each other.

'Nonsense. I like my independence. Besides, it was nothing for young John to collect me from the door and drop me here. I've told him to make sure he comes back for me at three.'

Ginny suspected that John, the community bus driver, had other thoughts on the matter, not least since it would've made him late for the rest of his route. But she doubted William could be convinced on that so she just smiled and asked if he would like a cup of tea.

'Oh yes, please. Three sugars, ta.'

Ginny reached the staff room just in time to see Cleo throwing her arms around Slim as she let out a sob.

Slim's whole body went rigid as his eyes semaphored to Ginny for urgent help.

Oh dear. Ginny had often dealt with crying people while working at Eric's surgery, and even since she'd started at the library, but she'd never had to deal with Cleo in tears before.

She hurried over. 'Is everything okay?' she asked, exchanging looks with Slim.

He gave her a bewildered shrug of his shoulders before untangling himself. 'Er, yes, there, there.'

Slim took a couple of steps back as Cleo hugged a small brass box close to her chest.

'Cleo, what's happened?' Ginny asked, now feeling as bewildered as Slim appeared to be.

But before the volunteer could answer, Andrea rushed into the staff room, then let out a huge sigh as her gaze settled on the box. 'Slim, you did it.' Andrea also burst into tears and went to throw her arms around him.

He took a terrified step backwards and held out his hands. 'Hey, no need to thank me. It was nothing.'

'Nothing? Of course it wasn't nothing. You should be knighted for this.' Cleo recovered her voice and held out the small box. There was a locking mechanism which now had a tiny pin sticking out of it. Cleo gave it a sharp twist and flipped open the lid. Inside were several small black and white photographs and two gold wedding bands. 'These belonged to my parents, but several years ago my sister's grandkid managed to lock it and hide the key. And I thought I'd lost them forever.'

'Forever,' Andrea echoed.

'Then Slim offered to open it. And—' At this point, she broke off and burst into tears again.

Ginny was grateful when Andrea put an arm around Cleo and persuaded her over to the couch by the window.

'Bloody hell. If I'd known how worked up she'd get, I wouldn't have bothered.' Slim gave a little shudder. 'I mean, I like Cleo, but no one needs crying at this time of the morning.'

'It was very kind of you,' Ginny said, relieved it wasn't anything more serious.

'It was nothing. I like to keep my hand in. Especially now I'm writing the book. I don't want to be one of those authors who makes things up and doesn't have a clue what they're doing. Speaking of which, I need to tell William. After seeing all those papers the old boy has been squirreling away, I thought he could help me look up some of my historic crimes. It's hard to remember them all. He immediately agreed. That man really does have the mind of a master criminal.'

Oh.

Ginny winced, feeling silly that she'd assumed William had brought them in to help her and her friends. And she'd offered him a cup of tea. Still, she could hardly rescind it now, so she put her bag away, checked on Cleo and then delivered William a cup of tea – though only with one sugar because she knew his doctor wanted him to lose weight. Then she joined Connor at the issues counter so she could actually start her day.

It was almost twelve by the time her friends walked into the library. JM was wearing navy leggings and an over-sized white T-shirt. Tuppence had on a bright purple tracksuit and Hen had on some loose-fitting linen trousers. Their cheeks were all red as if they'd been exercising.

'What a con-artist that woman is,' JM said, by way of greeting as Ginny joined them at the other end of the reading table.

'What woman? Did you speak to Gemma this morning?' Ginny frowned. 'I thought you were going there yesterday.'

'We did.' Tuppence extracted the address book and plonked it on the table before letting out a breath. 'And spoke to a girl with an unusual name... what was it?'

'Shadow Crescent,' Hen said, before wrinkling her nose. 'I'm not sure what it means.'

'Who says it means anything? But if that's the name she chooses, it's the one we will use,' JM said in a stern voice, before taking over the story. 'Anyway, Shadow Crescent told us that Gemma sometimes shows up halfway through a class and convinced us to all do it. Which we did, but Gemma never turned up. More concerning is that the girl's downward dogs were incorrect.'

'That's terrible – about the class,' Ginny quickly qualified, since she wouldn't know a good downward dog from a bad one. 'Is that why you went back this morning?'

'Yes, Shadow Crescent was positive Gemma would turn up today, so we decided to go in for round two, which was a mistake.' Hen winced and rubbed her arms.

'But we did take a video of the studio in case there were any clues that we overlooked. It's a lovely place, on Loom Lane.' Tuppence retrieved her phone and pressed play. It was in a new building with lots of lights and mirrors, and everyone in the class appeared to be tall, skinny and under the age of thirty. They even looked alike. By the time the video had finished, Ginny was heartily pleased she hadn't been there to feel inadequate. No one needed that kind of negativity.

'We also took it because I refused to throw good money after bad just to try and speak to the girl.' JM pointed to the address book that Tuppence had put on the table. 'Make a note of my official refusal to be involved in any further sham classes.'

'That's a good idea. Here, let me get that all down.'

Tuppence flicked open the small book. 'I'm going to put it down under "E" for evil yoga.'

'So did you find out anything?' Ginny asked, once Tuppence had finished writing out JM's complaints.

'Only that I'm neither flexible nor coordinated.' Hen sighed.

'Oh, and here's another thing to write down, Tuppence. At the end of the session, one of the students told us Gemma often advertised that she was taking the class but then wouldn't show up. Like I said, a total con,' JM growled.

'I don't suppose they mentioned when they last saw her?' Ginny asked, remembering all the comments that followed the 'Spill the Tea' video.

'You think something's happened to her?' JM's fierce glare softened and she almost looked contrite. 'I hadn't considered that. Tuppence, please retract my statements until further notice.'

'Oh dear.' Hen's mouth trembled. 'Surely it's just a misunderstanding. We only saw her on Saturday and while she wasn't that nice, it's dreadful to think something might have happened to her.'

'We don't even know where she lives to check she's okay.' Ginny sucked in a sharp breath. It *was* dreadful. Especially since they had absolutely no proof other than some social media comments and two yoga classes.

'And if DI Sterling is as bad-tempered as Wallace, I doubt she'd appreciate our help.' Hen fretted. 'But we have to do something.'

'What if I call Anita?' Ginny suggested. She didn't like the idea of causing trouble or alarm when there was every chance Gemma was fine. *But what if she wasn't?*

Her phone was in her office, so she retrieved it and made the call.

It was a short conversation and Anita said she'd look into it. 'Though I can't promise much. Sterling seems to be allergic to the case... and Little Shaw. But give me the name of the care-taker at St Luke's and I'll follow it up with him as well,' the young PC promised.

Ginny returned to her friends and relayed the conversation.

'At least it's something. And Ginny, you haven't told us what happened when you saw Theo,' Hen reminded her.

'He's missing Grace dreadfully.' She filled them in on her conversation with Theo, along with Annabel's obsession with collecting maps, and her angry outburst. 'There's clearly some tension there, and Theo was embarrassed to admit that Annabel seems to think of the Faulkner wealth as his inheritance. I thought we could do a bit more research on them.'

'Anything that doesn't involve bending or twisting sounds delicious to me.' Hen eased herself down into the chair, grimacing as she did so.

JM went to the other end of the table and had a quiet conversation with William before returning with several stacks of newspapers. 'He's agreed to let us look through ten at a time.'

'With gloves,' William called out, and JM gave him a forced smile.

'With gloves,' she agreed then sat down. 'Now, let's get to work.'

'I think there's about to be an argument,' Connor said, a little later. Ginny followed his gaze to where Tuppence was snatching a paper out of William's hands.

'Careful. That's a historic document,' William grumbled.

'Well, you shouldn't have sent your henchman over to steal it from me,' Tuppence retorted, hugging the paper close to her chest.

'I hardly stole it,' Slim protested, from the nearby shelves where he was tidying. 'Now, if I'd taken your wallet out of that backpack, *that* would have been stealing.'

Oh dear. Ginny, who had been in the middle of ordering audiobooks for the library, quickly made her way over. 'Is everything okay?'

'I'm not sure your friends understand the concept of sharing. But,' William said, his voice turning magnanimous, 'they can read the papers for ten more minutes. Then I need to pack up so I'm ready for young John to collect me. He's getting awful grumpy lately.'

'Thank you.' Ginny gathered up the teacups that now surrounded him and put them onto a tray before joining her friends. She'd had a reply from Anita an hour ago to say that they'd checked in on Gemma Murphy and that while she wasn't chatty, she was very much alive. Which was wonderful yet still left them back at square one. 'How's it going?'

'Not well. There are lots of articles on the glorious reign of the Faulkner dynasty and more opening day ceremonies than I'm prepared to stomach on a Tuesday afternoon. But nothing substantial.' JM pushed away a stack of newspapers. 'In the end I looked them up on the internet and found some interesting articles.'

'Rude,' William muttered, from the other end of the table. 'I'm sure you just weren't looking hard enough.'

'Yes, but we wouldn't have got very far without your lovely papers,' Hen reassured him. 'You really are a treasure, William.'

'Thank you,' he said gruffly.

JM let out an impatient sniff. 'As I was saying, I found some interesting articles. Apparently, Theo's father, Randal, was considered a bit of a catch back in the day. He was a sportsman and had a fair few knickers thrown at him before he married Annabel. I found one article that suggested it was a pity Randal wasn't born first because he would've made the perfect baronet.'

'I have to say that looking at them on YouTube, it's hard not to agree.' Tuppence brought up a carousel of photos that had been put into a video. They showed the two brothers together over the years and seemed to highlight their differences.

One had the Honourable Randal Faulkner wearing polo gear with an arm thrown around his older brother. At over six foot, with broad shoulders and a square jaw, Randal all but dwarfed the smaller Sir Spencer, who only came up to his ear and had a slight build. There were more shots of the brothers together, and while they appeared close, their wives tended to be on either side of them and facing away from each other. And of course, Annabel was always exquisitely dressed compared to Lady Kitty's haphazard style, which seemed based on whatever was at the front of the wardrobe.

'That's a bit mean.' Hen wrinkled her brows together. 'Poor Sir Spencer. Not that I'm a huge fan of inherited wealth, but hopefully he isn't aware of what people think.'

Ginny frowned. 'When I met Lady Kitty, she said something similar about Annabel making a better lady of the manor than she ever would.'

'I'm not sure about that.' Tuppence flattened out the newspaper she'd wrestled back from William and opened it. 'This is what I was looking at before it was rudely stolen from me.'

'Not stealing,' Slim's voice came from somewhere between the shelves.

'What have you found?' Ginny said, hoping to move on before another argument broke out.

'It's an article on Lady Kitty and all the work she's done to make the Faulkner estate so successful,' Tuppence said, and spun the newspaper around so they could all read it.

The Rise and Rise of Lady Kitty

Oldfield Hall has always been at the heart of the Faulkner fortune, ever since Sir Joseph Faulkner built it. But as most owners of historic estates will tell you, this isn't like the old days and between crumbling walls and rising taxes, many of our loveliest houses are struggling to stay afloat. Unless you're Lady Kitty, who is a breath of fresh air after stepping into the shoes of the late Mauve Faulkner, who died thirty years ago leaving behind a huge tax bill. Most new brides might have shied away from that, but not our Kitty.

Her commitment to the Faulkner Charitable Trust has meant that so many essential Walton-on-Marsh community projects have been able to receive vital funds. And as they say, a rising tide floats all boats. Part of the success of this philanthropic endeavour is thanks to Lady Kitty's shrewd business skills, which would have made even the first baronet proud, despite not being a blood relation. When asked what drives her, Walton-on-Marsh's first lady said she wanted to leave the estate in a better condition than she found it, so that the Faulkner legacy would live on. And so, it shall, and so it shall.

'She is very well known for her charity work,' Hen agreed, once they'd finished reading the article. 'But I'm not sure how this proves anything. Lady Kitty told Ginny that she and Sir Spencer were happy about the wedding, so why would she sabotage it?'

Ginny closed her eyes, trying to sift through all the information and see how it connected together, but Hen was right about it not making sense. Unless the fact that by making the estate more prosperous, Theo's inheritance had increased, which made Annabel more determined her son should have a wife who could continue the good work.

Or, have a wife who would let her mother-in-law control things.

It wasn't a nice thought and sounded more like something out of a historical novel than a real-life situation.

Brriiiiiilllll.

An alarm rang out and they all turned as William produced an old-fashioned clock from the sports bag by his chair. He banged it several times to turn it off. Then he looked around and realised everyone was staring at him.

'Sorry. It's my reminder about young John. He'll be here soon.'

'Nonsense, don't let that poor man make such a big detour.' JM got to her feet. 'I'll drive you and the newspapers home. We should probably leave and give Ginny some peace. Should we meet up tonight?'

'I can't,' Ginny admitted, and told them about her invitation to have a meal with Harold and Myles. 'But we could meet early tomorrow to work out a plan, since right now we seem to be going backwards.'

If this is my unpaid side hustle, I'm not doing a very good job of it.

EIGHTEEN

'Come through.' Harold gestured for Ginny to make her way into the Grade II listed cottage that had been lovingly restored to its full glory, complete with three dormer windows and gleaming stonework. Some of the tension in her shoulders lessened.

'Thank you.' Ginny handed over a small bouquet of flowers that she'd gathered from her garden, though with all the heat she'd had to fill it out with some of the wild mint that was about to bolt. She wasn't sure how traditional it was, but it did smell lovely.

'Aren't these glorious?' Myles appeared from the kitchen, a pristine apron over his shirt and trousers, while the mouth-watering scent of garlic and rosemary followed him out. He wrapped her up in a hug while Harold gave her a fond pat on the shoulder.

'I wouldn't go that far. Apart from Sunday's shower, the weather's been so hot that most of my flowers are flagging.' Ginny untangled herself and smiled at them both, pleased these two lovely men had become her friends. The fact she didn't have to cook was an added bonus. Her mood sobered as she thought of Grace, who was curled up watching a movie, the ancient toy rabbit tucked into the crook of her arm.

'Aren't we all? Still, we shouldn't complain since who knows how long it will last,' Myles said, as they walked through to the back of the house to the beautifully set table. Silver cutlery shone and crystal wine glasses glittered in the late afternoon sun.

'Oh, look at all the trouble you've gone to. It's lovely.'

'Thank you. It's nice to have someone else to cook for. This one would happily eat the same thing every night if given the chance,' Myles said.

'One less decision to make,' Harold defended himself, then kissed Myles on the cheek.

'Hmmm.' Myles raised a sceptical eyebrow and disappeared back into the kitchen, while Harold led Ginny through to the sitting room that overlooked the back garden. The French doors had been thrown open and Ginny gave a sigh of happiness.

The room itself was cosy, with exposed oak beams and pale grey walls and even paler carpet. The two sofas were covered in a heavy linen, with exposed legs, while old botanical prints were dotted around the place. Ginny let herself sink into the cushions.

'Now, dare I ask where you found your most recent volunteer?' Harold joined her on the sofa.

'Er, I met Slim when I was engaging with the community,' Ginny said, not wanting to go into too much detail about the murder she'd been investigating at the time. 'He's been really enjoying it and he gets on with everyone, which is refreshing.'

'I noticed that he'd made a conquest of Cleo and Andrea.' Harold shuddered. 'Not sure how he can bear all the chatter, but each to their own.'

'I hope you're not talking shop.' Myles reappeared with a

tray of thinly cut bruschetta. 'We have toasted goat cheese with basil and some of the onion marmalade you gave us. And before I forget, I've made up a plate for you to take to Grace. We heard she's called off the wedding, poor thing.'

Ginny thanked them both and the talk turned to more general things as they ate the appetisers and then moved to the table for the meal. But it wasn't until Ginny tried – and failed – to be allowed to do the dishes, that she ended up with Harold back in the sitting room.

He shifted a large pile of books, and several sheets of paper fluttered out. 'Oh dear. I really should have tidied this away before you arrived tonight. I usually work in the study, but this weather has been so lovely I couldn't resist coming through to this room. It's a bit of a suntrap. If England can have such a thing.'

'What are you working on?' Ginny studied the pile of books with interest. As well as being an ex-archivist, Harold was a vital part of the Little Shaw Historical Society and always had his nose buried deep in primary sources.

'I'm gathering information about the bedsit where Slim lives. Did you know it was originally called Regent's House, because it reminded someone of the Brighton Pavillon?'

'Goodness, that seems optimistic.' Ginny bit back a cough as she thought of the old building that had fallen on hard times. While there was no doubt it would've once been lovely, it was hardly comparable to the Prince Regent's pleasure palace. 'Why are you researching something for Slim? I got the impression you didn't get on.'

'He's a bit more casual than I would prefer,' Harold admitted, 'but he told me about the book he's working on, and I was concerned at the lack of historical accuracy. Though... he was surprisingly detailed with his descriptions of the ballroom in the manor house and some of the upstairs rooms – the ones that are out of bounds to the public.'

Ginny bit her lip, wondering if Harold was aware of just what Slim's former job had been and how he might have gained access to those particular areas. Still, it was nice of Harold to help.

She watched as he stacked up the rest of the papers and put them in a roll top desk. Hanging above it on the wall was a framed antique map. Ginny moved closer to study it and then let out a gasp.

'It's a Stanley.'

Harold raised an eyebrow. 'I'm impressed you recognise it. Not even my dear husband would know who the cartographer was.'

'Lies.' Myles returned to the room carrying a tea tray that was stacked high with plates of delicately crafted chocolates. 'I know exactly who Henry Stanley is and how many maps he produced in his lifetime. It's one hundred and seven, if you're curious. Which I presume is why the price tags are so extortionate. Things like that stick in my feeble mind.'

'Touché.' Harold gave his husband a warm smile then stood next to Ginny to examine the map. 'I have a particular interest in cartographers and surveyors. They had an incredible amount of power at the time and could often be responsible for entire villages being destroyed to reroute water or rail lines, which were so essential to the region's industry.'

'Old Jack,' Ginny exclaimed, remembering the story.

'Exactly. Jackson Fold was the perfect example of one small hamlet being stripped off the map with a single pen stroke. Or should I say off the copperplate engraving. And then of course there was all the bribery, the forgery and the downright cheating.' Harold's eyes glowed and Ginny resisted the urge to smile.

Myles, however, did no such thing. 'My love, I'm not sure Ginny came here for a history lesson. No matter how delightfully devious those fellows all sound.'

Harold let out a sigh. 'Sorry, I do tend to get carried away.

But I am impressed at how much your knowledge has increased. You've obviously been studying the local history books I suggested.'

Ginny winced. While she'd planned to do a lot more reading about the area, it seemed like all of her favourite fiction authors had conspired to publish new books so that her to-be-read pile was teetering. Besides, it was now literally her job to make sure she'd read the latest Lisa Jewell.

'Until Sunday I'd never heard of it, but when we were—' She broke off, suddenly remembering that Harold didn't know what they'd been doing. 'Er, when we were talking to *someone*, they also had a first edition print of it.'

Harold studied her. 'And who is this *someone*? Was it to do with Lesley Charlton?'

Ginny froze. Was it that obvious?

Her startled expression must have shown, and Myles laughed. 'Relax, he's teasing you. We assumed you would be looking into it. Someone needs to. But where does the Stanley map fit?'

'I must admit that I'm also intrigued.' Harold leaned forward.

'I'm not sure.' Ginny went over what Ross Mitchell had told them about Lesley, and the fact she had had a different map by someone called Malcolm Lawson. She also told him about Annabel's map collection.

Harold's face darkened. 'I've come up against her several times in the auction room.'

'She beat him to a particularly lovely globe recently,' Myles elaborated. 'Though personally I think she did us a favour since we wouldn't have anywhere to put it.'

'Hmmmm.' Harold didn't seem convinced.

'What about Malcolm Lawson?' Ginny quickly asked. 'Theo asked Annabel about it, but she denied any knowledge of it.'

'She could just be playing her cards close to her chest.' Harold stood up and strode across the room to retrieve a slim leather book from a shelf. He flicked it open. Then he frowned. 'No mention of it in here. Did he tell you where she got it from?'

'She inherited it. I believe it was considered an heirloom.' Ginny scrunched her brow trying to recall Lesley's maiden name, but Harold beat her to it.

'Lesley's family lived in Little Shaw for generations, which made her murder even sadder, since she was the last of her line.' He picked up a pen and made a few notes. 'Leave this with me and I'll see what I can find out.'

'Thank you. Right now, it's the only real clue we have. Until we can speak to Gemma Murphy again, we're short on ideas.'

'Having seen you in action, I'm sure that won't last long,' Harold said, then reached for one of the delicate chocolates. 'In the meantime, let me tell you about Emanuel Bowen who got himself into a right pickle by being the royal geographer to King George II and Louis XV at the same time. Talk about playing both sides...'

NINETEEN

Wednesday, 6th August

'What do you think, love?' Ginny knotted a soft mustard shirt at her waist the following morning. She tried not to be self-conscious about the singlet dress underneath. When Eric didn't answer, she turned to Edgar, who'd been curled up in a ball at the bottom of her bed. He blinked one amber eye and then yawned. 'Well, you're no help.'

She studied her own reflection but was still unsure.

It was a different colour for her, and while she wasn't by nature a risk-taker, she had been trying to broaden her think-ing... and her wardrobe. But maybe it was too much? She began to slip it off but before she could, her phone rang, Connor's name flashing up.

Ginny answered it, shirt all but forgotten.

'Sorry to call you so early, Mrs C. I know it's only eight.'

She suppressed a smile at what he considered early. 'It's fine. I've been up for a while.' She'd always been a morning bird but between widowhood and menopause, these days she was usually out of bed by five, which meant eight o'clock was what farmers and cats might call "second breakfast".

'Do you want to speak to Grace? Because I heard her leave the house ten minutes ago.' Ginny couldn't blame her for all the jogging, considering the food that people continued to leave on the doorstep.

'Actually, it's you I want to talk to. After the police spoke to Gemma, she started posting comments again, and so I thought I'd go snooping further into her Instagram account, and you'll never guess what I've found.'

'What?' Ginny stood up straight. It wasn't like Connor to be cryptic, and her heart pounded against her ribs.

'I've sent the link through to your email account, but basically, it's loads of photos of Gemma and Jacinta Theakston together. It looks like they're old friends.'

'Are you sure?' Ginny asked, not wanting to go downstairs and turn on her laptop and not trusting herself to check her email on her phone without losing the call. 'I did ask Theo if Jacinta and Gemma knew each other, but he wasn't sure.'

'Maybe Jacinta didn't tell him. She could've kept the friendship on the downlow. Sounds like something a snob would do.'

'We need to pay Jacinta another visit this morning,' Ginny said, firmly.

'I agree. I can cover the library if you and the detective club want to go there now.'

'I think that's a good idea. Hen's got a doctor's appointment and JM is meeting with her accountant, but if Tuppence is free, I could collect her on the way,' Ginny replied.

She'd called her friends the previous evening once she'd arrived home from Harold's house and had filled them in on what she'd discovered. It was also why she knew their schedule. They had taken to letting each other know what they were doing, since none of them wanted to be the one who slipped in the bathroom and was stuck there for days because no one had thought to check in.

'Really?' Connor let out a breath, a rare indication that he'd been worried. 'Thanks. I was around at Nan's last night and Joey's still determined to come over if we don't have an answer by Friday.'

Ginny swallowed. Her former worry about what might happen if there was a killer on the loose was nothing compared to the idea of Joey West going on the rampage.

'That colour looks wonderful on you.' Tuppence climbed into Ginny's car, clutching a map. 'It's somewhere between ochre and cadmium yellow. And look, I've taken a leaf out of JM's book and have charted a course so we can get to Walton-on-Marsh without going past the roadworks taking place.'

'We must be on the same wavelength.' Ginny pointed to her own paper map that was sitting in the console. 'It's not far from the turn off to Oldfield Hall, but we go right at Walton-on-Marsh College.'

'Actually, I was thinking we could do a detour via that farm shop.'

'But won't that take us longer to get there?' Ginny raised an eyebrow as she pulled onto Ten Mile Lane and headed through the village in the direction of Walton-on-Marsh.

'Well, yes, but it's such lovely scenery.' Tuppence began to fold and unfold her map in a very un-Tuppence-like way. Ginny didn't like to take her eyes off the road, but she could feel her friend's agitation radiating through the small car. Was something going on? Then she remembered Tuppence had done a very similar thing with the linen napkin on Saturday when they'd been in Weaver's Tearoom. It was after Hen had suggested Tuppence join her on a walk to Lesley Charlton's old neighbourhood, which was near the school she'd taught at.

And what had Ross Mitchell said to her about Tuppence's husband?

I met him a few times while he was working on the mural for Walton-on-Marsh College.

Oh. Understanding hit and pain swept through her on her friend's behalf. This was about Taron, and seeing his work. It was something Ginny could well understand. After all, didn't she have a suitcase of Eric's clothing still sitting in her loft because she couldn't bear to open it, afraid they would still smell too much like him? Or, even worse, that they wouldn't smell like him.

'I'm sorry. Let's take the scenic route,' Ginny said softly, not allowing herself to take her focus off the road.

Tuppence let out an audible sigh and shook her head. 'No, you're right. The other way is much faster. I'm guessing by the way you're clutching the steering wheel that you've figured out why I didn't want to go past the college. You must think I'm being so silly.'

'Hardly,' Ginny said in a fierce voice. 'I would never think that. And if you don't want to drive past the mural, we don't have to. Who cares if we're a few minutes late? In fact, if you would prefer, I can turn around.'

'Thank you for being so understanding.' Tuppence let out a small sniffle then blew her nose. 'But I don't want us to cancel. Besides, I think it's time I looked at it.'

'The mural? You haven't seen it before?' Ginny asked, as she turned onto a lovely tree-lined road and past the turn for Oldfield Hall, which looked regal from between the trees.

'I've seen the sketches and went out a few times while he was working on it, but he got very ill before the official unveiling, and I haven't dared visit it since. Which, to be fair, hasn't been hard, since I don't ever travel to Walton-on-Marsh. But I was his muse, you see. So, looking at the finished work just felt too difficult.'

'Oh, I'm so sorry. I didn't know that,' Ginny said, before frowning. 'Y-you don't think his death was related to the curse, do you?'

Tuppence shook her head, sending her wild curls dancing around her face. 'No. While there are several strange things that *might* have been caused by the curse, I don't think pancreatic cancer is one of them. And even though Taron moved to Little Shaw with me when he was twenty-five, he wasn't from here so thought the curse was nonsense. He would be furious if he thought I was blaming it for his death.'

'He sounds like he and JM would get on well.' Ginny pulled the car to a halt just outside the college and turned to Tuppence.

'Oh yes, they would both sit there declaring it was hogwash.' Tuppence laughed, sounding more like her usual self. Then she picked up the map and began to smooth it down, before twisting towards Ginny. 'Problem is, I wasn't just Taron's muse... he was mine. And since his death, I haven't really been able to paint much.'

A tear trickled down Tuppence's cheek and Ginny reached for her friend's hand, thinking of the restless energy that always surrounded Tuppence, and all the YouTube clips she watched. Was it because she'd been avoiding the space left behind by her husband's death?

'Have you told Hen or JM?' Ginny asked in a soft voice. She was naturally reserved, and she and Eric had led such a quiet life that it wasn't until she had moved to Little Shaw and met her friends that she'd been able to see how dangerous it had been to keep all of her feelings bottled up inside, where they became bars that kept her prisoner to her own grief.

'No.' Tuppence swallowed and used her spare hand to wipe away the tear. 'I wasn't hiding it from them. I just hadn't joined the dots of why I couldn't bear to go into the studio and lose myself in my art the way I once could. But on Friday, when

Hen mentioned she was going to go for a walk near the college, my whole body froze. So... I suppose I should be grateful to Walton-on-Marsh. Otherwise, I might not have known I was carrying this around with me. I'll talk to them both today. I don't like keeping things from my friends.'

'It was obviously ready to be released.' Ginny patted her hand and peered around. 'So, does that mean you would like to look at it?'

'Yes.' Tuppence squared her shoulders and climbed out of the car. 'It's just around the corner, at the main entrance to the college. And... thank you, Ginny.'

'To quote JM: nonsense,' Ginny told her in a firm voice. 'That's just what we do for each other.'

'It is indeed.' Tuppence smiled fondly at her. 'Now, let's go and see what my lovely husband created.'

The two of them walked through the empty car park and around to the front of the college. Thanks to the summer break, the place was deserted, which meant there was no one standing in the way as they reached the huge concrete wall that had been turned into a historyscape of Walton-on-Marsh that almost exploded from the wall.

Ginny recognised Taron's trademark creeping vines curling around its edges, while at the base of the mural were several steam trains, the trailing black steam seeping into the many waterways that had given the local mills their competitive edge. But the main focus of the painting were the everyday people who had built the town with their sweat and labour.

There was a woman bent over her lacemaking bones, while another controlled a spinning jenny, and another a hand loom. To the left was a man with a huge woolpack on his back, while a gaggle of young children covered in dust from work huddled around an old woman smoking a clay pipe. And in the middle was Sir Joseph Faulkner, the first baronet, looking more like his brass statue than a person as he clutched a roll of parchment, which Ginny presumed was his official confirmation into the peerage.

'Oh, jolly good, Taron. Look what he's done.' Tuppence let out a delighted laugh and pointed to thousands of tiny bones that were scattered at Sir Joseph's feet. 'He's made them look like grass, but in the linework, you can see them for what they really are. It's a political statement about money coming at the expense of those around you.'

'It's extraordinary,' Ginny gasped. She'd already seen his concern for the environment through the murals that enveloped Tuppence's cottage, but this was an even stronger statement. 'Why did he decide to conceal the bones as grass?'

'Because the funding for the mural came from the one and only Faulkner Charitable Trust, and it was to celebrate the glorious history of Walton-on-Marsh. He wanted to pay tribute to all the people who'd lived here, but didn't want to whitewash the history. He always did so much research before starting a piece.'

'He succeeded,' Ginny said, and they stood in silence for several more minutes before the alarm on her phone went, reminding them that it was five minutes to ten. She'd set it to ensure they had time to talk to Jacinta before it got busy. Ginny quickly turned it off. 'Just ignore that. It doesn't matter if we're late.'

'Yes, it does. I feel like I've just released a huge burden and am ready to paint.' Tuppence positively beamed, looking suddenly like a young woman again. 'But first let's go and talk to Jacinta Theakston and see what she has to say.'

Ginny nodded as they walked back to the car. She just hoped Jacinta would give them the answers they needed.

TWENTY

'Oh, they have some lovely things. I like that pink raincoat.' Tuppence pushed her face up to the front window of Coco and stared inside. Then she jumped back, her breath mark still visible on the glass. 'Goodness, it costs two hundred and sixty pounds. No wonder people from Little Shaw don't come shopping here. Imagine how much yarn Hen could get for that.'

'It's very expensive,' Ginny agreed, even though she suspected it wasn't just the price tags, but rather the frosty reception the shopkeepers continued to give them. She checked her watch and then looked back through the window to where Jacinta Theakston was standing.

The young woman scowled at them both, as if hoping they would disappear before she was forced to open her doors for the day.

'Someone woke up on the wrong side of the bed.' Tuppence gave Jacinta a cheery wave. 'I really must learn how to lip read, because I'm pretty sure she's swearing at us.'

'At least she's not running away,' Ginny said, as Jacinta

reluctantly drifted to the door and opened it, a phone clutched in her hand.

'You do realise this is harassment, don't you? Detective Sterling is a family friend and if you don't move away right now, I'll be calling her.'

'Excellent.' Tuppence beamed and walked to the door, clearly recovered from the shock. 'Maybe she could talk to you about your prices. They seem quite exorbitant.'

'My prices?' Jacinta's jaw dropped but by that time Tuppence had already stepped past her and was now at the central table where the red leather bags were still on display. 'How dare you?'

'We're not here to cause trouble. We just want to ask you a few questions about Gemma Murphy,' Ginny quickly explained.

'Who?' Jacinta said, but her mouth snapped together.

Tuppence's eyes gleamed. They both knew what that meant. Jacinta was lying.

'She's Lancashire's fifth largest paranormal investigator and influencer. And we have reason to believe she's the one who put Lesley Charlton's skull in the gardens at St Luke's,' Ginny explained, taking the opportunity to step inside. 'But, up until now, we could never work out *why* she would do it. Was it simply to get more likes?'

'Likes are a metric used to gauge popularity and engagement on social media,' Tuppence added in a helpful voice.

Jacinta's eyes filled with loathing as she shut the door and walked back to the counter.

'What's this got to do with me?' She busied herself with a pile of packing slips. 'Just because I didn't want Theo to marry *that* woman, it doesn't mean I did anything. I hoped that fate would intervene, and it did. I'm not going to pretend I'm not delighted.'

Ginny joined Tuppence by the red handbags and picked

one up. The leather was like butter against her fingers. It really was lovely, and she carried it over to the counter.

'We know you and Gemma are friends because we saw it on Instagram. And we know that Gemma had this exact same bag and the matching sandals. Is that how you convinced her to help you?'

'Oh my god. You're hilarious. You think that I *bribed* Gemma Murphy to bury a skull in St Luke's church? Just for a handbag?'

'Handbag *and* sandals,' Tuppence chimed in. 'Maybe you threw them in to sweeten the deal.'

'We know Gemma was the one who buried it in St Luke's, because someone saw her. Plus, they have a security camera in the kitchen window which looks straight out to the garden,' Ginny said, and was surprised to see Jacinta flush. Clearly, she wasn't made of the same stuff as Gemma, who seemed to have nerves of Teflon.

'B-but Gemma said it didn't work,' Jacinta stammered, then swore under her breath as her mouth settled into a sulky frown. 'Do you mean the police have the footage?'

Tuppence shrugged. 'I couldn't say.'

Ginny stared at her friend in awe. None of them were good liars, but Tuppence hadn't lied. And while it still felt dishonest, she had to keep remembering this was to help Grace.

'Yeah, but even if I *did* ask Gemma to help me, it's not illegal,' Jacinta suddenly said, and Ginny's stomach tightened.

So, it was true.

Jacinta and Gemma Murphy had been behind moving Lesley Charlton's skull. It was shocking to have it confirmed.

'I'm not sure if it's illegal or not.' Tuppence frowned. 'I wish we had JM here. She's very good with the legal stuff.'

'Yes, but I didn't know it was a real skull,' Jacinta protested. 'Gemma told me it was a fake, and it's not like I ever saw it myself.'

'So, you didn't go with her to the church?' Ginny asked and Jacinta hung her head, as if realising she'd gone too far to go back.

Sighing, she leaned against the counter. 'I didn't mean for it to happen. The night before the wedding I went out to the pub and had a few too many to drink. I bumped into Gemma. We've met a few times and get on really well and I told her about the wedding and how my life was ruined.'

'What did she say?'

'She wanted to know if it was being held at St Luke's. And when I said yes, she burst out laughing and said that if I wanted, she had the perfect way to stop it.'

'What was that?' Ginny's throat ached as she tried and failed to dredge up sympathy for the two young women. To hear the callous conversation while knowing how much Grace and Theo were suffering was difficult.

'She's been losing viewers to some influencer over in Pendle called 'Tabitha, Daughter of the Night' and was desperate to get a breaking story. Said it was unfair that Tabitha had the witch trials to fall back on, and all Gemma had was a curse and a couple of murders. That's when she found a fake skull. She decided to bury it so that she could "fake" find it and pretend it belonged to Lesley Charlton, which would give her channel a massive boost.'

'And ruin Grace and Theo's happiness.' Tuppence let out a strangled cry as grief tracked its way across her face. 'That's too bad of you both.'

Ginny reached out and squeezed her friend's hand. It was obvious the emotions from earlier were starting to take their toll.

'What happened after she told you about the skull?' Ginny forced herself to ask, though her own throat was tight. 'Did Gemma tell you where the skull was so you could plant enough dog treats in the hope Colin would find it?'

'The next morning she wasn't so sure, which is when she

asked me for some kind of payment. I couldn't just take cash out of the register, so I gave her the bag.'

'And sandals,' Tuppence reminded her for a second time.

Jacinta gave her a furious glare. 'So, what now? I suppose you'll go running to Theo and ruin my chances for a second time.'

Chances?

Ginny closed her eyes. There was no remorse in Jacinta's tone, or even acknowledgement that what she and Gemma had done was wrong. One had dug into the past merely to get more likes on her channel, and the other had used it to stop a wedding. Except it still didn't make sense.

Her eyes flew open and she studied Jacinta.

'You said Gemma thought the skull was a fake and that she was going to pretend it belonged to Lesley... are you seriously saying she didn't know?'

Jacinta shuddered. 'Of course not. That would be so messed up.'

'Yet that's exactly what happened.' Tuppence folded her arms. 'So why didn't you or Gemma say anything to the police once you both knew the truth about the skull?'

For the first time a flash of guilt filled Jacinta's dark eyes. 'Because we were worried we might get in trouble. But I swear she didn't know. Neither of us did.'

Ginny wasn't entirely convinced. 'Where did Gemma get the skull from?'

'She didn't tell me, and I didn't ask. God, you two really are gruesome.'

'Pots and kettles,' Tuppence retorted, before turning to Ginny. 'I think it's lucky JM *isn't* here – she would be furious.'

'She would,' Ginny agreed, feeling pretty furious herself. 'I'm going to ask you again. Where did Gemma find the skull?'

Tears formed in Jacinta's eyes as the enormity of what she'd done settled in on her like the dashing pink raincoat in the window. She began to shake. 'I don't know. I swear I don't. She wouldn't tell me.'

'And you didn't push?' Ginny pressed.

'No,' Jacinta admitted. 'I suppose I didn't want to know.'

Which was the whole problem. Even if they hadn't known the skull had once belonged to a living person, Gemma and Jacinta didn't seem to have thought through the consequences of their actions, and the impact it would have on Grace, Theo and both their families.

'When did you and Gemma last speak?'

'I don't know. It's not like we were *that* kind of friends.' She shrugged but when no one spoke, she sighed. 'I called her the day police released the forensic results. I was completely freaked out, but she told me not to be an idiot.' She swallowed. 'So, what happens now?'

Ginny and Tuppence exchanged a glance, but it was Tuppence who spoke. 'You said that DI Sterling is a friend of your family, which means she might not throw the book at you when you tell her what's happened.'

Jacinta's face drained of colour. 'You're not serious, are you? Besides, I can't leave my shop on a workday. There's a big event coming up and I have several people coming in to get outfits, including Cynthia Eagle-Edwards. And in case you're not aware, dressing her is a big deal around here.'

'Then you'd better hope that Sterling is nicer than DI Wallace. If he was here, you would be in *all* kinds of trouble,' Tuppence retorted.

'I know you're scared but you do need to tell the police immediately,' Ginny said, gently, and finally the young woman picked up her phone and made the call.

At least Maureen and Joey West have the answers they wanted, and Grace will know that it was nothing to do with the curse.

Just an ex-girlfriend who didn't want to let go.

TWENTY-ONE

Ginny walked to the counter of the pet shop, pleased it was still open. Despite waiting at Coco with Jacinta, the police hadn't had any interest in interviewing her and Tuppence, and they had been dismissed with barely a second look. So, Ginny had returned to the library and spent the afternoon wondering just what Jacinta and Gemma were saying.

Still, it was no longer her problem, which was why she'd remembered how long it had been since she'd gone shopping. And while she could happily survive a few more days with salad from the garden and homemade soup, Edgar apparently couldn't.

'Hello, how can I help?' The cheery girl minding the shop smiled in greeting.

'I was wondering what food you would recommend for a fussy cat?' Ginny asked, before listing all the brands she had tried.

'We have several options, but I think these are the best ones.' She pulled down some cans from the top shelf, which in

Ginny's limited experience as a cat owner, probably meant they were the most expensive. 'But there are several other things you can do as well. Like making sure the bowl is shallow enough so it doesn't brush their whiskers. And you could try keeping them company while they're eating.'

'I hadn't thought of that.' Ginny winced. Was this Edgar's way of protesting about her absence? 'But thank you. I'll take four of the cans, and make sure I have a dinner date with him.' Ginny had filled her cat in on most of the investigation so far, so it would be a good chance to finish the story.

Once she'd paid and put the food into her carrier basket, she headed out to the car park – and almost walked straight into a tall man coming out of the off-licence next door, a phone clamped to his ear and a bottle of wine tucked under his arm.

'Tell them I'm not that desperate yet,' he said, before coming to an abrupt halt to avoid the collision. Ginny caught her breath and took in the long cornrows and dark eyes. It was Ross Mitchell. His gaze swept over her and he winced with an apology. 'Oh, hell, Ginny, I didn't see you there,' he said, as he ended the call. 'Please tell me I didn't almost wipe you out.'

'Not quite.' She clutched at her basket so that it didn't swing into him. 'I hope your call wasn't bad news.'

'Depends on your point of view. The estate agent seemed to think he was offering me the deal of the century and was trying to convince me to sell the cottage for less than what I still owe on it.' Ross sighed and waved the bottle in the air. 'Which is why I'm going to drown my sorrows. Though from now on I won't attempt to walk and talk at the same time.'

'I'm sorry to hear about the offer. Hopefully the market shifts soon,' she said. It had been a while since she and Eric had bought Middle Cottage and she'd got out of the habit of tracking the market, though now she thought about it, the house across from Maureen West still hadn't sold. But she'd assumed that was because a murder had taken place in it, not because the value of the Little Shaw properties had gone down.

Hmm, maybe the two facts are related.

'Yeah, and in the meantime, I might as well invest in a flying-pig farm. It's my own fault for retiring early. I thought that between my savings and business, I'd be covered, but it seems not. I probably wouldn't be so bitter if yet another house at the other end of the road hadn't just sold for a ridiculous amount. Then again, Sterling always did fall on his feet.'

Ginny's brows pushed together. 'Do you mean Angela Sterling?'

'No, it's her father. Used to be a copper before he retired. Not that he ever spoke to the Little Shaw end of the road.' Then he sighed. 'I don't want to bore you with my problems.'

They said a quick goodbye and Ginny made her way home to find Edgar waiting at the front door. She glanced over to Wallace's white car, which was now covered in several weeks' worth of paw prints.

'Let me guess, it's now too dirty for you to give it your continued patronage?'

Edgar raised a brow at her and Ginny picked him up. Since when had her cat become so toplofty?

'Okay, let's forget about the car and get inside. I have a gourmet meal for you and so much to tell. Oh, and a brand new whisker-friendly cat bowl. What do you have to say to that?'

Edgar yawned, but didn't attempt to wriggle out of her arms, which she was certain in cat language meant that he enthusiastically agreed with her.

She entered the house and looked around, but there was no sign of Grace. Ginny wasn't surprised: after telling Connor what they'd discovered about Jacinta and Gemma, she'd let him break the news to his family, and she suspected they would be sitting on Maureen West's patio discussing it.

'Which means it will be just the two of us,' Ginny said.

But no sooner had she shut the door than there was a sharp knock.

Ginny frowned. Her friends always called before they came around, and her neighbours didn't pop in for no reason – they simply cornered her while she was taking out the bins if they wanted a chat. Reluctantly she put her cat down. Edgar would be much better in a fight than she was, if his vet-avoidance swiping skills were anything to go by, but she couldn't in good conscience put him in danger.

She probably shouldn't put herself in danger either, so she gripped her heavy handbag and peered through the small peephole. Then she blinked.

It was Annabel Faulkner.

The queen of Walton-on-Marsh, in Little Shaw.

Annabel's navy eyes were large in her face, though her expression had been softened by pink lipstick. Ginny loosened her grip on her handbag and cautiously opened the door. Why was she there? Did she know about their meeting with Jacinta? Or that Digby's sister hadn't been their only suspect written in the address book?

'I'm sorry for turning up without an appointment, but I'd like to speak to Grace. I heard she was staying here.'

'She's not in right now.' Ginny clutched the door, not sure if Grace would welcome a visit by her almost mother-in-law, or be pleased to have missed it.

'Would you mind if I wait for her? It would give us a chance to talk.' Annabel stretched out her hand.

Talk? Ginny swallowed and studied the outstretched hand. Annabel had a lovely manicure though some small calluses suggested that she tended to at least some of her beautiful garden. She thought of how rude Theo's mother had been on Monday, and at the wedding. And yet, Ginny didn't have it in her to act like that herself.

She sighed and opened the door further. 'Come in.'

'Thank you.' Annabel stepped forward, as if worried Ginny would change her mind. Edgar, who was perched on the bottom stair, watched their progress before following them through to the kitchen and sitting by his bowl.

'Let me feed the starving cat, then I'll make a cup of tea.' Ginny motioned to the large wooden table. She then rinsed the new bowl out and carefully spooned in the expensive food before lowering it down to Edgar's tray and staying there as the black cat gingerly sniffed it.

'Let me guess, a fussy eater?' Annabel asked, as she ignored the request to sit down and walked over to the sink and filled the kettle. 'This is a charming place, by the way. You have lovely taste.'

She did? Ginny didn't dare look around while she was in a squatting position, in case she toppled over, but she still blinked. Had she moved into an alternative universe?

'Thank you,' she finally answered, as Edgar sniffed the food again and, deeming it worthy, began to eat. *Thank goodness.* She joined Annabel in the kitchen to retrieve cups and saucers.

Once the tea tray was ready, they both returned to the table. 'So, what's this about?'

'I suppose you could say this is where I eat humble pie,' Annabel admitted, before taking a delicate sip of tea. 'I've just had a phone call from Jacinta Theakston, who admitted that she and a friend purposely put the skull there in the hope that Colin would find it. Theo and I have had a long, and rather frank conversation, and I admit my judgement was... flawed.'

Ginny sucked in a sharp breath. 'I take it that's why you want to speak to Grace?'

'Theo has made it abundantly clear that I owe her an apology.' Annabel closed her eyes and bowed her head. 'And I must also say thank you. You and your friends have been more considerate of my son's happiness than I seem to have been.'

A wave of sympathy rushed through Ginny at what

Annabel's apology must be costing her. 'How is Theo? Has he spoken to Grace yet?'

'They had a short phone call and he's feeling hopeful. It's the first time she's spoken to him since they broke up.' Annabel pushed away the tea and peered around. 'I don't suppose you have anything stronger? Don't worry, I came here in an Uber, since I'm not that familiar with the area.'

Ginny walked to the fridge and retrieved a bottle of wine, along with two glasses, and carried them back to the table. She poured out the drinks, then waited for Theo's mother to continue talking.

'Believe it or not, I do love my son.'

'No one ever doubted it.' Ginny took a small sip from her glass. 'But surely you could see how much he loved Grace, and how much she him.'

Annabel took a long drink and then sighed. 'When I first met Theo's father, Randal, he was the most glamorous man I'd ever seen. Very athletic and charming, and of course wealthy and well-respected. And along with that came all the gold-diggers. Women were always throwing themselves at him. I know what you're thinking... why would they bother with a younger son, when Spenny had the title?'

It was the last thing Ginny had been thinking, though she knew from their research that it had been a popular idea. 'That must have been difficult.'

'Thing is that Spenny, while being the sweetest man, doesn't have any of Randal's charisma, or his health. And of course, he and Kitty were already married, and it seemed unlikely there would be any children, so when I came along, Randal was considered a catch, and our children would inherit the title.'

'I see,' Ginny murmured. Randal and Theo were both very handsome. On cue, Edgar wandered over and jumped into her lap, purring.

Yes, you're handsome, too, she told him telepathically. He blinked twice and then curled up and promptly went to sleep. Would she ever understand cats?

'The irony is that their mother *hated* me because of my background. I wasn't born into this world, but I always knew where I wanted to end up. So, I won't deny that when I first met Randal, I was as infatuated by the future he could give me as much as anything. But that's not why I married him. We both fell hard.' Annabel sniffed, looking into the middle distance, and for the first time Ginny could relate to the conversation.

She knew that look.

Love.

Pushing back her own emotions, Ginny finally responded. 'Why were you so against Theo and Grace's marriage?'

'Because I've spent years watching women throw themselves at my husband. And some of them are *very* good. Oscar-worthy performances. So, while I know Theo seemed to love Grace... I was never one hundred per cent sure if she was genuine.'

Oh no. That was going too far. Ginny put down her glass and frowned. 'Grace is shy and reserved, and you mistook it for being calculating?'

Colour swept up Annabel's neck. 'Yes. I admit I did. Whereas I've known Jacinta Theakston for years. We're close friends with the entire family and Jacinta understands this world of ours.'

'Your world, that deems it acceptable to use human remains to its own ends?' Ginny said, a prickle of annoyance still dancing in her belly.

'Please believe I had no idea what she'd planned. I'm mortified. And to think she used my Colin to do it. I suppose it's karma coming back to bite me.'

'Karma? I'm not sure I follow.'

'One of the *women* who tried to take my Randal from me

was Cynthia Eagle-Edwards,' Annabel said, her whole body shuddering at the admission.

'That's why you don't like her?' Ginny said, remembering what Theo had told her.

Annabel nodded. 'She did her best to have an affair with Randal, but she didn't realise she'd have me to contend with. I protect what's mine. Unfortunately, by doing so, I pushed her straight into the path of Lenny Theakston – Digby and Jacinta's father.'

'I saw them at the wedding,' Ginny said, recalling Digby's parents at the church. They had been deep in conversation when she'd seen them.

'Like I said, they're good friends of ours and it almost destroyed the marriage. While Lenny denied it, there's been rumours for years that Vanessa is his daughter. He's never admitted it to poor Binks, and they've kept it from the children, but she's told me that large sums of money mysteriously go out of their joint account. It breaks her heart, but it's become an unspoken thing between them.'

Ginny pushed her glass away, trying to unravel this strange world that Annabel was part of. So, Cynthia had slept with Lenny Theakston, who likely fathered her child and currently paid her money while never publicly acknowledging it.

No wonder Theo had turned his back on so much of his world. Then she groaned as she thought of Vanessa and Digby. If it was true, then they'd be half-siblings. Was that the real reason Vanessa refused to date him?

It all seemed very complicated, and Ginny wasn't sure it was all a good enough reason to think badly of Grace West – and her family. Then again, she couldn't imagine that Donna, Jake or Maureen would give Annabel an easy time of it, and she almost felt sorry for the woman.

Just then, the front door opened and Grace appeared.

Ginny slipped discreetly from the room to let the two women resolve their differences.

TWENTY-TWO

'I knew it,' Maureen West announced the next morning as she walked into the library, just minutes after they'd opened. She was wearing heavy gold loops that dragged down on her earlobes and a pair of purple cargo pants that appeared to have been bought in a children's department. Behind her trailed Jake and Grace.

'Nan?' Connor frowned and hurried over. 'What are you doing here? We were going to come around after work to see you.'

'If you expect me to sit around twiddling my thumbs all day then you've got another think coming. Besides, Annabel Faulkner came skulking around to the house, her tail between her legs, which means it's time to celebrate,' Maureen retorted, before gesturing for him to bend down so she could kiss him on the cheek.

Connor obliged, then grimaced as his grandmother produced a bottle of champagne from the bag at her side. He gave Ginny an apologetic look just as Hen, JM and

Tuppence all appeared in the doorway holding a huge cake.

Ginny pressed her lips together. She, too, had told her friends they would catch up properly at Maureen's house later in the day, but it seemed like there was no show without punch.

Or, in this case, no show without cake and bubbles.

Not that she could blame them all for wanting to discuss it. Ginny had spent most of the evening going over everything Annabel had told her, but still wasn't clear what punishment Jacinta and Gemma would receive. And it still left the unanswered question of where Gemma had found the skull.

She presumed the influencer would eventually confess it to the police, but Ginny couldn't imagine DI Sterling would stop by to give them an update. So, after having a one-way conversation with Eric and Edgar, she'd forced herself to accept the situation for what it was.

Of course, she hadn't reckoned with a party in the library on what was usually a quiet morning.

Several of the regulars, including William, peered over with interest and Ginny decided she needed to get things under control. Doing a quick head count she made a few mental calculations, then gestured to the far end of the library.

'Why don't we go to the reading corner? The Raunchy Ramblers aren't in until eleven, so there will be time to get everything tidied up. I'll ask Cleo to cover the desk.'

'Thanks,' Connor said, and then put an arm around his nan. 'Right, come on, you lot. Let's go.' He herded them over, chatting as he went, much like he did with story time. He'd come a long way since the monosyllabic young man she'd first met.

They'd already set up the teacups and large hot water urn for the ramblers, and before Ginny could remind everyone that they weren't allowed to drink in the library, Maureen had popped the cork and commanded Jake to pour while Hen cut up generous slices of cake.

The next twenty minutes were chaotic as she and her friends answered all the questions and explained repeatedly what Gemma had told them. Maureen's instincts were to pay a *special* visit to the influencer and to Jacinta, but JM had managed to talk her out of it, and they were now deep in conversation, discussing something to do with the law.

Smiling, Ginny glanced over to the issues desk to make sure things were running smoothly and was just about to slip away when Grace appeared at her side. There was a brightness to her gaze that suggested she was feeling better.

'I wanted to say thank you.' Grace's soft voice perfectly matched her name and disposition. Then she bowed her head and fiddled with her ring finger, which was still minus the large sapphire.

'You don't need to. I'm pleased we found out the truth,' Ginny said, before nodding at Grace's hand. 'Annabel said you spoke to Theo last night. How did it go?'

'He still loves me and wants us to get married. But...' She broke off as tears glistened in her eyes. She hastily wiped them away, as if worried someone might see. 'I'm not sure anything has changed. Annabel was lovely when she came to see me last night, but there will always be people looking at me and judging me. I hate that we come from such different worlds.'

'Oh, love.' Ginny gently squeezed Grace's hand, not wanting to draw attention to the shy nanny. What had Eric always said? That people don't need to be the same, they just need to be the right fit. As she thought of her dearest husband, she returned Grace's troubled gaze and gave her an encouraging smile. 'I don't believe in giving advice, but if it's any help, Eric and I were nothing alike. He was brilliant and outgoing and could talk to anyone, while I still jump when I hear a police car. And yet we had the loveliest of marriages.'

'Really?' Grace frowned gently as if considering the idea.

'Really,' Ginny agreed, as warmth filled her at the thought

of Eric. 'I got to spend every day with the person I liked best in the world. So, if you and Theo feel like that... well, like I said, I'm sure you'll figure it out on your own.'

'Thank you.' Grace gave her a shy smile then kissed Ginny's cheek. 'I'm meeting Theo this afternoon, and there's nothing I want more than to spend every day with the person I like best in the world. I really—'

'William, they clearly don't want us there. Despite all the help we gave them with background information on the rivalry.' Cleo's tart voice broke into the conversation and Ginny turned to see Cleo, Andrea, William and Slim all staring at the half-eaten cake and the champagne bottle, which still seemed to be full.

Ginny winced and realised Maureen must have had more than one bottle with her.

'Exactly,' Andrea echoed, as William shuffled forward waving one of his newspapers like a white flag.

'Oh dear. Do you think Maureen would mind if they joined us?' Ginny asked Grace.

'Nan would say the more the merrier. She loves being around people... but ever since Uncle Joey went on the run, she's been locked up in that house of hers. Strangely, this is the happiest I've seen her in ages. Maybe that's the silver lining to this whole thing?'

Ginny gave her a grateful smile and hurried over to where William and the three volunteers were standing. 'You're right, of course. You go along and I'll mind the desk.'

'I'll help.' Connor joined her, his dark eyes filled with relief. 'That was way too much peopling for this time of day.'

'Would you like to do some shelf-checking to recover?'

'Thanks. The one hundreds are a mess after the Learn Computer at Any Age class we had here yesterday.'

Ginny watched him lope his way over to the non-fiction area that had once been his favourite hiding place. Then she hurried to help a young mother who was trying to balance a toddler and newborn as well as a big stack of picture books.

'Here, let me get those for you,' she said and carried them to the counter, where she issued them. After checking with the mother that it was okay to give the toddler a stamp on the back of their hand, she waved them off.

Apart from the growing din from the far end, the library was quiet, and Ginny was about to consult her to-do list when PC Anita Singh walked through the door.

'Oh, aye, are you here to arrest me for reading?' someone called out, but Anita, who was usually quick to smile, ignored the taunt and beelined straight to Ginny.

Oh dear. Her heart rate increased and her palms went moist. Was this about Jacinta and Gemma's confession yesterday? She took in Anita's tight jaw and the panic increased.

'PC Singh, is everything okay?'

'No, Mrs Cole, I'm afraid it's not,' Anita said, as a crowd gathered around her. 'I need you and Tuppence Wilde to come with me to the Walton-on-Marsh police station. We have some questions for you both about Gemma Murphy.'

Ginny sucked in her breath. So, it was about yesterday.

'What's she said now? Don't tell me she's posted another dreadful video,' JM demanded.

Anita shook her head, mouth set in a grim frown. 'She won't be doing anything again. Gemma Murphy is dead. There's been a murder.'

TWENTY-THREE

For someone who didn't like police stations, Ginny had become an uncomfortably frequent visitor to them over the last twelve months. But as she looked around the Walton-on-Marsh reception area, her nerves were momentarily forgotten. The floor was covered in grey wool carpet while a bank of comfortable black leather chairs lined the blond wood walls. Mood lighting gave the whole room a warm glow... and was that a proper coffee machine against the other wall?

She blinked and turned to Anita, who seemed to clearly read her thoughts.

'I know,' the PC whispered. 'It's nothing like Little Shaw. We don't even have enough in the budget to fix the hole in the wall where someone punched it while drunk. And sorry I couldn't speak to you in the car, but PC Stick in the Mud would've reported everything back to Sterling.'

Anita nodded to the PC in question who was walking ahead of them with Tuppence. It was the same officer who had been short with her at the church, and after recognising him, it hadn't surprised Ginny when Anita hadn't answered any of the questions they'd peppered at her. Instead, she and Tuppence had silently sat in the back of the vehicle clutching hands, trying not to think about Gemma Murphy.

It was heartbreaking. She was only twenty-five, and healthy, if all the talk of yoga was to be believed. It just wasn't right. Ginny was dragged back to the present by the realisation that the grumpy PC escorting Tuppence had peeled off in a different direction. Did that mean they would be interviewed separately, in a classic case of divide and conquer?

'I still can't believe someone murdered her.' Ginny lowered her voice. 'Is there anything you can tell me?'

Anita's lip twitched and she peered around before stepping closer. 'She was found in her flat yesterday evening at eight, and she was last seen at six that night, giving us the time of death somewhere in that window. Her head had been struck with a blunt instrument. There was no sign of forced entry, and forensics haven't released any details. But, off the record, it's similar to Lesley Charlton's murder. Which means it might be a copycat. Or—'

She broke off as another officer walked past, but she didn't need to finish the sentence. They were now considering that Terrence Charlton hadn't killed his wife. Someone else had.

It was the whole reason Ginny had called Anita the other day to make sure Gemma was safe.

Then her stomach dropped. Was this why they were here? Because they'd inadvertently led a killer straight to the young influencer? Horror drenched her.

'Anita, was this our fault?' Ginny gasped, trying to push down the looming dread.

'Definitely not. The only person whose fault it is, is whoever killed her.' Anita gave a fierce shake of her head in reassurance.

'Singh, if you've finished chatting, please escort Mrs Cole

into the second interview room,' a sharp voice said, and DI Sterling appeared in the doorway. Today's trouser suit was a heavy tartan. Sweat beaded on Ginny's forehead just from looking at it. 'I will be in there shortly.'

'Yes, ma'am.' Anita straightened her shoulders and they walked on in silence.

The interview room more closely resembled those in Little Shaw, and despite the circumstances, it helped ease some of Ginny's nerves, so that by the time Sterling reappeared, she was tolerably calm.

'Please tell me exactly why you and Mrs Tuppence Wilde were at Fresh Fields pub on Saturday afternoon having a conversation with Gemma Murphy,' Sterling said, once she'd switched on the recording device and gone through the formalities.

Ginny swallowed and tried not to stare at the red dot on the machine that indicated everything she said would be captured.

Wallace had once advised her not to conceal anything unless she wanted to get in more trouble than she was currently in. And since Ginny didn't want that, she gave the detective a full account, including the conversation with Jacinta Theakston, the multitude of video clips they'd watched which led them to Ross Mitchell, the mysterious map, the numerous yoga classes her friends had tried to attend, and of course the red bag and sandals that Gemma had been wearing.

Once she was finished, Sterling steepled her fingers, mouth impassive. 'So, with no evidence to prove that Gemma Murphy was involved in this business, you and your friend decided to interrogate her?'

Ginny opened her mouth to correct her. It had hardly been an 'interrogation', and it had turned out they had been right. But she quickly pressed her lips together. Clearly Sterling wasn't happy at having a murder linked to what she'd declared was a closed case. Ginny didn't blame her. She also couldn't help the guilt from rising again.

Should they have done more to make sure Gemma wasn't in danger? Or worked harder to discover who else might have killed Lesley Charlton, and what her murderer may have been trying to hide?

'Then on Tuesday you called PC Singh, concerned that something might have happened to Gemma Murphy, because... and I quote: "she isn't answering comments on her YouTube channel." This in turn took up valuable police time as they followed it up.' DI Sterling was now leaning forward, not a drop of sweat on her face despite the stifling heat of the tiny room.

Again, Ginny opened her mouth. But it was impossible to know how to answer when she had so many questions of her own. Had Gemma told the police where she'd found the skull? Or why she hadn't been answering any of her fans or filming content? And how had the killer found Gemma's flat? Ginny and her friends had been searching online for her address for days. Did that mean the killer knew her? Or had they followed her home?

Ginny shivered at the idea.

'Well?' Sterling jabbed a finger at her, and this time Ginny got the feeling she was expected to answer.

'It occurred to us that if Lesley Charlton's skull wasn't discovered with the rest of her body, then maybe there was a reason for it. Perhaps someone else killed her and kept it as a souvenir? Did your father consider that during his investigation?'

'Enough. This is my case, not yours.' Sterling's face turned a puce colour and, too late, Ginny realised her mistake. Despite Wallace's bad temper, he'd always been open to new ideas and questions. Well... nearly always. But clearly, he and Sterling weren't cut from the same cloth.

'I'm sorry, I spoke out of turn. I didn't mean to imply that your father—'

'You will leave my father out of it. That case is closed. Now, we're going to start again,' the detective said in a cool voice. 'Tell me exactly why you and Tuppence Wilde went to speak with Gemma Murphy...'

'Are you okay? I'm sorry that took so long.' Anita reappeared two hours later. 'I've just checked with Sterling and you're free to go, though you're not allowed to leave the area without informing us. I can drive you back to Little Shaw if you don't mind waiting ten minutes while I finish some paperwork.'

'Thank you,' Ginny said, as she peered around the pristine reception area that was now filled with the rich scent of freshly ground coffee. 'Do you know where Tuppence is?'

'She was released forty minutes ago, and PC Bent took her home on his way back to the station,' Anita said, just as Sterling appeared at the far end of the room and spoke in a low voice to someone sitting behind a decorative screen. The screen would have been as out of place in Little Shaw as a cow standing on water, but here it fitted into the upmarket décor.

Sterling gestured to whoever was behind the screen and, moments later, a weeping Jacinta stepped out. She was wearing a dramatic black outfit, right down to a black handkerchief that was pressed up to her bloodless lips. Digby had a protective arm around his sister's heaving shoulders.

Sterling quickly ushered them through a door before closing it behind her.

'Talk about special treatment. I don't see why *she* gets taken to the guv's office while you and Tuppence were stuck in the poxy interview rooms. Especially after what she did,' Anita muttered, then winced. 'Sorry, I probably shouldn't have said that. But now I get why Wallace refuses to work here. He can't stand the "special treatment" either.'

'Oh.' Ginny frowned, trying to imagine the grumpy Wallace walking across the soft carpet to get his freshly roasted double shot coffee instead of making do with the nineteen sixties brutalist waiting room that was the main feature of Little Shaw station. 'I didn't know he had the option to work here.'

'Well, technically he and Sterling work out of Preston, but they use other stations as a base, depending what investigations they're assigned.'

'I didn't realise,' Ginny admitted. She'd only recently discovered that the hardworking detective had several cases at any one time. It had given her a much better understanding of his grumpy persona. And his belief in justice. She couldn't imagine him giving anyone special treatment. And, up until now, she hadn't realised how much she admired that in him.

'Wallace isn't much for the small talk. And I don't think he gets on with Sterling.'

'Seems we have something in common.' Ginny sighed.

'I just keep reminding myself that Wallace will be flying back this weekend,' Anita said, then checked the time on her phone. 'Right. If you would like to wait here... or outside if you want some fresh air, I won't be long.'

Ginny agreed and after Anita disappeared into the bowels of the building, she stepped outside into the bright sunlight – and immediately regretted her decision. A crowd of young women had gathered, all holding up black candles and wearing over-sized T-shirts with a large skull and the words *Memento mori* blazed across them.

They spun to glare at Ginny, as if they somehow knew she might have been involved in Gemma's death. Deciding she didn't want to find out, she slipped around to the other side of the building and followed some planter boxes to a car park at the back. Then she let out a shuddering breath as Gemma's death really sunk in.

When someone passed it was never easy, but for someone so young to have been brutally murdered made it even more difficult to accept. Ginny rubbed her arms and tried to swallow down the lump in her throat at the dreadfulness of it all.

From the front of the building, a low chant rose in some kind of ritual. As the chanting reached a crescendo, she wondered if Gemma would have been gratified to have so many fans turn up and honour her, or been horrified that her favourite motto had in fact come to pass. *Remember you must die.*

The chanting stopped moments later and then came the sound of hurried footsteps, which made Ginny think one of the officers must have moved them on. She leaned back into the shade of the station wall, and sent Anita a quick text to let her know she was in the car park, in case the PC was worried she'd gone AWOL.

Anita pinged back to say she'd be another five minutes, and Ginny closed her eyes, trying to make sense of what had happened. But her meditations were cut off as another voice floated over.

'I've tried that, but Sterling won't listen. She said that we're not paid to look at old forensic evidence now the case is closed. Especially as we have a current murder to investigate. But I can't just leave this. Why was someone else's bone included in Lesley Charlton's remains? There is no mention of it in the notes, and while it's clear it's much older, without sending it off to be tested I can't be sure. And I know that Gemma was the one to find the skull, so why won't anyone tell me where she got it?'

Ginny held in her stomach as the pathologist Imogen Smith suddenly appeared from the back of the building. Her red hair was pulled back from her face and she had earbuds in, which suggested she was talking to someone on the phone. For Ginny, who was still mastering public phone calls, that was a step too far, but Imogen was obviously comfortable with the technology as she used her hands to juggle a large folder and a cup of coffee.

'Yes, but...' Imogen broke off as she noticed Ginny. Her face immediately drained of colour. 'James, I have to go.'

Ginny straightened and realised she was still holding her stomach in. Which was silly because she hadn't done anything wrong. *Well, apart from eavesdropping on a personal phone call about the Lesley Charlton case, between the pathologist and DI Wallace, who were apparently on a first-name basis with each other.*

Taking a gulp of air, Ginny waved politely as Imogen stared at her.

'Mrs Cole. I-I didn't see you there.' Two bright spots of colour now blazed on the pathologist's cheeks.

'Please, call me Ginny. And I'm sorry. I didn't mean to over-hear anything. I'm waiting for Anita... I mean, PC Singh, to give me a lift home.'

'I see. But why are you here? Surely it's not about the skull?' Imogen's eyebrows knitted together.

'Well, yes, I suppose you could say that. Tuppence and I spoke with Gemma Murphy on Saturday and then she seemed to disappear for a few days, so I called PC Singh to check on her.'

'What?' Imogen all but yelped. 'I have just finished the autopsy and am about to meet Sterling. But she hadn't mentioned your involvement.' Then she let out a soft sigh. 'I take it you heard my conversation with James?'

'I am ever so sorry. I wasn't trying to listen.'

'Don't apologise, it's my fault. I should've ended the call before I got out of my car.' Imogen juggled the pile of folders and the coffee cup around so that she could run a hand through her lovely hair. 'I should have taken that bet.'

'Bet?' Ginny blinked.

'James bet that you would somehow get yourself involved in this case.'

'I assume he wasn't smiling when he said it.' Ginny rolled her shoulders, trying to shake off the feeling of impending doom. 'Did he sound angry?'

'No, but I think that if he wasn't on the other side of the world, he'd be having a stern conversation with you,' Imogen admitted, before stepping into the shade and joining Ginny. 'Do I dare ask *why* you were talking with Gemma Murphy five days before she was murdered?'

'It's a little convoluted.' Ginny swallowed, but considering Imogen was probably going to hear it all from Sterling soon enough, she repeated what she'd told the detective, including her concern that there was more to Lesley Charlton's murder than first appeared, before adding Maureen and Joey West's interest in events.

Once she was done, Imogen leaned back against the brick wall and groaned. 'Oh dear. The idea of someone like Joey West getting involved is the only thing this case needed to take it to a Dantesque level of hell.'

Ginny raised an eyebrow. Thus far, her experiences with the police hadn't lent themselves to literary references, and she was almost tempted to ask if Imogen preferred the Botticelli or the Blake illustrations but thought better of it. Instead, she dared to look at the pathologist. 'Is that why you were calling Wallace... er, I mean, James? Because of the case?'

'Not exactly. It's because we are friends. We met about ten years ago in London, when I was dating a friend of his. It was before he moved up here. Anyway, the relationship' – she broke off and sharp colour flooded her cheeks – 'ended not that long ago and I needed a fresh start. I had no idea James was here until that last murder.'

'So, you're friends,' Ginny said, as things started to make

sense. She'd seen them several times together and while it hadn't looked romantic, it hadn't looked like a work conversation either. The thought made her smile. She'd lived next door to Wallace for almost a year, and she'd hardly ever seen him with other people. Or even relaxing. Maybe having a friend like Imogen, who seemed warm and ready to smile, might be just what the more serious Wallace needed.

'Yes, I suppose we are. Well, that is if he forgives me for waking him up at four in the morning. I got a bit muddled with the time difference. I just needed some advice.'

'I hope he gave it to you,' Ginny said, as Anita appeared at the far end of the car park. She swallowed, the overheard phone call still going around in her mind. 'You don't have to answer this if you don't want. But I couldn't help overhearing you talking about an extra bone.'

'I see what James means about your tenacity.'

'My husband used to say that I like to finish what I start,' Ginny admitted.

Imogen chewed her lip then leaned in closer. 'Please don't repeat this, but when I went back through the original forensic evidence for the Lesley Charlton case, I found a carpometacarpal joint that didn't belong to the rest of the victim's bones. Sterling didn't want me to follow it up. But in the light of this new murder, I'm hoping I'll be able to go ahead and get it tested.' Imogen broke off as Anita reached them.

'Doctor Smith,' Anita greeted the pathologist. 'DI Sterling will be pleased to see you. Though I warn you, she's on the warpath.'

TWENTY-FOUR

'At least we have a good reason to skip Senior Shake and Shuffle,' Tuppence said, as she opened her front door and beckoned Ginny inside, where Hen and JM were already waiting.

Ginny managed a weak smile. It had already been a long day, and it wasn't over yet.

By the time Anita had dropped her back at the library, all traces of the champagne and cake had been cleared away, and Connor promised that his nan had gone straight home instead of on a vengeance-soaked mission to make Jacinta Theakston pay.

After all, Gemma had already paid and, regardless of the special treatment Jacinta might have received at the Walton-on-Marsh police station, she'd still be upset.

'Now we're all here, let's get started,' JM said, but Tuppence shook her head.

'Actually, I think we should go out to the studio. I have something to show you.'

'The studio?' Hen made a squeaking noise, her gaze sweeping across Tuppence's face, as if checking to see if she was feeling well. Ginny wasn't surprised. As far as she knew, no one had been out there in years, not even Tuppence.

'It's time,' Tuppence announced, and led them through the cottage, across the garden and to the free-standing studio.

The three of them exchanged worried glances before stepping into the light-filled space. Brandon, who had accompanied Hen, gave a curious sniff and wagged his tail.

A stack of large canvases leaned against the back wall along with several easels and ladders, while the shelves were full of books and ephemera that Ginny suspected had belonged to Taron as part of his research. And on one of the easels was a large pencil sketch of the Walton-on-Marsh mural that Ginny and Tuppence had visited the previous day.

Ginny swallowed as she looked around. The heavy layers of dust suggested Tuppence had been avoiding the studio, in the same way she'd been avoiding Taron's final work. In the far corner was a collection of abstract paintings, some in primary colours, but many in unusual palettes of lavender and orange. They weren't like anything Ginny had seen before, and yet they also screamed *Tuppence*.

'Oh, how wonderful.' JM, who had once owned an art gallery, strode over. 'I love the mid-century influence and how you've fused it with a modern sensibility.'

'And the colour mix is dreamy,' Hen chimed in.

'When I look at them, I smile,' Ginny added, unable to stop the upturn of her mouth as she studied them.

'Thank you. That means a lot coming from you all.' Tuppence gave them a shy smile before squaring her shoulders and walking over to an easel that was covered with a sheet. 'But this isn't just a trip down memory lane. I realised that if we're going to solve this case, we needed to rethink the address book-cum-murder board.'

'Oh dear.' Hen's hand flew to her mouth. 'Is this because of what I said the other day? Tuppence, I didn't mean to upset you.'

'Nonsense, she doesn't look very upset,' JM corrected. 'But do get on with the big reveal. I have no time for dramatic pauses.'

'Ta-da.' Tuppence pulled back the sheet. Dust motes from the surrounding surfaces flew up, catching the late afternoon sun that was still pouring through the windows, but Ginny hardly noticed as she stared at the large poster board on the easel.

It was an explosion of colours, with smaller words written everywhere. In the centre it said 'M for murder' written in a pink swirling font. And underneath were two circles, one for Lesley Charlton and one for Gemma Murphy, with a perfectly rendered skull sitting between them.

From there twenty-five lines spiralled out like a mind map to all the other letters of the alphabet and, underneath each one, were the notes that Tuppence had been storing in the address book.

The studio was silent as they stared at it.

Finally, Tuppence made a small sound in the back of her throat. 'Why is no one speaking? Does this mean you hate it? Are you cross that I didn't consult with you all first? It's just while I was stuck in that interview room, my mind was trying to figure out how all the pieces fitted together and then my fingers twitched to hold a paintbrush. They haven't done that for such a long time. Anyway, I suppose I just got carried away.'

'Carried away? Well, that's an understatement,' JM retorted, and then grinned. 'This is wonderful.'

'Absolutely,' Hen agreed. 'It's so beautiful.'

'And it's exactly what we need,' Ginny added. 'Yesterday we weren't investigating a murder, but today we are.'

'So, you agree that we should look into it?' Hen checked.

'Well, of course we should.' JM picked up a long paintbrush and, holding it by its bristle end, started to use it as a pointer. 'Gemma Murphy was killed on our watch. We owe it to her to find out what's really going on since Sterling might be trying to bury the truth. What do we know?'

'The time of death was between six and eight p.m.,' Ginny said, as Tuppence picked up a fine brush and painted in the details. 'It takes Annabel Faulkner out of the picture, since she was at my house.'

'What about Jacinta? If Gemma was released from the station, Jacinta must have been as well? What if she was angry that Gemma lied to her about the skull being real?' Tuppence wondered.

'Seems a strange way to show it. Besides, Jacinta doesn't strike me as someone who likes to get her hands dirty,' Hen said. 'And we don't know if her murder is connected to Lesley's death.'

'But we can't rule it out.' JM began to pace the room. 'Especially now we know about the extra bone that Imogen found, which had been ignored in the initial investigation. What was it called?'

'A carpometacarpal joint,' Ginny said, as Tuppence painted the small bone in a blazing red. 'Imogen told me, off the record, that it was older than the other bones.'

'Sounds dodgy to me.' Tuppence looked up from her painting. There was a splodge of green on the tip of her nose, but her eyes were bright with the same gleam Hen got when she was knitting. 'Why wouldn't the police have investigated it more? And why won't Sterling let Imogen get it tested?'

'Same reason she bit Ginny's head off for suggesting that Sterling Senior might have ignored evidence.' JM turned on her heel as she continued pacing.

'I didn't say it quite like that.' Heat travelled up Ginny's neck, still not quite able to believe she'd said it out loud. 'Though I can't blame her for getting angry. It wasn't very nice of me to bring her father into it. We haven't met him and there's nothing to suggest he didn't do a good job.'

'Doesn't mean he did, either.' JM once again played devil's advocate. 'We've been so distracted that we never did any research on him. What do we even know?'

'We saw him having a conversation with DI Sterling at the coffee shop in Walton-on-Marsh. Do you think they were discussing the case?' Hen's eyes widened.

'I hope not. It wouldn't be appropriate since he's no longer on the force.' JM folded her arms. 'But it makes me wonder if he was mining her for information? If only we knew where he lived.'

Ginny's breath quickened as she recalled her meeting with Ross Mitchell. 'Actually, he lives up the Walton-on-Marsh end of Boundary Road, and he's just sold it, so all we have to do is look for the sign out the front.'

Tuppence put down her brush and smoothed her overalls. 'I think we should visit Stuart Sterling and see what he has to say.'

'Excellent. I'm in the mood for a shakedown.' JM joined her and cracked her knuckles, but shook her head when Ginny stood up. 'I don't think you should come, though, in case it gets back to DI Sterling.'

It was a good point and Ginny sat back down.

'We could stay here and research Sterling and Gemma.' Hen patted a sleeping Brandon on the head. 'It's a pity we don't have William's newspapers.'

'Nonsense. I think it's time we all improved our internet skills. You're lucky I have Edward's spare laptop with me.' JM gave them a stern look, retrieved a laptop from her bag and passed it over. 'See what you can find out and we can update the board as soon as we get back.'

Ginny gulped as they took the machine. This would be interesting.

An hour later, and Ginny was exhausted.

'Goodness, I had no idea so many of these sites existed,' Hen said, as they went onto yet another social media platform. 'And reading the comments was a jolly good trick. Lucky JM isn't here, though, she would probably say they're making her eyes bleed.'

'Yes, some of them seem very petty. We didn't have much luck with Stuart Sterling, but I was hopeful we'd find something else on Gemma, especially with the research hacks you found,' Ginny admitted.

'I have some more here.' Hen picked up her notebook and flicked through it. In the end they'd decided to first research how to get better search results on the internet and had been trying them out one at a time.

'Okay, let's try mentioning a location as well as her name,' Hen announced, and Ginny dutifully typed in Gemma Murphy and Walton-on-Marsh. Numerous articles populated the screen but most of them referred to Gemma's YouTube clips that they'd already seen.

'There's nothing new here. Oh dear.' Ginny scanned through the numerous articles.

Hen peered back at the notebook. 'Here, try using a minus sign directly before YouTube. That should stop any of the videos from coming up.'

Ginny did as directed and blinked in surprise when several articles about Gemma appeared, that they hadn't seen before. It took a few minutes for them to read the content, but there still wasn't anything that resembled a clue.

'I think we should move on to the next idea on the list.' Hen peered over Ginny's shoulder. 'It says we should use a photograph and then do a search.'

'I know how to do that.' Ginny brightened.

'Maybe we're getting better at this,' Hen said as Ginny managed to copy one of the many photographs of Gemma and put it into the search bar along with the location. They both stared at the results.

'Oh.' Ginny's eyes widened as a whole list of new articles flashed up. She clicked on the first one and began to read the headline: *Local Girl on Loom Lane Makes Good*. Next to it was a photo of Gemma Murphy, wearing one of her tight outfits, standing outside a large building with her hands up in the air.

Gemma Murphy is a girl on a mission. Not content with running a popular YouTube channel, this young entrepreneur is well on the way to global success with the purchase of her yoga studio in the newly built commercial building on Loom Lane. When asked what inspired her to make such a bold move at such a young age, she was quick to say that it was up to her generation to be the change they wanted to see in the world.

'I believe in creating an ethical brand that empowers young women like myself and this is just the start of my journey.'

'Wait. She *owned* that place?' Hen squeaked. 'But it was huge, and brand new. It would have been worth a fortune. How could a twenty-five-year-old girl afford it?'

'She was twenty-three when she bought it.' Ginny read further down the article to the comments section. 'Oh, this is interesting. Someone has called her a typical nepo baby. Maybe that's why she was killed?'

'What's a nepo baby when it's at home?' Hen frowned.

'It means nepotism baby,' Ginny explained, though she only knew about it because Connor had talked about them the other month. 'I think it's when children of wealthy parents get certain advantages because of their family name.'

'Ah. A new term but an old tradition.' Hen sighed. 'Things

like that have been happening throughout the ages. But how does Gemma Murphy fit in? I thought her mother had died, and she didn't have any other relatives.'

'According to this commentator, she had a big trust fund.' Ginny scrolled down to see what else she could find, but the other comments were more focused on Gemma's outfit and make-up.

'Big enough to buy a yoga studio?' Hen was still astounded. 'I suppose it explains why she and Jacinta were friends. They both had businesses bought for them.'

They were cut off by the sound of Brandon barking as JM and Tuppence strode back in. Their hair was wet and their shirts were clinging to their skin.

Ginny's brow furrowed and she peered out of the window. It wasn't raining.

'You're back.' Hen looked up and gasped. 'Um. How did it go?'

Tuppence wrinkled her nose and walked over to the murder board painting. 'I'm not sure it was our best work.'

'I'm definitely losing my shakedown powers.' JM frowned. 'From now on we can only take on cases in Little Shaw.'

'Oh dear.' Hen's face fell. 'Did he get angry at you?'

'I wouldn't say angry exactly. But I also wouldn't say he'd be happy to see us again,' JM admitted, as Tuppence painted a large cross through Sterling's name and then put a rain cloud above it. 'He turned the hose on us.'

'Jolly rude, too,' Tuppence added. 'Thankfully it's quite a hot day so I found it refreshing.'

'His manners are severely lacking,' JM retorted, before squaring her shoulders. 'How did you both go?'

'We have this.' Ginny showed them the article and the comment section.

'A nepo baby?' Tuppence said, and painted a tiara above

Gemma's name. 'Do you think someone might have resented Gemma for her money?'

'We need to keep our options open,' JM said, holding up her fingers. 'We have money as one motive. But we also have the Lesley connection. Stuart Sterling worked on the case twenty years ago – apparently rather sloppily, given the extra bone – and now his daughter is also working on it. They could be covering something up.'

'Ross Mitchell told us that Lesley had been obsessed with the Lawson map. Could that be part of it?'

'Quite possibly,' Hen agreed. 'Except Ross also said he couldn't find any information on the map and had never seen it. So, unless someone else had one, how could it be so contentious?'

'I don't suppose you've heard back from Harold about it all?' Tuppence asked, in a hopeful voice.

'Not yet.' Ginny pressed her lips together as she studied the murder board Tuppence had painted. Her gaze kept going back to the carpometacarpal joint. Who did it belong to, and did it mean there was yet another skeleton in someone's closet?

'Woof.' Brandon suddenly started kicking out in his sleep, dreaming of goodness knew what as he air-galloped, wriggling off his cushion in the process.

'Oh no, my love. Don't do that, there's not enough room.' Hen reached for his collar.

'And far too much dust.' Tuppence coughed.

'Not to mention all the precariously placed paintings,' JM added, as the still-dreaming Brandon sent one of the easels crashing over. She reached out just in time to save the large pencil sketch of Taron's mural from falling to the floor.

'Oh, JM, thank you.' Tuppence's face had gone pale at the idea such a precious piece of her husband's legacy might have been damaged. She took it – then let out a soft cry. 'I don't believe it.'

'What's wrong? I hope it's not damaged.' Hen settled down a sleepy-looking Brandon, then hurried over to see what had upset Tuppence so much.

'No, but look at this.' Tuppence's hand shook as she pointed to the pencil sketch of Sir Joseph Faulkner, Baronet. It was the same as on the mural but without all the colour and details, and on a much smaller scale.

Ginny's gaze drifted down to the scroll in his hands. In the mural it appeared like a piece of paper, perhaps to suggest the royal decree of lineage. But in this sketch, it was a map.

'No, it can't be.' JM was the first to speak. 'This is different from the Stanley map.'

Hen gasped. 'You don't think it's a sketch of the Lawson one, do you?'

'We can soon find out.' Tuppence put the sketch back on the easel and hurried over to the crammed shelves. There were several boxes, all labelled with years and project names, and it didn't take Tuppence long to return with one. She delved inside, before lifting something out, her eyes bright with pride. 'My Taron never did anything by halves.'

'No indeed.' JM grinned as Tuppence smoothed out the old parchment so they could see it properly. It was a map, but unlike the Stanley map that hadn't been hand-coloured, this was shaded in parts, though the colours had faded with time. But it was beautiful nonetheless, with the lakes and rivers all thatched in a careful hand as well as intricate details around the hills and lanes.

'Do you think it's the same one that belonged to Lesley?' Hen asked.

'No, look, you can see that Taron's written a note to go with it. He bought it at an auction thirty years ago, and we know Lesley had hers until twenty years ago.' Tuppence studied a small piece of paper that had been rolled up with the map.

'It makes sense that there was more than one copy of the map,' JM admitted.

'The main thing is that we have it. Well done,' Hen agreed.

'Absolutely.' Ginny joined them, still not able to comprehend that they finally had the key to this whole mystery. The same map that Lesley Charlton had been so protective of. Created by the unknown Malcolm Lawson.

TWENTY-FIVE

'Please tell me you all washed your hands before touching this,' Harold said the following morning, unable to look up as he stared at the map.

Ginny had called him the previous evening in the hopes they could go around to his house immediately, but had been thwarted by getting no reply, and it wasn't until eight the following morning that he'd sent her a text explaining he and Myles had been at a classical music recital.

Once again, Connor had agreed to open the library. When this was over, Ginny really needed to see about getting him a raise.

'Absolutely,' they all chorused, and then exchanged a guilty look. Even Ginny had been too excited at the discovery to remember how careful people needed to be around such old parchments.

'You're all terrible liars,' Harold retorted, gaze still trans-fixed on the Lawson map, laid on the table next to the framed

Stanley map, which had been taken down from the wall. He reached for a large magnifying glass and moved closer.

'He means that in a loving way,' Myles assured them as he came into the room with a tea tray and a plate of delicate biscuits. 'I'll leave this over here, so no one is tempted to spill anything on the new treasure.'

'I hope you haven't learnt that lesson the hard way,' JM asked.

'Let's just say it was a near-miss.' A smile danced in Myles' eyes as he beckoned them over. 'It's probably best if we give him some space. Though considering this turn of events, I'm sure he won't mind if I steal his glory and share the other news he discovered.'

'Steal away,' Harold called out from across the room, and Myles smiled.

'He couldn't find out much about Malcolm Lawson; however, he did look into Lesley's family tree and found something interesting. There was an ordnance surveyor hired by a gentleman not far from Jackson Fold.'

'The area that was flooded so that the Faulkners could expand their textile business,' Ginny gasped, recalling what she'd been told about the start of the feud between the two villages.

'Correct. They were worried about the proposed sale to the Faulkners in case this happened, since it would destroy their own road access.'

'Someone tried to stop Old Jack from being killed off?' Tuppence marvelled.

'Yes.' Harold suddenly turned to them, the magnifying glass still held up to his face, making one eye appear enormous. Myles gestured at it and Harold lowered it before continuing the story. 'From what I could discover, the surveyor, a chap named Gareth Davies, moved to the area to do the survey and fell in love with Lesley Charlton's fifth great-grandmother. However, despite promising marriage, he abruptly left the area and moved to Newcastle, leaving her pregnant, and never completing the survey. But he did leave behind the map by Malcolm Lawson, which he might have been using as a reference.'

'What about the Henry Stanley map? Would he have used that as well?' JM asked.

'It's entirely possible. The Lawson map is dated 1743 and the Stanley map was done in 1745, so I imagine he referred to both. And that his equipment might have also been left behind. However, it's impossible to say, and I'm surprised that even one map managed to get passed down through the generations.'

'That's so sad.' Hen's eyes misted up.

'I agree, it's very sad.' Harold beckoned them over to the two maps. 'Not because he deserted her, but because I suspect he was murdered.'

'What?' Ginny gasped, surprised at how quickly she found her voice. But even as she said it, she thought of the carpometacarpal joint that Imogen had found. Was it possible that it had belonged to Gareth Davies? But why would someone murder him? And Jackson Fold had been sold almost two hundred years ago, so how could they possibly solve something like this now?

However, as she studied the tight smile around Harold's mouth, she quickly got to her feet.

'Oh, you clever man. You've found something, haven't you?' Myles joined his husband.

'I have,' Harold agreed as they all crowded around, and he pointed to the eastern corner of Lancashire on the Stanley map, an expectant gleam in his eyes.

'Eh?' JM peered closer. 'What are we looking at? Is it the skull marker, where Lesley's bones were discovered? Because we already know about that.'

'And we know all about Jackson Fold,' Tuppence added.

'Not to mention how much Walton-on-Marsh grew after it was flooded,' Hen chimed in.

Ginny's brows pressed together as she stared at the place on the Stanley map that Hen was pointing to. Walton-on-Marsh was there, as was the tiny hamlet of Jackson Fold. Further along was Little Shaw.

She turned her attention back to the Lawson map and let out a gasp.

Harold began to laugh. 'I take it you've seen what the issue is?'

'Yes, but how is it possible?' Ginny's heart thundered in her chest.

'How is *what* possible?' JM demanded. 'Was I not clear on what I think of dramatic pauses?'

'Sorry, you're right.' Harold's smile fell away. 'What the Lawson map is showing us is that Walton-on-Marsh does not exist.'

'That makes no sense.' Hen's gaze went from one map to another. 'Did Lawson just forget to put it in?'

'Can't say I blame him. Maybe he visited the place and thought better of it?' Tuppence offered up. 'It does have that effect on people.'

'Tempting but doubtful.' Harold pointed to the two dates the maps were made. 'Remember that Lawson did his map two years earlier and, considering how thorough it is, I would suggest there's only one reason he didn't include it. Because it wasn't there.'

'I still don't follow,' Tuppence admitted.

'It's a cartographer's folly... a copyright trap,' Harold explained, before turning to Ginny. 'Remember I was telling you about all the double dealings and underhanded things that went on back then when it came to boundaries and map making?'

'Yes. But I don't know what a copyright trap is,' Ginny admitted.

'They're made-up places.' Myles let out a short bark of laughter. 'And words. They were sometimes put into maps or dictionaries as a way of proving if someone was copying the work.'

'Like a honey-trap.' JM's eyes widened. 'But if Walton-on-Marsh isn't a real town, how do you explain it suddenly appearing?'

'That's the thing. These copyright traps... or paper towns, as they're also known, can end up becoming real. I suspect someone might have set up a shop in the area after seeing the Stanley map, and so it began.' Harold's eyes sparkled with the excitement of a historical discovery.

Ginny stepped away to work through what it meant. Ross Mitchell had said Lesley was fascinated by his copy of the Stanley map. Did that mean she'd also noticed the discrepancy? And then what? Had she told someone, who then murdered her for it? But why?

She turned back to Harold. 'What are the implications if it was discovered Walton-on-Marsh wasn't a real town? Does it even matter?'

'I can assure you it matters.' Harold's eyes darkened and he folded his arms. 'It would affect everything. Parish boundaries for a start. And then there are property claims and inheritance rights, not to mention tax.'

Ginny's throat tightened as she thought of what Ross said about the cost of property and how his cottage was only worth half as much as those on the Walton-on-Marsh side of the boundary.

It would be more lovely if it was a mile down the road.

How many other properties had been affected by the copyright trick, and how many had benefited?

Such as Stuart Sterling's house.

Then there were so many other things to consider. The implications could be huge. Not to mention the humiliation for everyone in the village. Especially for the most powerful, well-known family in the area, who had benefited the most.

'Ginny, are you thinking that someone killed Lesley Charlton because she discovered this?' JM asked, her shrewd gaze fixed on Ginny's face.

'Yes,' she admitted, her words sounding hollow. 'Remember that Stuart Sterling has just sold his own property on the Walton-on-Marsh side of Boundary Road.'

'You think he killed Lesley to protect the price of his house?' Hen said, but Ginny shook her head.

'No. Lesley was killed twenty years ago, and there would be no reason for her to take the map discrepancy to the police. If I found it, the first person I'd think of taking it to would be the ones most involved in the history of the town. And the only people I can think of are—' She broke off, not wanting to say it out loud.

'—Sir Spencer and Lady Faulkner,' JM finished.

There was silence as they all considered it. The worst of it was that Ginny had liked Lady Kitty. She was down to earth and energetic and had done so much for her community and for the Faulkner estate.

But at what cost?

'Whatever you do, you can't outright accuse them of anything,' Harold reminded them. 'Not until I do more research. There's still a chance we're wrong about the copyright trap. May I suggest that you wait until I have more conclusive proof?'

'No, you may not. There's a killer out there and I've had quite enough of these Walton-on-Marsh people lording it up over the likes of us,' JM retorted as she gathered up her bag and fumbled for her car keys. 'We'll leave the research to you and you leave the shaking down to us. I'm feeling my powers return. Now, let's pay Lady Kitty a visit.'

Ginny's stomach tightened but JM was right. It had to be done. She collected her handbag as Hen picked up the address book – still in use when they were out and about – and handed it to Tuppence.

'I think you need to put this under "O" for Oh dear.'

TWENTY-SIX

'I wondered how long it would take for someone to work it out,' Lady Kitty said an hour later, as Ginny and her friends stood on her doorstep, holding a printed copy of the Lawson map.

They'd considered bringing the original with them, but Harold had been horrified and refused to allow them to. He hadn't even let them put it through the scanner, instead insisting they take a photograph and print it out that way.

'Eh?' JM blinked, lost for words.

'Not the reception I was expecting,' Hen admitted.

'Definitely anti-climactic,' Tuppence agreed, before peering over Lady Kitty's shoulder into the formal entranceway of Oldfield House.

Ginny was equally confused. Despite spending the drive going over ways the encounter might play out, none of them had considered a full confession as being on the table.

'I take it you've seen this map before,' Ginny said, scanning Lady Kitty's face, trying to get a read on what she was thinking.

Her countenance was placid and open, though her brown eyes were filled with... *is that remorse?*

'I have. I think you'd better all come inside.'

'Oh, do you just? Well, we'll be the judge of that,' JM retorted, before turning to her friends and lowering her voice. 'What do you think? Do we risk it?'

'Yes,' Tuppence said. 'It might be my only chance to look around.'

'I have always wanted to see inside,' Hen admitted, and they turned to Ginny.

She swallowed. They'd gone there to confront Lady Kitty about what they'd discovered, but her acquiescence was disconcerting. Did that mean it was a trap? It wouldn't be the first time she'd walked into something dangerous, and she didn't like making the same mistake twice.

'Okay,' she agreed. 'But on no account drink any tea or eat the cakes. Just in case they're poison.'

'They're not,' Lady Kitty assured them in a calm voice from the doorstep. 'But Cynthia isn't here right now, and she usually makes the tea for guests, so I'm happy to go without. Now, let's get this over and done with.'

It was a wide entrance with slate floors and a wooden stairway that housed several gold-framed portraits of the first baronet, Sir John Faulkner, while an oak table had a visitor's book and numerous leaflets, suggesting that they regularly did house tours. It was grand but not very personal, and didn't seem to match the weather-blown Lady Kitty.

She led them through to a smaller, less formal room with a threadbare sofa, three or four armchairs, a stack of gardening books and a large open fire that had been swept and stacked with logs for when the cooler weather hit. On a small console table, there were several pill bottles and scrawled phone messages, as well as a TV guide and a remote control.

'Please, have a seat.' Lady Kitty motioned them to the sofa

and armchairs, and then sat down herself. A couple of cats who had been sprawled on the carpet immediately planted themselves on either side of their human.

Ginny cautiously sank into an armchair. 'Why do you think we're here?' she asked, not sure how to start the conversation. 'What is it that you think we've worked out about Lesley's death?'

For the first time Lady Kitty showed a hint of surprise and lifted an eyebrow. 'Lesley Charlton? What's there to work out? The poor woman was murdered by her husband.'

'Or was she?' JM said in an ominous voice, as she reached for the map that Ginny had put on the crowded coffee table. 'We know that Lesley had a copy of this... and that she most likely worked out what was on it.'

'She did,' Lady Kitty affirmed and closed her eyes, as if gathering her strength. 'Twenty years ago, Lesley came to visit me and showed me the Lawson map. I'd never heard of him, though we do have the Stanley version. When she told me Walton-on-Marsh was a copyright trap, I didn't believe her. I mean, Spenny's family have been here forever. We're not some backwater village that no one knows of—'

'Objection. Witness is suggesting that Little Shaw *is* a backwater village.' JM jumped to her feet. But at Lady Kitty's startled expression she waved her on. 'You may continue.'

'O-kay.' Lady Kitty swallowed as shame filled her eyes. 'Like I said at first, I didn't believe her so decided to do some research through our own archives. There wasn't anything in the study, but there were older boxes down in the cellars and that's where I found... it.'

'Found what?' Tuppence leaned forward, eyes wide.

Ginny's own heart was pounding, and her skin prickled with discomfort for the obvious pain Lady Kitty was experiencing.

'Sir Joseph's diary. You might be aware he was the first baronet of Faulkner—?'

'It has been brought to our attention once or twice,' JM's reply was dry.

Lady Kitty sighed. 'No one is more aware than I am of how much this village has lorded it over Little Shaw, and the rest of the area. And while there's no denying Sir Joseph did remarkable things, especially in Parliament, some of his *other* actions were not so commendable.'

'What did the diary say?' Ginny asked, her heart still beating fast.

Lady Kitty swallowed hard. 'A young surveyor called Gareth Davies confronted him. He'd been hired by a landowner near Jackson Fold to contest the sale, knowing that if the area was flooded it would unfavourably affect his land, and the industry of the nearby villages. He had several maps with him as proof that Walton-on-Marsh was nothing more than a publisher's copyright trap put in to protect Lawson's map.'

Ginny sucked in her breath. 'Did you know that Gareth Davies was related to Lesley?'

'I suspected as much. Lesley told me she'd inherited the map and had never understood why it had been in the family.'

'Did the diary mention what happened to Davies?' Tuppence wanted to know, the little address book in her hand. 'We were told he moved away from the area and left a woman high and dry, and expecting a child.'

Lady Kitty sighed heavily. 'Unfortunately, that's not true. Joseph wrote that he couldn't bear the idea of facing the shame that the village he was so proud of had merely been a cartographer's folly, not to mention possibly losing his water and property rights. There was a fight and while I like to believe it was an accident, the result is what matters. Joseph buried the body out on Harris Hill, near the lime caves. There had been an accident there some years earlier.'

Ginny swallowed. It was the same place Lesley's body had been buried. Had someone done it on purpose? And *was* that who the carpometacarpal joint belonged to?

The room was silent, everyone turning over the same thought.

The much famed and lauded first baronet of Faulkner had murdered Gareth Davies.

TWENTY-SEVEN

For a long time no one spoke.

But finally, Tuppence stood and left the room and marched out to her car, returning several minutes later with the murder board that she'd painted. She dragged over a stunning Louis XV chair covered in plain blue fabric and perched the painting across the polished oak arms.

It seemed to shake Lady Kitty out of her reverie and she leaned forward. 'What is that?'

'A murder board,' Hen said, with pride. 'It's what we used to figure things out. Though maybe you shouldn't look at all the entries that include your family.'

'Yes, sometimes we are only speculating. Think of it like mind-mapping,' Tuppence added quickly.

'And sometimes we're *not*.' JM gave them all a stern look before getting to her feet and standing next to Tuppence. 'Lady Kitty, please answer truthfully. What happened when you found out that Lesley Charlton's claims were correct? Did you murder her and set up her husband to take the fall?'

'Murder her?' Lady Kitty stiffened so quickly that one of the cats made a hissing sound. She bent over and soothed it before returning JM's penetrating gaze. 'Of course I didn't. How can you even think that?'

JM opened her mouth as if to give several reasons, but Hen quickly jumped in. 'So, what did you do? Did you try and talk to her about it?'

'The day I went to visit her was the day the news broke about her disappearance. I felt terrible because she'd seemed a lovely woman.'

'Yet, it also solved a big problem for you. With her out of the way, the family skeletons could go safely back into the closet.' JM still didn't seem happy.

'I know it must look like that.' Colour stung the baroness's cheeks, and she sagged back in her chair. 'And I suppose in a way you're right. But if I went public it would have destroyed the Faulkner legacy. And poor Spenny. His health has never been marvellous, even back then. Despite all the chatter about Randal being better suited, Spenny's always done his best, so to have this happen on his watch would've been disastrous.'

'Did you even tell him?'

'Goodness, no. It would have killed him. But I've tried to make sure we're giving back to people. Everything I've done since then has been to make amends.'

'Make amends to who? From what I could see, all your work was purely for Walton-on-Marsh, and excuse me for being crass, but I think they've already had quite enough,' Tuppence replied, and Lady Kitty seemed to sink even further back into her chair.

Ginny's heart was caught between sympathy and outrage at what had happened to Gareth Davies. *And to Lesley Charlton.* She rubbed her arms as something else occurred to her.

'When you found out Lesley had disappeared, did you consider that it was due to what she'd discovered?'

Her friends all went still as they stared at Lady Kitty, waiting for her reaction.

'No. Never. I swear to you. Besides, three days later her husband was found dead with a confession note, written in his own handwriting, so I had no reason to.' Lady Kitty suddenly looked up, face drained of colour. 'You don't really think it's connected? How could that be?'

'You tell us,' JM said. 'Did you ever meet Gemma Murphy?'

'Yes, numerous times,' Lady Kitty said, and they all turned to her. She flushed at the attention. 'She came to the house once a week to run yoga classes for some of the staff. I tried to attend one of them, but they weren't for me. However, some of the younger workers enjoyed them.'

Ginny exchanged a glance with her friends. Gemma Murphy had been to the house numerous times. Had she found the diary and tried to bribe them over it? Or... the skull itself? It would explain how she came to be in possession of it. But it didn't explain Lady Kitty's adamant denial.

'You said you didn't tell Sir Spencer, but did someone else know about it? What about Randal or Annabel?' Ginny asked.

'No. Randal, for all his peacocking, isn't much more robust than his brother. As for Annabel, I didn't tell her for concern about what she might have done. I'm sure she loves this place more than I do.'

'So, you didn't tell *anyone*?' Ginny pressed, unease creeping up her throat.

'No... well, yes. But only Cynthia, and I trust her completely. She's worked with me for thirty years and she'd never do anything to hurt the estate.'

Never do anything to hurt the estate.

The words echoed in Ginny's mind. It was strange phrasing considering they were such close friends. Shouldn't she have said *hurt me*? Alarm bells began to ring in her mind.

'Did Cynthia attend Gemma's yoga classes?'

'Why, yes. And I think she paid her for private lessons at her own house, too,' Lady Kitty said, as the door swung open and Annabel Faulkner marched in.

She was wearing what Ginny had started to call the Walton-on-Marsh uniform: an expensive skirt and equally expensive silk shirt that didn't show any signs of sweat despite the heat outside. The only concession to the weather was a hat, in her right hand.

'Honestly, Kitty, you could have bloody well called me. I got caught in the most shocking traffic on the way to pick up Spenny from his appointment, and when I got there, they told me you'd already collected him. *Oh.*' Annabel took in the occupants of the room. Her brow was drawn, but the familiar scowl was nowhere in sight, and her mouth softened into a faint smile. 'I didn't realise you had company.'

'Never mind that.' Lady Kitty got to her feet, the pain in her eyes replaced by worry as she hurried over to Annabel. 'I didn't collect him because I had an appointment with the gallery about next month's fundraiser.'

'Well, why did they say you'd been there?' Annabel snapped, clearly frustrated from a wasted trip.

'No idea. This is his first time at that clinic. It was to check a growth on his hand,' Kitty said, before her mouth tightened in worry. 'I don't understand this. Here, where's my phone? I need to call them.'

Ginny and her friends exchanged worried looks.

'Should we leave?' Hen whispered.

'Definitely not. We still have unanswered questions,' JM said firmly, as Annabel stalked over to them.

'What unanswered questions? Why are you here? I hope you're not hashing over what happened with the wedding. I have explained myself to the Wests – and damn uncomfortable it was, too. So, there's really no need to bring Kitty into this. She has enough things to worry about with Spenny's health—'

'Clearly I didn't pick him up since I'm calling you about it,' Lady Kitty's voice cut them off as she paced at the back of the room. 'Please describe what they looked like.'

No one spoke as Lady Kitty's face drained of colour and the phone dropped from her hand.

'What happened?' Annabel was immediately on her feet and guiding her sister-in-law into a chair. She then waved a hand. 'One of you get some water. Quickly.'

'I'll do it.' JM marched out of the room while Annabel knelt beside a trembling Lady Kitty. She didn't try to speak other to utter soothing words until JM reappeared with a jug of water and a glass.

Lady Kitty swallowed a couple of gulps, but the colour still hadn't returned to her face. 'I think they must have made a mistake.'

'Why? Who collected him? I'm sure it couldn't have been Randal because you'd hardly react like this. Plus, you know he hates to interrupt his golf game.'

'It's Cynthia.'

Ginny's heart slammed against her chest. Cynthia Eagle-Edwards was the only person Lady Kitty had told about Lesley Charlton's discovery. But she'd said she'd never do anything to hurt the estate, and even that kind of loyalty didn't usually end in murder. Someone would need a very good reason to do that.

Oh. Her throat tightened as she remembered her conversation with Annabel and her ongoing feud with Cynthia. Because Cynthia tried to have an affair with Randal before moving on to Digby's father, Lenny Theakston, who Annabel believed to be Vanessa's father.

But was it possible that Vanessa's father wasn't either of those men?

Annabel let out a soft groan as if suddenly coming to the same conclusion. 'Kitty... no. Please tell me that Cynthia didn't have an affair with Spenny—?'

'It was a long time ago,' Kitty whispered, her strong frame unravelling under the truth. 'And he was sorry. So very sorry about it.'

'I can understand you forgiving your husband. I can *even* understand you forgiving Cynthia, since you're much nicer than I am. But why in all things glorious did you let her continue to work for you? If it was me, I would have fired her arse and made sure she never crossed my threshold again,' Annabel raged, eyes glittering with fury.

'Exactly.' Kitty let out a feeble laugh. 'You always did know how to act the lady of the manor. But I didn't want people to see me like that. B-besides, she was excellent at her job, and part of our success is down to her.'

'Oh yes.' Annabel let out a bitter laugh and got to her feet. 'And you know why that is? Because technically Vanessa Eagle-Edwards is Spenny's only child and once he dies, you can bet this stupid hat that Cynthia will be at her lawyer's office trying to cut out my Theo.'

Kitty began to shake. 'No, that's not possible. Cynthia's never asked him to acknowledge Vanessa legally, even though he pays her money that he thinks I don't know about. But the estate will still go to Theo.'

'I'm afraid that Annabel's correct.' JM got to her feet. 'Edward Tait is dealing with a case like this right now.'

'What are you saying? That Cynthia has kidnapped my husband? But what about his medicines? They're all here. And he doesn't do well when his routine is changed. W-what can she be thinking?'

No one answered as Tuppence retrieved her phone from her pocket. 'I saw a YouTube clip that said the first twenty-four hours in a missing person's case are the most important, which means we should call the police.'

'Do it now,' Annabel snapped. 'Before it's too late.'

TWENTY-EIGHT

Friday, 8th August

'Any news?' Cleo asked later that afternoon, as they all stood around the issues counter.

'Not since last time you asked,' Connor said, which earned him a dark glare from the feisty volunteer before she flounced off, Andrea trailing in her wake. He grimaced. 'Sorry, Mrs C.'

'It's fine. I'll go and speak to her,' Ginny assured him, not wanting to admit she was feeling a bit like Cleo.

It seemed like a lifetime ago since the police had shown up at Oldfield Hall. After a quick conversation, it was decided that Ginny and her friends were surplus to requirements so they had come back to Little Shaw, with the strict instructions not to leave town.

Again.

By the time she'd walked back into the library the news had already spread about the manhunt for Cynthia Eagle-Edwards, and the growing concerns for Sir Spencer Faulkner. Her friends had decided to go back to Harold's house to see what else he had discovered, and Ginny had tried to settle into the demands of the day. But her mind kept going through all the pieces.

Twenty years ago, Cynthia must have killed Lesley and Terrence to protect her daughter's inheritance.

The buzz of Connor's phone made her jump.

'It's from Grace.' He swiped the screen and pulled up a text. 'Theo's joining a group of volunteers looking through the area around Harris Hill. There are lime caves there, and the police think that's where she might have taken him.'

'We know there was an explosion in one of the caves in the seventeen hundreds, but apparently there are several others in the area. Though the trail is challenging, so I'm not sure how she'd get a frail man through.' Ginny didn't want to think what would happen if Cynthia did manage to get him into one of the caves.

Is that what she'd done to Lesley Charlton? Had she decided to take matters into her own hands after Lady Kitty had confided in her about the copyright trap? And what then? Had she threatened Terrence Charlton and forced him to write a suicide letter before killing him? It was hard to imagine someone as petite and refined as Cynthia doing anything like that. But she'd read about what happened when a woman thought their child was in danger. It could lend them strength to do impossible things.

Did the same apply when they were at risk of losing an inheritance?

So, what happened then? Had Gemma somehow found the skull while giving Cynthia a private yoga lesson, and she'd either taken it thinking it was a fake... or she'd known who it belonged to and was using it to grow her channel? Or blackmail Cynthia?

Then she'd run into Jacinta at the pub, and decided to let Colin find the skull to attract more followers to her channel.

Ginny recalled Cynthia's sharp glare while they'd been

waiting in the church for the police. And if Sam told the police that he'd seen Gemma with a spade, it wouldn't have taken Cynthia long to put two and two together.

Terrible grief swept over her and Ginny gripped the counter so she wouldn't get lost in it. Had it been their fault? Had their poking around forced Cynthia into acting as she had done now?

'Yeah, that's what Grace said. Apparently, she and Theo often walk around there. She's going to join him.'

Ginny looked up at him. 'Are they back together?'

He nodded. 'She called this morning but with all this going on, I doubt she wants to tell anyone. Theo's super close with his uncle, so right now they're just concentrating on that.'

Ginny's throat tightened. She hated to think how the sensitive Grace would feel if their ill-fated wedding ended up being responsible for Sir Spencer's death.

'It's too awful.'

'Yeah,' Connor said, in a bleak voice. 'I guess bad things really do happen to good people. I told Grace I'd join them once we finish.'

'Why don't you head off now? And I'll call Hen, Tuppence and JM. I'm sure they'll want to help.'

'Theo said the more the better. Do you really think they'd go?'

'I know it,' Ginny assured him, and she did. Because in the last year she'd learnt that her friends could always be depended on. 'If you call Hen, she'll drive you there.'

'She drives faster than my brother does.' His eyes filled with relief. 'Thanks, Mrs C.'

'Don't thank me yet. I feel terrible that this might have happened because of us.'

'You were only doing what Nan asked you to do. So, if it's anyone's fault, it's mine.' Connor bowed his head.

'Let's save the blame for later,' Ginny quickly assured him, realising it wouldn't help the situation. 'But keep me posted and I'll join you as soon as I've closed the library.'

He nodded and picked up the latest book he was reading, and she smiled despite the terrible situation. Connor had been a self-confessed non-reader but had recently discovered the *Rivers of London* series and was devouring them at a fast pace.

'Where's he going?' Cleo demanded, hurrying over to the issues counter. 'I told you he had news. What is it? What's happened? Oh, that poor man.'

'Poor man,' Andrea echoed, and Ginny looked up in surprise. She'd assumed Cleo had been pestering Connor for news because she liked gossip, not because she was worried about Sir Spencer.

'Did you know him?' she asked cautiously.

'Of course not. I refuse to step foot in that village. But that doesn't mean I want anyone to get hurt. All this waiting is terrible. I wish there was something I could do. Even if it's just making sandwiches for the police.'

A lump formed in Ginny's throat as other patrons gathered around the issues counter, expressing similar sentiments. Once again, she felt truly grateful to have moved to such a lovely village.

She quickly told them about the volunteer search party that was heading out to Harris Hill and wasn't surprised when the library all but emptied out, leaving just her and Slim to close.

'We should shut up sooner; it's not like anyone will come in.' Slim joined her at the issues counter.

'We can't do that. Imagine how annoyed you would be if you travelled in by bus because you needed something... only to find us closed,' Ginny said, and Slim grinned.

'You're a good one, you know that?'

Ginny returned the smile, but she didn't feel remotely good as she kept thinking of poor Sir Spencer. Logically, she knew they weren't responsible, but it didn't make the heavy sensation in the pit of her stomach lessen.

It only got worse as the afternoon wore on and by the time she and Slim stepped outside, her nerves were jangling. When her phone rang, the shrill sound caused her heart to pound. It was JM.

'Is there any news?' Ginny asked, without formality.

'No, sorry to give you false hope. I just wanted to let you know we've been moved to another part of the marsh. I don't want you to arrive and not be able to find us.'

'That's good timing. I'm locking up now and will get changed before heading out there. Do you need anything?'

'No, though would you believe that Cleo, Andrea and two dozen other people from Little Shaw turned up with sandwiches and flasks of tea?'

'I'm so pleased.' Ginny couldn't hide her pride. 'How is everyone? Have you seen Theo or Lady Kitty?'

'No, I think they're staying closer to home in case there's any news, but everyone's terribly worried, especially because of his medication.'

'And what about Vanessa? Has anyone told her?'

There was a pause and JM let out a soft sigh. 'It turns out the poor woman had no idea that Sir Spencer was her father, so it's been a terrible shock. I think Digby Theakston has gone around to see her. He'll know what to say, being a vet and all.'

Ginny wasn't surprised that Vanessa had taken it badly. Not just to find out the truth about her paternity, but to discover her mother was a killer... It was all too terrible.

They said a quick goodbye and Ginny dropped her phone back into her handbag, before remembering she still needed to lock the library door. *It's like my mind's turned to marshmallow,* she thought, as she frantically searched for the key.

'Any news?' Slim asked, as she finally located it in one of the pockets of her black handbag. She really needed to get something smaller, or with a brighter lining in it, so that things didn't constantly get lost in there.

'No, but they're moving the search.' She locked the door and double-checked it while Slim gave her an approving nod. He'd once told them that people often thought they'd locked the door but hadn't. 'Would you like a lift home? Or did you want to come with me?'

'Nah.' He shook his head and gave her a sheepish look. 'I'm not that great around coppers. Besides, I'm meeting a buddy for a game of pool. But William might like one. Young John's not speaking to him right now, says he's been taking liberties with all the lifts.'

Turning, Ginny saw the familiar figure of William sitting on a nearby bench with his pile of newspapers and a large back-pack by his white trainers. She bit back her frustration. She would've preferred to go straight home and get changed so she could join the search party. But she could hardly leave William stranded.

'I didn't realise he was still here. Of course I'll take him home. I was worried John might be getting annoyed at all the detours.'

'I think it's more about the pontifications about the best way to make a right-hand turn,' Slim replied. Then said proudly, 'I've been using the thesaurus for my book, hence the fancy word. It's a good one.'

'It is that.' She smiled and said goodbye to Slim before joining William. He quickly agreed to the lift and after bustling him into her small car, and stacking the newspapers in the back-seat, she headed to the cottage where he lived.

'Thanks, Ginny.' He mopped his brow and settled into the front seat. 'Dragging these newspapers around is hard work. And now that young John refuses to pick me up at the door, it's making things difficult.'

'Maybe you shouldn't bring in so many of the newspapers

each day,' Ginny said in a cautious voice. She didn't want to interfere, but she also didn't want William to lose his main mode of transport. 'It's been lovely of you to help us out, and everything you've done for Slim, but if you didn't have to carry them you could walk to the bus stop.'

'Did young John put you up to this?' he demanded, as she reached his home and helped him out.

'No, I just don't like the idea of you fighting with him.' She waited until he retrieved his key and unlocked the front door, before passing over the large pile. 'Just think about it.'

'Hmmm,' William said in a non-committal voice as he hugged the papers and shuffled inside, leaving Ginny to hurry back to her car and make the short drive home.

There were no more messages from JM on how the search was going, and her stomach tightened at how long the detour had taken. It was illogical to think she could make a difference, but all the same, her flicking pulse was like a ticking time bomb telling her to get there quickly.

TWENTY-NINE

The drive to Walton-on-Marsh involved being stuck behind a lorry before Ginny hit roadworks that sent her around the outskirts of the village. As the traffic moved sluggishly on, she wished she *had* closed the library early and left with her friends.

Her fingers tapped against the steering wheel at the slow progress. She was usually patient, but the longer it took for her to arrive, the more worried she was becoming. None of it was helped by the instructions her phone was giving her.

'Turn left at the roundabout,' it said in a bossy voice. 'No, I said left. Left. Left.'

'I *am* turning left,' Ginny protested. No wonder JM preferred using a paper map instead of the very judgy app.

'Now take the second right at Loom Lane,' the voice continued, and Ginny made the turn, only to join another queue, which was moving at a snail's pace. The car in front of her slowed and its horn honked as a modern building came into sight on the lefthand side.

The horn blasted again, and someone leaned out of the

passenger side window. 'Rest in peace, Gemma, you were a queen.'

It earned them a huge roar from the group of people gathered on the grass verge. Another car honked as it went past and several women in the crowd waved at them, holding lighters up in the air.

Others clutched large banners adorned with photos of Gemma Murphy, much like the day Ginny had been at the police station.

She looked again at the building and smothered a gasp. This was where Gemma's yoga studio was. Then she groaned. Of course. The article they'd found had mentioned Loom Lane. Another car horn blasted but this time it was directed at a woman in a black dress and platform sandals, who came to a halt in the middle of the road as she stared directly at Ginny.

It was Vanessa Eagle-Edwards. But not as Ginny had seen her before. Mascara was streaking down her cheeks, and her hair was flying out around her, as if it had been charged with electricity. She'd clearly been crying.

What was she doing there? Had she been a friend of Gemma's? It seemed unlikely considering the age difference, and surely Vanessa wouldn't be at Gemma's vigil when there was a manhunt on for her mother and biological father. Especially considering her distraught appearance. And where was Digby? Wasn't he meant to be comforting her?

The car honked again, which seemed to snap Vanessa out of her trance, and she dragged her gaze away from Ginny and turned to the driver, who was half hanging out of the car window.

'Move it, love. I don't have all day.'

'I'm sorry,' Vanessa sobbed as she stumbled her way to the curb. The driver shouted an obscenity at her before screeching off. *Oh dear.* On instinct, Ginny searched around for somewhere to park. There was a space further along, so she slowed down and reversed into it, then she climbed out and hurried over to the still sobbing photographer.

'There, I've got you.' Ginny put an arm around her and led her to the safety of the grass verge.

Vanessa let out another shuddering cry but finally looked up, lashes loaded with tears. 'Thank you. What are you doing here?'

'I'm on my way to help the search party. But why are you here?'

'It's my studio.' Vanessa pointed to the top floor of the building. 'Digby was meant to come and collect me, but he never showed, and it's impossible to think with all the people. I just need to get out of here. Then I saw you and got such a shock—' She broke off and buried her face in her hands. 'What am I going to do?'

'Let me help you. Would you like a lift?' Ginny said, still trying to process everything.

How had they not known that Vanessa and Gemma both worked out of the same building?

'Actually, that would be lovely.' Vanessa suddenly straightened, the tears gone. In her hand was a knife and a twisted smile had spread out across her face. 'Now, climb into your car and we'll head back to your house.'

'My house?' Ginny's limbs turned to stone. 'I don't understand.'

'Of course you don't.' Vanessa pressed the knife against Ginny's shirt, the sharp blade slicing through the thin fabric and nicking her skin. A spike of pain shot through her, as Vanessa pushed her towards the driver's side of the car. 'Then again, neither did Gemma. Which is what happens when you stick your nose into things that don't concern you. Now, get in, please, and drive.'

Cold steel pressed against her stomach and Ginny's mouth went dry as she managed to climb in and start the engine. Frantically, she looked at the vigil for Gemma Murphy, but the gathered crowd was facing towards the building, all bent over in what seemed like a mob downward dog moment.

Her vision blurred as she pulled out onto the street and headed back to Little Shaw. Next to her Vanessa reached into her bag and retrieved a heavy balaclava, which she pulled down over her head, concealing her features. Then she tugged a hoodie out, and shrugged it open, using the hood to further conceal her identity. As she moved, some of the contents of the bag spilled out. It was packets of noodles, crisps and several bottles of water.

Supplies.

Ginny groaned. Too late, she realised Vanessa hadn't been leaving the building at all, but crossing the road towards it. With a bag full of supplies.

Was that where Cynthia and Sir Spencer were? Did it mean he was still alive?

Ginny cautiously reached for her hazard lights, wondering if she could put them on to attract attention. But would it be enough? Would people guess she was being held under duress, or would they just see someone with a hoodie pulled over their face?

'Don't even think about it,' Vanessa hissed. 'This will go a lot better if you assume I'm not stupid.'

'I don't think that,' Ginny finally managed to speak as she clutched the steering wheel, her palms slick with sweat. 'After all, if you managed to kill Gemma, you must know what you're doing.'

'I know enough not to get dragged into a touching confessional moment with a menopausal librarian. Now, shut up and drive,' Vanessa snapped, and began to check her phone messages, her black fingernails clacking against the screen. Was she texting Cynthia?

Ginny swallowed as they left Walton-on-Marsh proper,

speeding past the sun-dried fields and the wide river, where Jackson Fold had once been. Out of the corner of her eye the dark water continued to flow, oblivious to all the pain and betrayal it had caused.

Ginny suddenly realised that some of her fear had been replaced by anger. Vanessa had said she hated people who traded on their last name as if it was a currency, but wasn't that exactly what this was about?

Her mother had killed Lesley and now Vanessa had killed Gemma. All to keep their secrets, and thus save Vanessa's inheritance. But why had Cynthia kidnapped Sir Spencer? Had she done it in a spurt of anger? Ginny shuddered. And if the police didn't find Cynthia soon, then Sir Spencer would also be killed.

And so will I.

The heavy tightness in Ginny's stomach increased as she tried to piece it all together. She'd assumed the skull had been at Cynthia's house, but had it been in Vanessa's photography studio instead? If they were neighbours, it made sense that Gemma might have seen it. Then Ginny remembered the break-in. Vanessa said someone had destroyed equipment and started a fire. Had that been Gemma doing it to cover up the fact she'd stolen the skull? It would explain Vanessa's hysterical reaction when Colin appeared with it.

Ginny turned into Little Shaw, the familiar landscape flashing by until she reached Middle Cottage. All without Vanessa saying a word.

Finally, the photographer pocketed her phone and gestured for Ginny to get out of the vehicle.

'Remember, no screaming or I will gut you in the street,' she hissed, as Ginny's heart thundered in her ears.

Her legs shook as she climbed out and walked to the pink front door that usually made her smile. Edgar was waiting on the mat, next to a bouquet of flowers and another vial of what looked like Heather's curse buster.

Her heart plummeted at the sight of all the gifts for Grace. What hope did the young couple have of a happy ending, if Vanessa got away with it? And to what end? Both mother and daughter seemed to be taking huge risks that were hard to understand.

Her cat gave her an expectant stare, but Ginny just swallowed and tried not to fumble the house keys as she twisted the doorknob.

'That's it.' As Vanessa kicked the flowers to one side, she knocked over the potion, which harmlessly leaked out across Ginny's bottom step. *So much for magic.* Vanessa ignored the mess and hissed at Edgar, which sent him scampering over the fence.

Ginny's panic lessened as the blade of the knife gleamed in the late afternoon sun. At least her cat would be safe, even if she wasn't.

As soon as the door was open, Vanessa pushed her inside.

'Isn't this risky? Wouldn't it have been better to take me up to the studio where you're holding Sir Spencer?'

'Never you mind where we're stashing that miserable prick who's meant to be my father. Besides, I'd say you've got bigger things to worry about.'

Ginny's breathing increased and the room began to spin. Oh dear, she was hyperventilating. She had to calm down. She could panic later. She just had to imagine she was back at the surgery, that time a wee boy had come in with a broken bone. Or when that poor woman had given herself third degree burns. Thinking of the familiar scents and sounds of her old life helped slow down her breathing and she finally managed to look up at Vanessa's steely glare.

'Have you finished with the dramatics?' the photographer snapped. 'Because we're on the clock. Now, we're going to walk upstairs to your bedroom.'

'Why are you doing this?' she asked, her voice strained as the panic began to rise again.

Vanessa seemed to have forgotten her no-talking policy and made a snarling sound at the back of her throat. 'Let's see. Is it because that miserable man impregnated my mother and then refused to acknowledge me? Or is it because my mother has always promised that we'd get what we deserve from that family... and we were so *close,* before that stupid cow broke into my workroom and stole Lesley Charlton's skull?'

Ginny's mouth dropped open. She'd been right. Gemma had taken the skull. 'But why did you have it? Did your mother keep it as a souvenir?'

'Souvenir? Please, what do you take us for? The only reason my mother had it was because she knew that the wounds on the skull didn't match the hammer she'd left with Terrence, when she killed him. We moved it to my studio several years ago, thinking it would be safer if people just thought it was some dramatic prop.'

Ginny shuddered at the callous explanation. 'But why did Gemma take it? Did she know who it belonged to?'

'Doubtful. As for why she took it, it's because she was an entitled princess who never worked for anything in her life. I did some photography for her, and she was a total nightmare who tried to rip me off. When I sent her an email about it, she had the cheek to come up to my space and tear shreds off me. She must have seen the skull then and decided that what was mine was hers.'

Ginny recalled Gemma's attitude to the poor photographer she'd booked the day they spoke to her. *He needs to get over his inflated sense of self and accept that his best days are behind him.* Was that how she'd treated Vanessa as well?

'So, you killed her because you didn't like her attitude?'

'I killed her because I didn't want her telling the police where she'd found the skull. Which is what would've happened thanks to your interference. Imagine my delight when I saw you in the car parked outside my studio.'

'What happens now?' Ginny surprised herself with the steadiness of her voice. 'You kill me and Sir Spencer, and what? You can't do that and still claim your inheritance.'

'Ah, but as far as the police are concerned, I'm not involved in my mother's terrible schemes. They'll think I'm an innocent victim whose mother killed five people then went on the run.'

'Five?'

Vanessa gave her a wolfish grin. 'We can't forget you and my father. Of course, I will be the distraught daughter who had no idea of what was going on.' Her eyes gleamed with malice and Ginny struggled to see how she would act distraught, when she clearly didn't know what the word meant.

'And your mother?'

'A new identity, some surgery and a villa in Greece. Not such a bad option. I'll join her when I can.'

Brring. Brrring. Brrring.

The sound of the front doorbell cut through Ginny's shattered nerves, and even Vanessa stiffened, tightening her grip on the knife.

'If you try *anything* I will slice you,' she whispered, the cool tip of the blade pressing into Ginny's neck. Fear sluiced off her as the doorbell went again. This time it was accompanied by a thumping sound.

'Should I answer it?' Ginny asked, as the person had now started stabbing at the bell, causing it to sound out a trilly anthem. *Brr. Brr. Brr. Brr.*

'Should you answer it? Have you heard nothing I've said?' The knife tip pressed deeper into the fleshy part of Ginny's neck, causing another wave of nausea to sweep over her. 'You will leave the door until they go away.'

'This is Little Shaw... people don't tend to do that. It might be more presents for Grace.'

From beneath the balaclava Vanessa growled. 'Yet another reason to hate this damn village. And listen... it's stopped, which means they've pissed off. Now, let's get this over and done with.' Vanessa pushed her through into the hallway.

'You won't get away with it,' Ginny whispered.

'Could you be more of a cliché? You and your friends are just stupid old women who think they can investigate crime. It's embarrassing,' Vanessa snapped.

'My friends don't have anything to do with this,' Ginny said, fear now drenching her. She couldn't bear the thought of anything happening to JM, Tuppence or Hen because of something she'd done.

She opened her mouth but was cut off as a high-pitched sound echoed around the kitchen.

Wahwahwah.

'What the hell?' Vanessa yelled, her voice hardly reaching above the blaring noise that continued to assault their eardrums. The only positive was that it released the frozen thrall Ginny had been under, and she managed to take a wobbly step backwards, her mind rapidly assessing the noise. 'What did you do?'

She had no idea. It didn't quite sound like a police siren, or an ambulance, and it wasn't getting any closer, or further away. In fact... *Oh.* Her eyes widened.

'I think it's my car alarm.' Her voice was half lost below the din. Wallace and his father had insisted she get one, but it had never gone off on its own before. 'Maybe the person knocking on the door set it off by accident?'

Ginny gulped as a figure appeared in her house, between the dining room and the conservatory. He was in his late thirties with dark hair and a cranky expression on his face, clad only in pyjama bottoms and an All-Blacks rugby shirt. In his arms was a black cat with amber eyes, who didn't seem in a hurry to move.

For a moment no one spoke as his sharp gaze went from Ginny to Vanessa, who was now pointing the knife in his direction. 'Fifteen hours. I've only been back in the country for fifteen hours, and I'm already rescuing you? Not to mention finding out that your cat has made himself quite at home on my car,' Wallace growled in an exasperated voice, and thrust the cat to Slim, who had stepped in behind the detective, a guilty expression on his face. 'Slim, find the keys for the car and turn that damn thing off, then open the front door.'

'Slim,' Vanessa snapped. 'Don't move a muscle.'

'Slim, fix the alarm. And you might as well bring William back with you.'

Ginny's mouth hung open as she tried to take it all in. Wallace she could understand, just about. But where had Slim and William come from? However, Wallace didn't seem inclined to answer any questions and just glared at Vanessa, irritation rolling off him like a wave.

'I don't think so.' Vanessa's voice went up an octave to be heard over the piercing blare of the alarm. 'And who the hell are you?'

'He's my neighbour,' Ginny explained, wondering if she was having an out-of-body experience.

'I am,' Wallace agreed. 'I'm also DI James Wallace and since you don't seem to be aware of it, let me give you an update. Your mother has been caught at your photography studio, Sir Spencer Faulkner is recovering in hospital and, unless I'm very much mistaken, DI Sterling will be here in under five minutes.'

'You're lying. It's not true,' Vanessa howled as she waved the knife in the air, but her hand was beginning to shake.

'I think it's true. Wallace isn't great on the lying,' Slim told her.

'Terrible at it,' Wallace agreed, as he took a step closer. 'Oh, and you're holding that knife the wrong way.' As her eyes went to the knife in her grasp, in one fluid motion he closed the distance on Vanessa and clamped a strong hand around her wrist, forcing her to release the weapon. He kicked it away and reached for a set of handcuffs hanging out of his pyjama pocket.

He cuffed Vanessa and forced her into the closest chair, as the alarm continued to blare. 'SLIM.'

'On it, guv.' Slim reached into Ginny's black hole of a handbag and plucked out her car keys without pausing. Then he pressed a button and the blaring noise ceased.

Ginny felt like she'd just stopped walking in a hurricane as her senses settled.

Slim disappeared down the hallway, before he reappeared, a surprised William trailing him, a newspaper clutched in his arms.

Ginny's mouth opened and closed as she tried to force her spinning thoughts into order. First, she turned to Slim and William. 'What are you both doing here?'

'It's a long story,' Slim started, but Wallace made a growling noise, as if to suggest what would happen if he did start telling any kind of story. Slim got the message and shrugged. Ginny turned to Wallace instead.

'How did you know to come over here?'

'You mean between the cat trying to break into my house, the car alarm blaring and the phone call from my least favourite work colleague telling me to stop someone from killing my neighbour? I'll leave it to you to decide which version you prefer,' he growled – then sighed, as if remembering his manners. 'Sorry for yelling. I'm very jet lagged. Are you okay?'

'Yes, but I think we could all use a cup of tea.'

'Tea? You've been held at knifepoint and you just want tea?' Wallace stared at her.

'Well, she wasn't holding it the right way,' she said meekly, before taking in his tired face and smudges under his eyes. 'And you know alcohol wouldn't be appropriate if you're still jet lagged.'

'Why do I even bother arguing?' Then he turned his attention back to Vanessa, who was attempting to stand up. 'I don't think so.'

He blocked her path just as DI Sterling raced into the room, followed by PC Singh.

'Wallace, you're back. It's so good to see you.' Anita beamed.

Sterling's face was a tight mask as she stared at Wallace. It was clear she didn't share the sentiment.

'Thank you for your assistance,' Sterling said, sounding like she was swallowing thumb tacks. 'I can take it from here.'

'Be my guest,' Wallace retorted. 'I haven't read her her rights yet.'

'Leave it to me,' Sterling snapped, then spun and faced Ginny, eyes blazing. 'And let me assure you *and* your friends that I won't be cutting any corners. Just like my father didn't when he was working the Charlton case.'

Wallace raised a bemused eyebrow. 'Do I even want to know what that's about?'

'No,' Ginny quickly assured him. Little could be gained from telling him about JM and Tuppence's visit to Stuart Sterling.

His mouth twitched with the hint of a smile and Sterling gave them all a loathing-filled glare before dragging Vanessa to her feet and pushing her towards the front door. 'God, but I really *hate* coming to Little Shaw.'

There was a short silence on her departure, broken by William. 'Well, I say, that wasn't very nice. She didn't even thank us for helping apprehend a criminal.' He narrowed his eyes. 'I don't like her.'

'Neither do I,' Slim agreed. 'Especially since she's nicked me more than once. But she was so pissed off at Wallace and Ginny I don't think she even noticed me. Fading into the background has always been a talent of mine.'

Ginny wasn't sure how to answer that so decided to ignore it. 'Tell me what you're both doing here—?'

Slim raised an eyebrow and nodded at William. 'Turns out the old boy left one of his papers in your car and was worried it might fall into the wrong hands. He was fretting about it, so I walked here with him, but then when no one answered, I told him I'd get into your car and rescue it. I like to keep in practice. Except it's been a while and I haven't come across one of those alarm systems before.'

'Clearly,' Wallace snapped, as the sound of police sirens came closer. Then he turned to William and held out his hand. 'Show me the paper.'

Slim gave William a reassuring nod. 'I think it's time you came clean. Especially since the scumbag's dead.'

Scumbag? Ginny exchanged a glance with Slim, who wrinkled his nose.

'Who died?' Wallace demanded.

'Sid Clement. But don't go looking like that,' Slim instructed the detective, before holding up his hands. 'Er, I mean, you don't need to worry it's anything dodgy. He died of natural causes.' Then he wiped his brow and turned to William. 'Just show it to him before I get myself into a muddle.'

'Sid Clement was married to my sister, but he didn't treat her right. Broke my parents' hearts and she was too scared to go to the police. Worried that no one would believe her.'

'Oh, William.' Ginny's hands flew to her mouth. He'd never mentioned having a sister before. 'What happened to her?'

'I did what I could to keep her safe.' William handed over the paper and Wallace unfolded it so he and Ginny could read the front page.

Have you seen Ida?

Little Shaw resident, Ida Clement, was last seen five days ago, in the village of Walton-on-Marsh, buying a cabbage. However, after she failed to come home, her distraught husband, Sid Clement, contacted the police, desperate for any news.

'Please. I love my wife and just want her to come home, where she knows I'll be waiting for her.'

Police have asked for anyone with information on Ida's whereabouts to contact them.

'What do you mean, you did what you could?' Wallace's brows pushed together. 'And why have I never heard of this case?'

'Because it was the best way to keep her safe.' William looked directly at the detective. 'The cabbage was just a ruse, you see. I followed her to Walton-on-Marsh and gave her enough money to leave, along with some things in a suitcase to see her through. She went to Leeds and started a new life. For the first few years I didn't risk seeing her in case Sid caught wind of it, but after his health got worse, we started meeting up. She was happy in the end, though, and she died two years ago.'

'I'm so sorry you both went through that.' Ginny dabbed at her eyes, hating the look of pain on William's face. It was clear he and his sister had been close. And it meant that what she'd assumed was a ridiculous story about someone disappearing after a trip to Walton-on-Marsh was actually true.

'I am as well. I don't like to think you were let down by the police.' Wallace folded up the newspaper and handed it back to him. William took it and hugged it to his chest.

Ginny frowned. 'I still don't understand why you have all the newspapers... and if both Ida and Sid have died, why were you so worried?'

'I think that's clear. No one wants their sister to be known as the woman who went to buy a cabbage,' Slim retorted.

William shook his head. 'It's nothing to do with that. The cabbage is a noble vegetable and Ida was mighty fond of them. I suppose I'm just so used to covering my tracks. For years I kept buying the *Walton-on-Marsh Gazette* to make sure that no witnesses had gone to the press about her escape. Because if Sid ever found out—'

He broke off and they were all silent. Even Wallace seemed lost for words, until Slim coughed.

'Don't bear thinking about. Sid Clement was a nasty piece of work, and the fact you got your Ida out of his clutches just proves you really do have the makings of a mastermind criminal.'

'Thank you, Slim, I have often thought that if things had turned out differently, I might have wandered down the darker path. But it was too risky while Ida was alive.'

'Fair point. Though it doesn't mean you have to forget about your dreams. It's never too late to fully explore your particular talents.'

Ginny opened her mouth and shut it again as she stared at Wallace, who was starting to look like he wished he was still in New Zealand.

For once she knew how he felt.

THIRTY

It was a beautiful day for a wedding. The sky was blue, the grass was green, and the rest of Maureen West's garden was an explosion of colour, from the bright orange velvet cushions on each of the chairs through to the fuchsia awning that the bride and groom were standing under. But the most colourful of all was Grace West's shimmering dress. It changed from deep purple to a delicate shade of cerulean as she moved to her new husband's side.

Theo Faulkner had on a pair of jeans, a white linen shirt and bare feet, and his eyes were bright as he laughed at something Grace said. An excited Colin danced and jumped at their side while Brandon lazily watched from over by the bar where he'd managed to drag one of the orange cushions and was hugging it like a teddy bear.

'I'm pleased that's over.' Connor appeared next to Ginny holding a tray of lurid yellow cocktails. 'Nan says you need to try one of these. She invented it especially for today. It's called The Wedding Bomb.'

'I'm so happy she got to see Grace's wedding.' Ginny took the drink, feeling a little tipsy just from the smell of it. Still, the strong drinks seemed to have broken down the final barriers between the two families, and she looked to where Lady Kitty and Sir Spencer were chatting to Nina, while Theo's father was laughing at something Slim was telling him.

'Yeah, me too,' Connor admitted, taking one of the glasses and handing the tray to his brother who was walking past.

'Who died and made you the boss?' Jake scowled. 'Honestly, it's like I have to do everything in this family.'

'Actually, I was going to ask you to take a drink to Theo's cousin, Bridget. She couldn't make it to the last wedding and doesn't know anyone.' Connor nodded in the direction of a shy-looking girl with thick pink hair and a wide-eyed expression. 'But if you're too busy...'

Jake's jaw dropped and he blinked several times before snatching the tray and beelining for Bridget.

Ginny suppressed a smile. 'Wests and Faulkners talking together. What a lovely sight to see,' she said, then glanced to where Annabel and Maureen were deep in conversation. 'Can you believe that Theo's mother asked your grandmother to join the Walton Marshigolds? Now that Cynthia Eagle-Edwards isn't there, Annabel has taken over and wants some fresh volunteers.'

Connor's eyes flickered. 'Yeah, so I heard. Should we be scared?'

'I believe your nan could surprise us all. Grace told me she's been locking herself away since your uncle went on the run. This could be good for her, because she obviously loves being around people.'

'She loves many things, some of which might shock the almighty Faulkners.' Connor's mouth was still set in a worried line. 'I think I'd better go over and break it up before Nan starts telling stories of what things were like in the seventies. Especially the one with the strip club.'

Ginny bit back a smile as he disappeared into the crowd just as JM, Hen and Tuppence joined her, all clutching their own cocktails.

'Well, that was a perfectly lovely wedding,' Hen said with a contented sigh. 'I do love a happy ending.'

'A happy ending?' Tuppence growled. 'How can you say that after the article in the newspaper today? Can you believe Walton-on-Marsh are now marketing themselves as the town that never was? Apparently, the tourists have been flooding there ever since we officially put them on the map. *And* they're trying to claim that they've had more murders than we have.'

'I'm not sure either of our villages should be proud of that,' Ginny reminded her friends, and Tuppence reluctantly nodded.

'Yes, I suppose that's fair. But, still, I have a good mind to talk to Harold about this. Ah, there he is.' Tuppence marched off, her Crocs bright against the soft grass.

JM sighed. 'As her legal representative I'd better make sure she doesn't say anything too outrageous.'

'Yes, we don't want any fighting at this wedding,' Hen agreed, before wandering in the direction of Ross Mitchell, who was in the process of selling his cottage to Grace and Theo and had been invited along to the wedding.

Ginny was wondering whether to check on the young flower girls who were hiding under the table, playing with the cocktail umbrellas, when Wallace appeared next to her. She hadn't seen a lot of him in the month since he'd returned, apart from the occasional updates on the case. And while the *Walton-on-Marsh Gazette* continued to refer to it as a tragic event, the rest of the country had dubbed Cynthia and Vanessa the 'Mother/Daughter Murder Club'.

Except, Ginny couldn't find the humour in it. All she could

think of was the life Lesley and Terrence Charlton and Gemma Murphy might have had, as well as the long-dead Gareth Davies. Though at least his body had been excavated from a nearby site, and Harold was planning a memorial in his honour.

'You're looking contemplative,' Wallace said, his gaze dropping to the yellow cocktail before taking a sip of his beer. 'Or are you worried that stuff has turned your mouth a funny colour?'

'Goodness, I hadn't thought of that,' Ginny said, deciding it best not to have another sip. 'And you're right. I shouldn't be thinking about murder in the middle of a wedding.'

'Well, you're probably allowed to give it a few minutes of your time. After all, the wedding might not have gone ahead if you hadn't thought about it.'

'You mean if I hadn't stuck my nose in where it doesn't belong?' Ginny turned to face him.

'Your words, not mine.' He shrugged and drained his beer. 'Now, if you'll excuse me. I'd better go and offer my congratulations to the happy couple. And say thank you for convincing Joey West not to attempt to turn up.'

Ginny was about to follow him when Colin barked and began to dig up something at the bottom of one of Maureen's rose bushes.

The entire wedding party fell silent before Colin emerged from the hole, a tennis ball clutched firmly in his mouth.

Ginny burst out laughing. It really was the perfect wedding.

A LETTER FROM THE AUTHOR

Huge thanks for reading *The Widows' Guide to Skullduggery* – I hope you were hooked on Ginny's journey. If you want to join other readers in hearing all about my new releases and bonus content, you can sign up for my newsletter.

www.stormpublishing.co/amanda-ashby

If you enjoyed this book and could spare a few moments to leave a review that would be hugely appreciated. Even a short review can make all the difference in encouraging a reader to discover my books for the first time. Thank you so much.

I originally planned to include the fictional rival village of Walton-on-Marsh in the first book of this series, but the plot took a different turn, which meant Walton-on-Marsh had to simmer in the background. I then tried to use it in the second book, but it still didn't work out, so I was determined to make sure it took centre stage in the current story. I also wanted to have a variety of reasons for the rivalry, with no one really knowing the truth, so that Ginny and her friends had more of a mystery to unravel.

Thanks again for being part of this amazing journey with me and I hope you'll stay in touch – I have so many more stories and ideas to entertain you with!

Amanda

KEEP IN TOUCH WITH THE AUTHOR

www.amandaashby.com

instagram.com/authoramandaashby

ACKNOWLEDGEMENTS

A big shout out to the readers who have taken the time to leave reviews and comments about my books: it means the world to me! I'd also like to thank everyone at Storm for making me feel so welcome, especially Emily Gowers, who has done so much to bring Ginny and her friends into the world. Also, a special thanks to Belinda Jones and her brilliant attention to detail. As always, I'm grateful to have Sally Rigby, Christina Phillips and Rachel Bailey in my corner. Oh, and special thanks to my mother for telling me about the backroom fake CCTV camera used to stop chocolate-biscuit thieving in the charity shop where she volunteers. *I told you it would end up in a book!*

www.ingramcontent.com/pod-product-compliance
Lightning Source LLC
Chambersburg PA
CBHW010434170726
48283CB00011B/3202